Dream Date

Johns Hopkins Poetry and Fiction
JOHN T. IRWIN, GENERAL EDITOR

Dream Date

STORIES BY

Jean McGarry

The Johns Hopkins University Press

BALTIMORE AND LONDON

This book has been brought to publication with the generous
assistance of the G. Harry Pouder Fund.

The Johns Hopkins University Press
2715 North Charles Street
Baltimore, Maryland 21218-4363
www.press.jhu.edu

Library of Congress Cataloging-in-Publication Data

McGarry, Jean.
Dream date : stories / by Jean McGarry.
p. cm. — (Johns Hopkins, poetry and fiction)
ISBN 0-8018-6937-4
1. Man-woman relationships—Fiction.   I. Title.   II. Series.
PS3563.C3636 D74 2002
813'.54—dc21

2001007188

A catalog record for this book is available from the British Library.

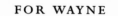

FOR WAYNE

Contents

His

Among the Philistines

The waitress was studying them. With one sweeping glance, she stripped his wife, Daria, of salient features and ornaments: the heavy rings, tanned hands, the bronzed face and black hair loosely piled up on her head. Then him: straight back and thick, dark hair, silver at the temples, but only there. In the waitress's eyes—caramel-colored and lustrous—he saw respect. He touched her sleeve and she saw his slim hands, his fine watch.

The girl returned with a wooden boat that held two steaming cloths, and as she was extracting them with tongs, she smiled with her face a little closer to his than it needed to be. She held the boat out for his cloth. First he wiped his face, then dampened his hands, and then rolled up the cloth, not smiling, as he collected his wife's cloth and dropped both in the boat.

"Did you see that?" he asked Daria, when the waitress (a Eurasian, he figured; nothing else could account for that coloring) had floated away from their table.

"Do you think she's pretty?" Daria asked, lifting her black bowl and swallowing a mouthful of the fishy soup.

"Beautiful. That's not what I meant. Did you see how she looked at you?"

"She wasn't looking at *me*."

"She noticed your rings."

"Maybe she did, but she was looking at you."

"If she was, I didn't notice."

3

"What were you going to say before?" his wife asked him.

"Nothing. It's not important."

"What was it? If you don't say it, you'll just be angry later."

Alex sighed. Daria was his gift from God; there's no way he could have done better, but they'd been married twelve years now, and she was taking a few things (like his patience) for granted. He stifled the impulse to push air out through his teeth the way he did (she could imitate it) when he was frustrated.

"Forget it," he said.

"Okay. Drink your soup. It's delicious. Don't let it get cold."

He removed the lid and smoke rolled up over the pearly broth, flecked with scallion curls. He loved good food and relished the thin, savory liquid as it steamed his throat. He drank the whole bowl. And here she was again, the waitress, laughing. Why was she laughing?

"Your face," said Daria. "It's all red."

"Take these," he said, pointing to the bowls. He wouldn't look at her. "We're finished." Then he looked. Her hair was like a fall of black water. As she left, he pulled from his shirt pocket his notepad and a tiny pencil. "Gorge," he wrote. "Torrent. Stream of inky water." (No.) "Fall of ebon water. Ebony fall." (No.) He scratched it all out, replaced pencil and pad, and took a long drink of his beer, clicking Daria's glass. "Cheers! Sorry," he said.

"What are you working on?" she asked. "You didn't tell me already, did you?"

"How could I tell you, if I don't know myself?"

"Does it have a title?"

"No." Here was the boxed eel dish and Daria's tempura. How, he thought, gazing at the puffy chicken limbs, dripping with oil, can she eat that?

"Stop making faces," she said.

He lifted the lid of his eel box. Steam rose from the bed of eels. "Miss," he signaled. She looked at him again. "This isn't hot enough."

"You haven't even *tasted* it," said Daria, but he shot her a look.

The waitress didn't understand. She had brought the *unaju* straight from the kitchen. She had watched while the chef layered it into the hot box.

"Take it back," he said. "Please."

The waitress looked at Daria's yellow chicken.

"Mine's fine," Daria said.

The waitress picked up the eel box—but without her potholders—and dropped the scalding dish on the table. Some sauce splashed Alex's shirt sleeve and wrist. He cried out. Soon the owner was standing over the Morgans' table. He offered free beers, sake, dinner on the house next time they came in? Alex was adamant. He refused to pay the check and said so then. At first the owner, too, was adamant but—seeing the hubbub table four had caused already, and other tables were now noticing—he gave in.

Alex took a second box of eels, although—he explained to the owner—he had no more appetite for dinner. Daria had already finished her tempura. Alex ate in silence.

"I like my food hot," was all he said.

"It was hot," Daria replied.

"Not hot enough."

*H*e was teaching his class. Every head was bent (he could hear the light scratch of pens on cheap paper) but one. That head, with its greasy blond hair, was level with his own. Eyebrows raised, the professor faced his opponent, and the student, a physical coward, looked down. But there was nothing—no pad or pen—on the desk.

This seemed to be the student's comment on Professor Morgan's class in Latin poetry of the Augustan age. He was a pleasant boy; when addressed, he was polite, but he didn't appreciate (this was so clear) the value of a symbolic gesture. He was no Latinist; like Professor Morgan, he was a *writer,* and it was enough to let the beautiful lines—recited first in Latin, then in translation—wash over him. Alex had seen the boy close his eyes as the pleasure of cadence or figure struck him. But to this student there seemed nothing of interest in the nation whence this verse had flowered, so quickly borne its perfect fruit, then perished—in its history, its representative men, its codes and politics. This student was there for the verse. But verse was the reason Professor Morgan taught the course. To understand the verse, and to give it its rightful place in twenty-seven-hundred years of the art of poetry; to see how it reflected, masked, or distorted its culture—these lessons, which Professor Morgan prepared for alternate weeks, were requisite. Notes must be taken. Otherwise, how would one draw on the fine lore of Olympians and mortals, of battles, civic life, dress, harvests, rites, diseases, and the weakness of great men for foolish ideas, to illuminate the elegies, epic, and pastorals? The boy would listen, yes—he didn't cut every second class— but he would listen only. Yet Alex felt that he listened closer than the scribblers, for whom transcription was all.

Alex had his pocket watch cushioned in a walnut box that also contained pens, pencils, and a knife. He glanced at it but didn't fail to notice that the blond student, in the interval, had glanced at his own watch. Five minutes remained. Alex closed the four small books laid out in front of him. He closed his notepad. He asked for questions.

The blond student started to talk. It was not a question. Thinking through the last several lectures, he had found a thread—beyond those Professor Morgan had teased out for them—that tied each poet to the age and, more interesting, tied each poet (especially where the greatest literature was concerned) to the ineluctable: corruption, decline, silence.

Alex listened. Without noticing, he had flipped open to the ribbon-marked page where he'd inscribed the notes for class. At the bottom of the unlined page, he jotted down the student's idea.

Next week, he told them, when he'd had time to reflect, he would challenge—and possibly (he smiled) wouldn't be able to quite defeat—this clever hunch. What was beautiful, he said, was not just the student's sharp sight and close readings but how shrewd a listener he was, how well he'd guessed what Professor Morgan had been leading up to. This was a fresh link in a story he thought he knew by heart. Thank you, he said. This doesn't happen often in a teacher's life.

The blond boy sat still. He hadn't quite finished what he was saying, but the teacher's notebook was slapped shut. The other students' books had long been packed away, and Alex pointed to his watch, shrugged—he had another class after this one—but they'd talk, he wanted to, and soon. I've forgotten your name, he said. You're not registered, are you? And Professor Morgan, pads and books and case in hand, fled.

In his office, he took the time to copy out the student's argument—that the poet had encapsulated in his longest work a portent of catastrophe and the drift of sterile centuries to follow. He wouldn't use it, no—that would be despicable—but he would insert it, proleptically, in his foreword. That way, it would shimmer as one of the many rewarding paths the author might have followed. Such notions—ludicrous, fantastically original—should be entertained; they could lead anywhere; they might undo fifty, a hundred years of diligent work. They were blinding for the moment, intoxicating. But they were, finally, immature, atopic. He slapped the book shut and decided that he needed a swim, a shower, maybe even a run. His body was overheated; his shirt was clinging to his armpits, to his waist. Luckily, he kept some fresh ones in his desk drawer.

*H*e stepped off the train. He was alone. The train had been fast and clean for an American train, but underground, the filth and stench—even in winter—made him draw his silk-lined scarf across his mouth and nose. In his satchel were poems, letters, books, the notepad, and the watch box. His wallet was in his pocket. Where were his gloves? Here. He was gloved, the scarf over his mouth; only his eyes were open lo the cold, damp cave, which he did not care to describe even in his head. Undercity Manhattan. It was all disease. Upstairs in the dismal terminal he unwrapped his face and stripped off his gloves, but the air was chilly, so he put them on again. He thought ahead to his afternoon and evening and gripped the handles of his satchel a little tighter. First would come . . . what? He'd enter the hotel. He'd be early. What would he do? Check in, unpack, wash his face and hands. Then what? Down to the bar for coffee, a light drink, nothing to cloud his head or jangle the nerves.

Sitting at a window in the hotel bar, a view of the doorman across the street, he opened his notepad and there was a first line in pencil. He ordered a somewhat stronger drink than planned and copied the line so as to feel the words under his pen. The line was bitter for all its excellence, and he wondered how someone so in harmony with himself (as he felt he was) could produce such darkness. And thinking, enjoying the solitary moment, here she was.

Without looking up, he knew she was there. He didn't hear *her* but, rather, the hubbub around her: the desk clerks, the bell, the suitcase rolling away on the cart, the startled voices. Next thing he knew, a wave of cold air swept over him and the soft fingers were on his neck.

She picked up his drink, sniffed it, and swallowed a mouthful, her eyes holding his. They were serious. Her mouth stayed shut. She was an actress—not professionally, but her entrances were stagey and you had to wait and see what would evolve. She'd flare up if she felt unappreciated. That he didn't need.

Finally she was seated, arranged. How many wraps did she have on? The Persian lamb, but something thrown over that, a shawl with a fringe, and underneath would be a sleek dress, black silk, something. She was tall with wide shoulders, full breasts, and muscular hips and legs; even her head was modeled on a noble scale. The hair was shoulder-length and wavy, a rich brown; her face was strong, with large hazel eyes and olive skin. And—he touched her chin to rotate the head—a classically pure nose, straight and slender. Djuna was a beautiful woman, ferocious, self-possessed, and all his. When she turned her head to order, he laughed.

No, thank God, not *all* his. (Djuna, as Daria liked to say, "could eat you alive!" He didn't care for the presumption, and she never said it again. She was right, though.)

They kissed. He gave himself up to the warmth, the layered scent (flowers, spice, something metallic), the lush mouth. For a moment. Then his eyes whisked, his head jerked, as he reassured them both that no one they knew—no one at all, to be honest—was in the bar watching them.

"Morgan!" Djuna warned, kissing him again, then resumed her air of being alone and content to be.

"Djuna," he said, trying to recover the tone of an earlier moment, when his need for her had been as great as his desire.

"What?" she said. The waiter took her order for a martini with Bombay Sapphire.

"I love you," he said. "You keep me aloft!"

This was the kind of talk she liked. They could both feel something building. This was the art of it.

She opened her billfold to show him recent birthday pictures of her daughter, Lucinda. "*She*'s the one *I* love," she said.

"That's so trite," he said, without thinking, and she flared up.

"I'm sorry," he said, "but it is somewhat trite for a parent to say."

"How would you know? Having only yourself to think about. And Daria," she added. "Don't you think that might make a bit of a difference?"

"I don't know," he said. "It's very tactful of you to point it out."

"Sorry."

"I didn't mean to hurt."

9

"Well," she said, "neither did I."

He smiled and then she smiled. Their hands clasped on the table. There was too much at stake to quarrel for long. A bit of meanness, name-calling—it was always like this. Something would flare up between them. They couldn't find his room— or tear their clothes off—fast enough.

Afterward it took her forever to wash, to do her make-up, and to dress. He read the hotel magazine. Finally she was wrapping the shawl around the curly, black-haired coat. He jumped out of bed and (in what must be—as he wrote later— an "erotic whirry") embraced her, his own thick-wrapped Aphrodite, but she stood firm. She wouldn't even open her lips. "I'm late!" she said.

"Call me tonight," he said, lying on his back. "Here." He wasn't angry. Some things didn't make him angry.

She was unlocking the door. And then the door, closing between them, clicked shut. He heard no steps on the hallway carpet. It was an old hotel, solidly built. That's why he liked it.

When she had really gone—ten minutes had elapsed—Alex lay on his back and mentally blocked the stage of tonight's dinner, with its players, props, and movement. He opened his eyes: it was bad luck to project. What, though, would he do to fill the time between now and then? He could make a few calls. He dialed three numbers and got three machines.

"Hello, this is Alex. I'm in the city—just for a day. I'm going back tomorrow morning—early. Just wanted to say hi. I'm at the Gramercy Park, Room 551. Call me, although I'll be out tonight. Ciao."

"Hello, Ted and Luc. This is Alex. I'm not at home. I'm at the Gramercy Park. Just calling to say hi. I hope your cold is better, Luc. And Ted, I loved your piece in *Harper's*. Wish I had written it. Great ending—so touching. Hope the trip home went okay. These things are always hard. At least it wasn't too drawn out. Well, love from me."

"Hi!" Alex had gotten a third machine, and then the beep, and was starting to say the minimum. Diana Harbison, curator of ancient coins at the Met, was someone who phoned often—sometimes it was business, sometimes not—but Alex, bored with this woman, her job, and her troubles, returned her calls only during work hours when the machine was on.

"Alex Morgan!" he heard. "Are you back from the dead?" She laughed.

"I can't talk, Diana. I'm in a pay phone."

"Oh."

"Diana, I meant to call you last week, but work piled up and I haven't been feeling all that well."

"Oh?"

"Nothing tragic. Slight swimmer's ear, but I'm on an antibiotic. It makes me feel very weak is all, which is why I've got to run. Daria's meeting me at the Dia Center and —."

"You're in Manhattan?"

"Unfortunately. I have to leave tomorrow."

"Oh. I have some things I wanted you to look over. Are you sure you won't have even twenty minutes—today or tomorrow, even late tonight? The fee's good."

"You know I would, Diana, if I could."

"Love to Daria."

Diana Bloody Harbison, oh God! To think that she'd picked up! It was 2:30 on a Friday. What the Christ was she doing home!

His mood—propped all day, through the trip and into the city, and past the first part of what should have been a flawless day and night—was sunk just by the sound of that woman's voice. He kicked off the sheet and blankets and just lay there, his arms flung out, half freezing, on the naked bed. He had to cleanse himself of this irritant.

A scalding shower, two glasses of water, and a speed walk to Spring Street bookstore and back—some forty blocks in toto, as he told himself—put that harpy, bursting onto the scene, out of his mind. It was a physical thing. His body was healthy, the male element, and he used it to discipline the weaker anima. It was darker now, lights coming on, and his coat was not thick enough, so he jogged the last four blocks, and that felt great, although now he'd need a third shower. There was time.

First he picked up his messages at the front desk. There were several, and his heart stopped at the thought of a cancellation. But no. It was just the people he'd rung earlier, returning his calls—hi, no need to call back. There was a third message, stuck to the second. Would his heart stop? It was who he thought it was. Was it a confirmation? No, it was (he couldn't *believe* this!) a summons (relayed by the department secretary) to join M/Mrs. J.C.R. LeDuc for cocktails, if he was free. "Free!" he moaned, and the deskmen looked up. "Sorry," he said. "I'm all right. It's just——." The clerks waited. "Nothing," he said, his hand brushing the air toward them. "Wait a minute. Could you dial this (handing over the pink slip)? Please, it's an emergency. Is there a phone I could take it on?

"Bring me a very cold beer. I don't care what kind. Please." He rushed to the sofa. While he waited for the ring, he composed himself. He was forty, he had a right to some self-command. The phone rang. Then the beer arrived on a tray, but he didn't drink it.

"Professor LeDuc? Alex Morgan here. Thank you so much for the kind invitation. Yes, very much. It would take me" (he glanced at his watch—he wasn't wearing it) "no more than, say, an hour. Oh, really? That's too late, is it? No, that's all right. No problem at all. I'll see you then at 7:30. Great. I can't tell you how happy I am to finally meet you. And your wife, too. Mrs. LeDuc. Timothea, yes. The Barrons, Geoff and Eleanor, speak so well of her. Yes, we know them. Well, *a presto,* then."

He hung up, lay back on the couch, caught his breath,

touched the beer bottle—not nearly cold enough. "Excuse me," he called to the barman, but if the man could hear, he pretended not to. When Alex turned to the desk, one of the clerks was on the phone, the others were gone. Alex closed his eyes; he didn't want to waste energy fighting them. He sipped the beer. What was it? Kronenberg. He drank half of it, left a five, and raced up the steps to the fifth floor. He only had an hour and there was much to prepare.

When he got to his room, unlocked and pushed open the door, he nearly dropped dead. "What are you *doing* here?"

Daria was sitting on the bed, pulling on ballet flats. Her high-heeled boots were tossed on the floor.

She smiled. "Don't be mad," she said, rising, reaching to touch his shoulders, kissing him on the cheek. "I took a later train. Everything I wanted to do today was done. I missed you." Daria smiled at her tall and so bewildered husband—but he was always bewildered. The smallest oddity, the slightest surprise, even a change in customary wording, and he was flummoxed. But this was more. His face was brick-colored and his bewilderment was not a mask for something else. Daria knew her husband: she watched him regather his wits. His welcoming grin faded, the brick color cooled, and she had the sense, for a moment, that she could look right through his head. His eyes were like clear tunnels. Slowly, painfully (it looked like pain to her—she could almost see his bones contracting, the brain signaling in all directions), he was back again. His mouth hardened into shape. He blinked.

"God!" she said. "I really scared you, didn't I? I'm sorry."

Alex folded his wife in his arms to avoid looking into those curious eyes. Instead, he saw the bed stripped bare. He told himself to wait and, if she asked, to say the simplest thing. ("I took a nap. When I tell you what just happened, you'll understand.") But she didn't ask, so he drew her over to the chairs near the window and showed her the pink slip with the invitation. His mind and face were clear now: she'd know what this meant. Nothing else mattered.

Daria glanced at the message. At first, she didn't recognize the name. Alex had referred to today's dignitary only as "the Burton-Rothschild Professor." When she'd asked who exactly this was, he just glared. So this "M/Mrs. J.L.R. LeDuc" meant nothing at all. But she'd learned never to show Alex a trace of her bewilderment. It threw him into a rage. He'd never hit her, but he could be abusive with words. And then it never amounted to anything. After an hour, he'd forget. He'd be shocked to find (in the earliest days) her overnight bag packed or to see her perched on the bathtub rim sobbing or staring out the bedroom window.

His reaction—so out of proportion to the cause—*had* to be avoided. It cost too much in anxiety and stomach acid. So Daria had learned, after a month of marriage—perhaps even earlier, when still dating the Rhodes scholar, Yale Younger Poet, and classics student—to present a composed face: awake, calm, disinterested, no matter what. His own face might be contorted, jaws grinding, eyes popping, but he still didn't need any extra stimulation from his wife (or girlfriend), even when they were making love. It was odd, but it was his only major flaw. No, she corrected herself, he had a few others. He was a snob, moody, and snapped at people whenever he felt like it, yet all his faults, totaled, amounted to very little. She loved him. She'd do anything to keep him happy—of course, he was never really happy, but just to keep him from being too *un*happy.

So, when she read the script on the pink slip and didn't get it, she took the second or two to prepare herself before facing him. "I'm sorry, darling, but I don't recognize the name."

He snapped. *Why* didn't she? Was she a fool? What had he been talking about these last weeks practically twenty-four hours a day? He got up to pace, but by then she had it.

"Alex," she said, "is this guy the Burton-Rothschild?" She braced herself for the look she got.

"Who do you think? What planet have you been on?"

"You never mentioned him by name."

He flared, but it blew over. He knew he'd said it, spelled it out, chanted it. She just hadn't bothered to take it in, like everything else that mattered to him.

He cooled fast; then he nearly laughed. "You know, I think you're right. I probably didn't mention the name. That's what they call him at school—can you believe it?—'the Burton-Rothschild chair.' Isn't that inane?"

Daria was silent.

"*Now* do you see?" he asked, and without rereading the message, she got up to console him for the missed opportunity to join the Burton-Rothschild, and wife, for cocktails. He accepted the solacing words.

She had not been invited to his dinner. She would come anyway. This is what he was thinking. Daria was reading the other pink slips. Alex walked to the bathroom, closed and locked the door behind him. His thoughts had been arranged for days. He didn't know the restaurant—that much would be uncharted— but he had already blocked out the principal actions. There were three things (compliments about the Burton-Rothschild's latest book and Professor Archivault's monograph, the inquiry about the Lexicon) he must find time and occasion to say— perhaps even to say twice. There were unknown factors: how the others would be feeling, and what they would say, and how much of their time would be eaten up by dinner and wines, service and ritual. There should be time for everything, but it had all been arrayed—a dress rehearsal played out in his mind—without calculating the presence of his wife. Should she—he lowered his head almost to his knees, knocking his skull with his fists—attend? What exactly would be her effect?

But already she was interrupting, tapping on the bathroom door. "Are you all right? Alex?"

He didn't answer.

"Alex, I think you're worried about the dinner, aren't you? I'm not going to it. I just wanted to come up to New York. I'll take a long walk in the morning. I needed a change of scene. Alex?"

"What?"

"Did you hear what I said?"

" . . . "

"Are you going to answer me?"

"I'm thinking."

" . . . "

"Daria? Are you there? I can't decide. Can you give me a minute?"

"I don't even want to go, Alex," she said. "I brought clothes, though, so don't worry. I brought clothes *and* jewelry, so I'll leave it up to you."

Daria heard no more. But after 10 minutes, when the toilet flushed and water from the shower broke into the tub, she guessed what he wanted, so she began to lay out clothes and three sets of necklaces and earrings. Alex liked to pick the jewelry.

And, sure enough, when he emerged from the bathroom, steam rolling out from the opened door, he walked over to the strings of silver, gold, and pearl, looked them over, and brushed aside all but the silver necklace and ear drops.

She knew enough not to break his concentration with an idle question, but she watched to see what he would wear. He had packed his best jacket and three shirts, two ties, and a black cashmere sweater. He tried on jacket and tie, shirt and sweater. Then he sat on the bed with his head in his hand until, she expected, he could picture the exact effect.

What would it be? Shirt and tie, but then he added a scarf—

the green silk jacquard—and just hung it, like a priest's stole, around his neck. His wet hair was combed, then brushed, his cheeks were freshly shaved. There was the lightest of scents— aftershave, maybe, or just bath soap. He was—she looked out of the corner of her eye—the picture of careless hauteur. He could be other pictures, but he had chosen that one, so she took her cue and piled her back hair in a loose knot on her head and removed the jacket from her sheath to display her neck and throat. Without having to ask, she clasped the pearls—not the silver—around her heck and inserted pearl studs. When he inspected her (if he got the chance, and had the peace of mind), he'd be pleased.

But he rushed her out ("Where's your coat?"), down the elevator, and into a taxi before she'd even put on lipstick. She carried one in her purse and would use the taxi window as a mirror. She watched while mid- and upper Madison Avenue flew by.

Before the taxi turned right on 72d, Alex took her wrist, stripped off the glove, and pressed her hand against his shirt. Yes, she felt his heart racing. She caught his eye for the first time since surprising him in the hotel room. Seeing those fierce, glassy eyes and clamped jaw, she knew he wanted to push all that *he* had thought and planned from his head into hers. He squeezed her hand. With her eyes she tried to say that everything was understood.

He had already dropped her hand and was reaching for his wallet.

The restaurant was Tuscan gold and greens. The furniture was light wood, the table cloths a reddish Italian weave. There were weavings and pottery hung on the walls. Straw flowers were massed in burnished tubs. As they entered there was a ripple of attention, but Daria could tell that—in the clusters of still faces, sumptuous fabrics, and cool gems—the scholar-poet, suave and shapely though he was, caused no head to turn. His jacket was three years old, too narrow in the body for fashion. He was a bit narrow himself, and elegant New York had by now fattened and toned. There was too much tension in his face. She knew this even though she couldn't see his face as Alex paced ahead, spotting his party in a corner. Only when he had arrived there at the oval table, did he stop and—before shaking hands—turn, track back, and guide his partner, in her velvet sheath—dark and lush, with the blackest hair and golden skin, a princess (heads turned ever so slightly)—to the spot.

There, both men had risen. There was a bustle to find the choicest place for this divine. Even the wives seemed struck.

Only one of them—Timothea LeDuc—knew enough to appraise the newcomer: dress, bones, gems, scent, nails; and then: voice, age, teeth, neck, graces of manner, gesture, speech. It was the work of hours, really, and Timmy felt invited to return the newcomer's gaze. She was no longer stifled, bored. The dinner began.

At first, nothing. Noise. Bread torn from the loaf, wine circling in glasses, slop-over of a salsa verde on the woven tablecloth, the nerve-shattering scratch of a heavy fork on ceramic. Alex's face flamed as conversations sputtered and went out or bubbled with an unknown heat or passed over his head like mountain weather. In each of these, he worked to fashion an opening: sometimes he managed; more often his fashioning was on the wrong scale or too fussy or not fussy enough, and it was ignored, or put to one side while the talk continued. Once, twice at most, he said the right thing and the conversation paused. Daria noticed faces starting to relax, and something like an opening made for her husband, who had been blocked by turned shoulders and backs of heads, dead eyes and hands held up to halt his entry into something far too intriguing to be interrupted.

Alex scarcely touched the food—carpaccio, pappardelle, veal chop—but he was forever reaching for wine, although

LeDuc had clearly assigned himself (speaking twice to the waiter) the honors of wine-pourer and had flashed the younger scholar a fierce look. Daria noticed and tapped Alex's leg. He brushed off her hand but then clutched it, squeezing. His hand was clammy.

Then, swallowing more wine and the dregs of his iced cocktail, which—since he'd ordered late—was melting in the glass, he leapt in.

At first, they wouldn't hear him. He raised his voice. It was too loud, Daria thought, noticing that diners nearby had heard, and stopped chewing to look.

"I don't know that anyone here is aware of the fact," he restarted, once he'd caught their ears, "that I've been working on a kind of project—"

"Congratulations," Timmy said. Her husband had written and published twelve such projects. (She was the other diner at the table who poured her own wine.)

"Thank you," said Alex. "I wasn't fishing. The project treats—" he went on. "It doesn't really matter," he quickly added, when he saw that this was exactly what they wouldn't want to hear—from him. Their eyes said it. Didn't he know? He'd been invited, singled out, because they thought he *did* know.

"And a night student has come up with . . ." Now he had their attention.

"—the thesis!" shrilled Timmy. Everybody laughed. This was the beginning of the kind of story they liked.

"What I'm trying to say is, an auditor in my seminar, a boy from the writing program, has produced a reading of the Augustan poets that precisely" (his hands were working—*now* he had them) "bombs scholarship of the last fifty, maybe a hundred years, right back to the Stone Age."

"Who is this?" asked the Burton-Rothschild. "Maybe I know him."

"I don't know the name. He's an auditor."

"What is he—or she—it *could* be a she," said Professor Archivault, "going to do with this thesis?"

Alex waited. The busboy was pouring ice water. He poured a splash into each goblet. Alex drank his water and the busboy returned with the pitcher.

"The question is: what am *I* going to do with it? The boy's a writer, a poet. it's of no value to him."

"No *value!*" said Archivault.

"It's happened before, Professor Morgan," said the Burton-Rothschild. ("Please call me Alex," Alex could have said once more, but even he could see that the chaired eminence preferred formality.)

"Don't I know!" replied Alex. He was flaring, Daria could see. Don't flare up here, she telegraphed with her eyes. Not here.

"Excuse me," said Archivault, listening intently but signaling the wine steward to bring the fourth and fifth bottles he had preordered.

The bottles arrived with fresh glasses. Plates were removed and salad plates set on a table swept of crumbs and laid with individual white cloths.

All eyes were on Alex, no more than fifteen years out of grad school, freshly tenured, in a department that meant little to anybody, so depleted was it, through retirement or death, of great names. The Burton-Rothschild was part of the old greatness that had been American classics. He would retire himself in a year. So little was left. This was plain when a chap like Morgan—a trivialist, a politician—stood for a generation of students of the ancient worlds. He had the credentials, yes, the looks and the money—but he was shallow, mean (everyone could see how he treated his inferiors), and corrupt to boot. The Burton-Rothschild closed his eyes. This was something he liked to do. People at his table knew what it meant.

Seeing this, Timothea excused herself. Archivault tried to engage Daria in talk—anything at all—about herself. When LeDuc ducked inside like this, it was, all his intimates knew, best to let him find his own way back. And then not to call attention to it.

Before Timothea returned, bright-eyed, restored, the Burton-Rothschild had reemerged. Not looking at Morgan, he said to the air: "I'd still like to know, if you'd have the kindness—or maybe I should say the 'brass'—to tell us, what you're going to do with this student's gem. Or would you prefer not to say?" he added. Out of the corner of his eye, he glimpsed his tipsy wife making her way back to the table.

Alex, after moving bottle number four (a nice Barolo) to his place mat, with number five (not as good) in arm's reach, laid his hands on the table and leaned in. "Dr. LeDuc, you seem to have forgotten that I was *telling* this story on myself, so your sarcasm is wholly unwarranted and untimely." He addressed the table: "May I continue?"

But here (the salad plates had been gathered and replaced with small menus on cards) was a call for dessert. The maître d' had attached himself to their table and stood ready to recite the specials with basic ingredients and garnishes.

"Is it too much to ask," Alex said to the maître d', but including the waiters circling the table, handing and unhanding china, flicking out their metal scrapers to collect crumbs, "to be left in peace for five minutes? You don't seem to comprehend," he continued. "We didn't come here to share our meal with you! Or them!" he said, indicating with his knuckles, the wine and table staff.

"Now just one moment, if you please," Professor Archivault was saying. He'd plucked the maître d's sleeve, preventing his retreat.

"These kind people have been gracious to you, Mr. Morgan. There's no reason to insult them. Come back a minute, Eric," he signaled to the maître d', but Eric had, by then, pulled off the table's crew and was making for the swing doors. He'd send the busboy for desserts.

"I won't have this, Morgan," continued Professor Archivault.

He rarely found his tongue in company, but fortified by the rich dinner and wines, he recollected that this was his turf, *his* restaurant—his head waiter, as it were.

"This is just a restaurant," Alex said testily. "We're paying, don't you see, for the privilege of eating in public, unmolested! Food is brought, drinks, and the table attended to, by strangers, who should stay strangers. That's the bargain. It's sheer masochism—although all too common here—to let the service staff march right in and sit down. As *these* have."

"That's right," said Timmy, who moved bottle number five onto *her* place mat.

"Can we change the subject, please?" said Mrs. Archivault. Skinny, pale, thirty years younger than her illustrious husband, Anne Archivault never spoke on these occasions, although she was often spoken about, and for. "I, for one, don't need this."

Now it was Daria's turn to flee to the ladies' room. Alex tried to stop her, first by looks, then by a rap on the table. "Where are you going?" he hissed. "Can't you wait till I've finished my story? We haven't even ordered dessert."

Daria eased back into her chair, then stood up again. "I'm sorry. I'll be back."

"Don't go!" he said.

"Let your wife go to the bathroom," said Timmy. "Who do you think you are, King Tut? Go ahead, dear. I'll take care of this bully boy," and with this, Timmy moved into Daria's chair.

"Timothea," Dr. LeDuc said, "come back to your own place, please."

"No, thank you," Timmy said, exchanging water glasses and attempting to move her wine bottle, so that it stood near, and available to, Alex.

Alex rested his head on his hands, elbows on the table. This was inconceivable. This was a nightmare.

*A*fter the long silence at table, Daria returned, dessert menus were collected, and their waiter—not a busboy—was ready to take orders. At first no one wanted any, but seeing that politeness required a show of normalcy, the ladies ordered poached pears with blackberries and the gentlemen flourless cake, grapefruit sorbetto, and panna cotta. There were decaf espressos, decaf cappucinos, and tea for Alex.

The LeDucs had just purchased land in Rhode Island and planned to build this summer. (The Burton-Rothschild tried this out, while awaiting their orders.)

"How wonderful. My family has a place at Watch Hill," Daria said. "We love Rhode Island. Where is the land exactly?"

"Where is it?" the Burton-Rothschild asked Timothea, who, luckily, was paying attention.

" 'Little Something,' " she said.

"It *is* called Little Rhody," the Burton-Rothschild joked. "We just bought the property. Twenty acres of grazing land overlooking the ocean."

"Little something," repeated Daria, "on grazing land overlooking the ocean." She closed her eyes. "That would be . . ." Her inner eye traveled up the coast from Westerly. "Is it Little Compton?" she asked. Little Compton was beautiful.

"Yes," said Timmy, "that sounds right. What did you say it was?"

"Little Compton."

"Is there," Dr. Archivault asked, smiling, "a '*Big* Compton'?"

"I don't think so," said Daria. "To tell the truth, I don't know why it's called Little Compton, because most everything near the water is Narragansett Indian. Except Watch Hill, of course."

"I've heard of Watch Hill," said Timmy. "That's quite the nice address. Did the Kennedys live there? Or was it the Auchinclosses?"

"So," said Alex (who hated name-dropping), "you're planning to build."

Then Timmy nearly knocked over her wine glass, reaching for the sugar bowl.

"Timothea," her husband said, "I think you've had enough

wine. Eat your fruit," he commanded, then added in a friend-
lier tone: "It looks good. What is it? Blackberries, raspberries?"

Timothea didn't answer.

"There are lots of wild berries in Rhode Island," Daria said,
"and the air smells of honeysuckle and wild roses. You'll love
it. We've gone there since we were kids."

"That's very interesting," the Burton-Rothschild said. "I
thought Rhode Island was mostly immigrant Irish or Yankee.
You're not either one, are you?"

"I'm not," said Daria, smiling at this absurdity, "Irish or Yankee. I'm not Italian either. Half the state is Italian."

"What does that leave?" the Burton-Rothschild said, smiling
back at this beautiful girl. "You're not Native American or
Canadian French, I don't think."

"I don't think," she replied.

Alex wanted to get in on this friendliness but didn't know
where it was leading. "What does it matter?" he said "By their
standards, she's not a native Rhode Islander. Virtually no one
is, except the Indians."

There was a lull. The waiter brought them vin santo and bis-
cotti. "Tell me, Daria, then, what are you?" the Burton-Rothschild persisted. "You're not Indian, not Canadian, not Yankee. You're not Italian, although you look Italian."

"What's your maiden name?" said Timmy, plunging in.

"It won't help you," said Daria.

"Try us," said Timmy.

But the Burton-Rothschild didn't want his wife butting in
on this fun. He knew, in any case, that Alex and his wife,
Daria—even if their name was Morgan—were both Jewish.
How did he know? He just knew. How her family came to own
property—a summer home in Watch Hill, no less—in Rhode
Island, he didn't know, but things had changed everywhere.
It was pretty damn plucky of them to pull it off *before* things
had changed. He was finished with his dessert, and the con-
versational gambit had grown stale. It was time to settle up.

He turned to Archivault. "Would you ask for the check, Archie?"

Then it dawned on him. "You never finished your story, Morgan. You teased us with the opening. Tell all," He then pulled the check from Archie's hand. "The department will pay. Now sing for your supper!" he commanded.

"No," said Alex, "Daria and I would like to take *you* to dinner. The check is ours."

"Not if I have it to hand," said the Burton-Rothschild.

"Absolutely not!" said Alex. "I'd always thought of this as our treat for you—and the Archivaults. So please hand it over." He paused. He'd let himself go a little; half his sails were stiff with wind. "Unless you want me to take it by force. I don't think you'd want that, Professor LeDuc?" he said, smiling.

Was this supposed to be funny? Everyone knew that the Burton-Rothschild had a heart condition and a withered arm. He had back trouble, diabetes, and was overweight. But he wouldn't give over the check. "Sing for your supper," he said.

Alex pushed out from the table. "What are you doing?" his wife asked him.

"I'm going to get another check."

But, of course, the maître d', the waiter, the owner—who was never too far off the scene—wouldn't, in a million years, release the tab to this grotesque, although to a man they were polite.

Alex was cornered. He stood in the middle of the restaurant. It was quiet now. Only three tables were occupied. The smell of roast meat, garlic, and ground coffee was less intense. Now there was the faintest odor of detergent, as the staff had begun to clean the kitchen.

Alex stood still.

At the table, Daria thanked the LeDucs for the fine dinner, offering to sing for *her* supper. That's what Alex would discover in future days. She looked the endowed chair in the eye and said, "Is that just as good?" and yes, he said, it was.

"Latvia was where my father's family started out. But naturally Latvia was no place for Jews in the late thirties, so they came via Cuba to Manhattan. My mother's family," she went on, "has been in America since the early 1600s."

"And your mother's people are . . . ?" Timmy asked.

"They were originally from Holland."

"Holland?" the LeDucs said together.

"Yes."

"Your mother is from a Dutch colonial family?" asked LeDuc.

"My mother's family is Dutch."

"Oh, how nice," said Timmy. "Dutch and Latvian." And with that she checked with all eyes at the table. "Now *that's* a combination!"

Alex was by then reseated. He'd accepted his defeat. The air was thinner, less poisonous, although it smelled—because of the cleaning fluids—*more* poisonous.

"Well," the Burton-Rothschild was saying, as he signed for dinner. "I've enjoyed myself tonight, no question about it." He was smiling. He was patting Mrs. Archivault on the back. "I like a little tilt, a good scrap. I hate to be bored.

"Dr. Morgan," he said across the table, "you're a most fortunate man."

Alex looked up, alert. "In what way?" he asked.

"For one, you have for a wife a Dutch royal princess—with the eyes of a gypsy." He continued, without pause. "*And,* I've been meaning to ask you all night, Alex—may I call you Alex?—about a project of my own. The working title—perhaps you've heard of it—-is the Burton-Rothschild Lexicon Latinitatis. I'm not sure you have the time, what with your teaching duties and your research. But perhaps you'd give me a call one day, at the university, and we could discuss this further."

Bewildered, flooded with feeling, Alex couldn't speak, but he listened as his wife answered for him, speaking his eagerness and gratitude. Then, still in a fever, Alex found his words. "Professor LeDuc, Professor Archivault," he nodded to each, "and ladies."

"Here, here!" said Timmy, knocking the side of her water glass with a fork.

Alex let fall a hand onto Timmy's wrist, drawing it close to him and clamping it to the table. "My friends," he said.

Timothea felt the goose flesh rising up her leg (or was it a run in her stocking?). She fixed her eyes on this bumptious young god, "a genius," her husband had said—or was he speaking of some other young lexical assistant? There must be twenty of them, and each a rising academic star—like her own Jackie, forty years ago, bounding out of Harvard College, out of Princeton, on to All Souls', then back. Timmy (or "Timmo," as they called her at Oxford) would have raised her glass in a toast, if her neighbor wasn't squeezing her wrist so tight! How dare you! she would have said, if she trusted her voice.

But he was talking. Timmy tried to listen. There was so much going on—in her head, at the table, behind her chair, to the left, to the right. It was hard to focus her attention on that grating voice. Why *was* it so grating?

"Thrilled and grateful," she heard. "Incredibly delighted!" What could be so delightful? Why was he making her so angry? Her wrist was still bound by his hand, clamped to the table. Her fingers were starting to tingle.

What now? Titles of her husband's twelve books, *The Pergamus, Ilium on the Tiber, Horace: The Complete Works, An Annotated Translation*. Each book she had read. In fact she'd typed some of them, using that special typewriter with the italic typeface. She'd typed them out in all the different houses—first there'd been the carriage house, then a row house where they boarded that art historian, and three real houses with gardens, four children; three boys, then Claudia eight years later. Life, *this* was life. What did this loud, grating voice know about life? He didn't have any children that she had heard about.

Her arm ached, the fingers stinging from the steady pressure, the blood stopped at the wrist. Then, with all her might, she wrenched the fettered arm free, just as his own hand was relaxing its grip. Up flew the arm, striking with the oversized watch Dr. Morgan's right eye. He cried out. Something flashed in his head, then a tunnel extended from the eyeball to the white table.

Waiters rushed in. Ice was wrapped in towels and napkins. Packs were laid on his head, cold water dripping down his cheek.

Was his eye still there? He couldn't feel it. Slowly, he opened the good eye and saw, first, the ring of bodies with heads pitched forward, the strain in those faces. Daria was not there. Where was Daria? "Daria!" he shouted, and pain stabbed his face. Still his hand was cupping his hurt eye. He removed the hand, but the eyelid wouldn't open.

"Here I am," Daria was saying. She was holding him in his chair. He was all right; he'd be all right soon. They were taking him to the hospital. New York had the finest eye clinics in the world. The eye, someone was saying, is a strong organ, resilient for all its sensitivity.

Tears flushed Alex's uninjured eye. Daria had sunk into a chair next to his. She stroked his damp head—the hair streaked with blood and ice water.

In the cave of pain that Alex had entered, there was nothing but chaos and blinding light. But when the medics rushed in, and he heard that the eye was intact—they ought to be able to save it, even some sight—he finally closed the other eye. He let Daria watch over him; he let Daria forgive and dismiss the panicky professor and the weeping wife. There'd be a price to pay, of course, but he didn't need to think about that yet. He let himself settle into this much-desired cone of quiet, of whiteness.

In the ambulance, medicine coursing through his veins sheathed the pain. Now they were at the hospital. Even before he had fallen asleep on the gurney, rolled under the hot lights, he knew that his suffering was but a small price to pay for the Latin house that the duke (the medicine ushered him into a realm beyond pain), the barons, and the Caesar-Rothschilds were renting for him. Was it a house or a horse? Would he be in the horse, or on it? No answer to be found, standing impotent with glaring eye, sealed off from the mob.

The Thin Man

In one year I lost a hundred pounds. Another seventy-five came off and I could see my feet. My hands were like x-rays. Even my tongue was reduced: in my mouth there was now room for it to loll within its ivory colonnade. My face, lately so tight-packed with meat, became a different face: the eyes had room to open, the mouth to spread. In time my rosy skin tightened around facial bones lost to me all those years, just as they had been lost to my family, because it was my father's face, and his father's—too late, though, for him to see and love.

I discarded the tent-like shirts, the jumbo suits. My shoes were so wide and shapeless that I was embarrassed to turn them over to Goodwill; instead, I wrapped them in newspaper, like garbage, and dropped them—one pair every few days—in the trash can. The two cashmere coats and camel-hair jacket I kept. Seamed up the back, up the sleeves, and at the neck, they were wearable, even stylishly roomy.

I changed apartments, taking a bigger place higher in the building, with a view to the Hudson. The big chairs and four-seater couch, reupholstered and restuffed, and with new springs, looked marooned in the lofty living room, all windows on the west.

I kept the bed, but threw out the mattress with the deep gulley on the left, where I always sleep so my arm can hang over the side. I bought a new one, extra-hard, and enjoyed stretching myself across its rigid coils, space under the arch of my back and under my knees and ankles. Space was still a fresh sensation. There was so much more of it, and of the world, and I fit into it, or so I thought, like an old-fashioned latchkey.

How fat is fat? I smoked too. Never for more than minutes at a time was my mouth empty or my arms slack at my sides. It was a whole life—there was no break in the smooth flow of activity, all of it aimed at procurement and consumption.

But how fat is fat? Doctors would say that the limit is set by the elasticity of the skin, the flexibility of the joints, and, of course, the strength of the heart, weakened by its huge house-keeping task and by the rings of adipose that squeeze and clog its valves and hoses.

Death is a limit and so is genetic inheritance. But I exceeded the latter and eluded the former, turning my doctors into gamblers. I stretched the limit of their training, their prudence. I was more than an experiment: I was the rat and scientist, and also the funding arm. I discovered, in the process, what most people outside the profession don't know: that doctors are bored with health. What interests them is the contest between the body, a slave, and its slave driver, or that between the slave and the world, so often an aggressor.

Today is my birthday. I'm forty, but I look younger—or at least I did when I was fat. The loss has caused my skin to crinkle. On the back of my hand is, up close, a pattern of squares that, were it not for the peach color, might seem a reptile's hide. Thin, fine, loose, patterned.

Actually, I'm forty-one. When I was forty, and still fat, my friends threw me a birthday party in a roof garden. They surprised me by appearing, late afternoon, at the door of my ground-floor apartment: Terence, Caroline, Isabel, Philip, and Mona; others, too. They were not all fat, but each had a pe-culiarity that, I suspect, was the real basis of our attachment.

Sipping cocktails, we looked the way odd-looking or afflicted people often do, as if our clothes were picked to magnify our defects. Mona, almost as fat as I, was normally proportioned, with enormous curvy legs. She favored a high-heeled Mary Jane whose strap cut off the foot and framed the delicate joint that blossomed into that huge limb. She wore the thinnest nylon stockings.

Philip, her husband, had no shoulders to speak of. His chest narrowed into his neck, so that the arms appeared to sprout directly from the spine. Philip favored jackets with no padding, their slack lines offering no relief from the sight of his puddling torso.

But that was age forty, when I was prized for the loving comfort that, most think, is lodged by nature in a fat person, whose sociability can, therefore, never be exhausted. However, I did not exactly have that nature. Or, if I did, things had changed. I would describe myself as the opposite of inexhaustible. I am nut-like, with a rich complex surface and savory odor. My covering is almost as various as my meats.

But, at forty-one, here is my birthday cake: angel food with white icing. Diet beverages poured into goblets and low-fat vanilla yogurt. I've always loved white. White peaches are heaped in a bowl, and there's a plate of artificially sweetened white chocolate. These are mine. For my guests I've bought my old favorite, Autumn Rose— layers of raspberry and chocolate mousse, with a great bittersweet chocolate rose, heavy and sumptuous, spread over the top. Then coffee and cream, chocolate truffles, and fresh raspberries to cleanse the palate.

"Happy birthday, dear Las," they're just about to say, and to wish me well. All normal-sized men and women, slight acquaintances, their luster is illusion. They disturb nothing, break no chairs, crowd no rooms, crack no toilet seats, suffocate no brides. The Autumn Rose is, to them, dark-hearted and oppressive. They can eat but a sliver of its richness. For them, consuming is nugatory, even to those who call themselves gourmands. They could never eat their weight in pig, or in apples.

*I*t is eventide. I say it that way because, as a torpid youth, I sang the evensong at John the Divine's before my voice, thin as a reed, broke in the tough organ of my throat. My party is over. The Autumn Rose, missing but an 18-degree wedge, has been sliced and plated by the sisters of St. James and fed to the orphans for supper. The truffles are with the concierge, the saccharine-sweetened angel cake is refrigerated in my own kitchen (a first!), and the carton of yogurt stands alone in my freezer. I'm walking the West Side streets, one day into forty-one, my thin soles slapping the sidewalks, strewn here with broken glass, there with the TV page of the *Times,* and, drifted against walls, the sand that's left over at the end of winter, but gone by spring, although no one sweeps it.

In my pocket, as I flank the park at Seventy-second, is a telephone number and a birthday handkerchief. Now that I've whittled my life down, people are already slipping things into it. This is the idea: a fat person's life is his fat, its maintenance, its carriage and deployment, its sign value among the ordinary, the normal. It's a full and satisfying life, free of questions, doubts, that swelling emptiness that fills the normal with despair.

Now *I* am normal, or am I not? This, on my forty-first birthday, is the question, now that the festivities are over and I face the coming years in my shrinkage.

A woman spots me from the park side of the street. At the end of her lead is a black-and-white dog, busy with his trees. I cross the street, the dog sniffs me, and the girl hurries along, yanking at the dog's muscular neck. I watch them approach the corner, turn, and disappear in the canyon of gray buildings. When I reach the crossing, I look, and she's turned back, holding the dog still. Then she shouts from a block away: "LaSalle, is that you?" She shields her eyes, but there's no sun in the street.

I don't answer, so she's nearly turned back, and the dog is already on the trot, then she whirls back again. "It is! I know it is!" she shouts, and I'm still looking. Something roots me to the ground, but no greeting, no sound comes from my mouth.

The dog barks, tugs, saves the day. She's again tracking behind him toward Amsterdam, then left. I watch—the slender back whose ribs I once numbered, whose spine like a string of freshwater pearls I fingered, whose neck could be clasped by one hand. She lived—there was no spotted dog then—in a one-bedroom flat, walls and ceiling painted the tenderest yellow. The furniture was white wicker on a blue cloth rug, a wrought-iron bedstead piled with quilts and curtains of dotted swiss. I liked to visit her—Marguerite, now I remember—although there was no place for me to sit. My first visit, I lowered myself onto the cloth rug, legs straight out, back against the wall, but getting up was hard, or maybe—I'd thought for a moment—impossible. I asked her to get me a glass of water, and while she was gone, I began my maneuvers, tucking up my legs, bracing my arms, and hoisting—only to slump back down. I was too heavy for my arms. She returned with the water and, seeing me, excused herself again. I rolled onto my side and with one hand on the arm of the couch and one on the floor, I knelt, straightened my back (aching from its rigid position); then, with an effort that brought tears to my eyes, I launched: pulled one kneeling leg up and positioned it on its foot, then—my hands like plungers—balancing on one foot, drew the other bent knee forward, pressing its shoe to the floor, then—with the greatest effort—I lifted myself onto my legs, half-asleep, stinging and trembling.

It was then that Marguerite reappeared with two glasses of wine and, on her pretty face, a smile—the sweetest I'd seen since last my father, presenting me with the featherweight of his glance, spread his lips over ivory teeth, each with its own slant.

I drank the wine standing. We looked through Marguerite's sheer curtains onto Murray Hill. It was a warm night, breezy, and strolling couples, coming from dinner, were bathed in light from the full moon.

From that day forward, and for three months, I spent every night at Marguerite's, or occasionally Marguerite spent the night with me. I can still feel her slim form rolled next to mine, her face pressed into my arm, her feet squeezed under my shins; sometimes her hands wormed themselves under the arch of my back, until my weight stopped her circulation. When I woke, her arms would be laced around my head.

That the filigreed bedstead supported my weight and hers seemed a miracle, until I happened to notice, stooping to pick up a cufflink, that one of its legs had bent, canted inward, and when I reached under to grasp the springs and shook, perhaps yanked, the bed out of alignment, or stressed the point where the metal fatigue was greatest, the bed collapsed onto my hand. Marguerite was at work. I left, walked the forty blocks north, and then across the park, with the deafening sound ringing in my ears and another set of fiery rings coiling up my arm.

By the weekend Marguerite had installed a large new wooden bed, which rested on its square frame, and an extra: a down-filled loveseat, made to last sixty lifetimes, just for me. I could sit, I could lie (I can hear her saying: "LaSalle, you can sit, you can lie"), but although I did come back and sleep at Marguerite's, or she with me, an extra month, it was never the same. I still have the half-moon scar on my palm where a spring gouged me. I didn't even notice until I got to my own place and saw the rivulets of blood, from my raincoat pocket over my pants cuff, falling into the well of one of my bowl-like and broken-down shoes.

At the edge of the park, evensong long over, darkness already filled the cross streets and was now stretching over the park.

My feet in their thin shoes were nearly frozen to the ground, but I pried them loose and continued north, watching the last wands of light pierce the high windows of the east. The twenty-block walk was surprisingly easy, although it was bitter cold and no blubber between my black coat and backbone.

I refused to pad myself with sweater, vest or jacket, preferring to feel the linen of my shirt sliding against the silk lining of my coat, the heft of this coat slung on the hard heels of my shoulders. I liked to rub my toe joints or grind my ankle caps against shoe leather, to remind myself of what was there and what wasn't.

But it *was* cold, and when I arrived at the club on Ninety-fourth, my feet were stiff and bloodless, the cold had penetrated my body, and my teeth were chattering. Luckily, I saw no one I knew and handed over my coat, took a spare jacket and tie from the rack, and proceeded to an armchair next to the fire, but not too near. Coolness, or chill, reminded me of who I now was.

There were papers to read, magazines and books, but I preferred, at forty-one, 6-foot-2, and 185 pounds, to sit on my flattened rump, surrounded by comfort, silence, and blissful solitude. I had this number in my pocket and later I might use it.

My beer was brought to me with ice cubes. A second glass filled with ice, an ashtray, and the box of clove cigarettes.

The beer, with its extra dilution, was a gift to myself for arriving, on my forty-first birthday, at a lightness I had never known. To achieve what I had been, I had sacrificed vocation and hobbies. Of course, I had cooked like an angel, and of course I drank. But I had not restricted myself to savory dishes, succulent fruit, and delicate sauces. I ate anything: penny candy, packaged cupcakes, hot dogs, loaves of fluffy white bread, brown beans, frozen vegetables, dough, marinated mushrooms, rolls of pink bubblegum, fast food, stick food, finger food, diet food, baby food, cookies of all kinds, puddings, ice milk and cream, frozen candy bars, bags of candy corn, brown bananas, cured meats, sponge cake, eggs in any style, even raw. Anything.

It started at two days old, when my mother handed me, screaming, to my father. My father filled my bottle with sugar water and an eyedropperful of whiskey; then, sugar water and paregoric, or barley water and rum; molasses, tea, and port wine. Every bottle was different. I was never bored. I lived, an infant with nothing but urges, for the insertion of that brown nipple between my toothless gums. I slept for the first three months.

My father hired a half-dozen girls to wheel me—for those forty-five minutes when I was awake, filled, flaccid—to the Common where I could ride the swanboats or slump against a tree in my angora suit and hat and feel the sun and shadow, hear the pigeons, the children on roller skates, the calls from the peanut sellers. Otherwise, I was doped and stuffed, spared the agony of infancy, its hungers, its loneliness, its frights and stabbing pain.

Infancy set the gold standard for my life. I kept up with my bottles, moved from spiked formula to whole milk to fine-milled cereals laced with syrup and melted butter. To sleep, I needed to suck—not just for the half-or quarter-hour, but off and on through the full night. First, my mother refilled my bottle several times, tucking it into a special padded holder. Then she had made for me a special quart bottle, so that when I fell into my milky sleep, a nighttime supply—tepid, separating, and sometimes spoiling—was in place.

After that year of babyhood, everything with me was extra, jumbo, hefty; "husky" was the size I wore until, at ten, I needed a man's shirttail and skivvies, and boys' extra-wide trousers. Thence, in prep school, for a short space, to the Big and Tall, and thence to the tailor.

Of him to whom so much is given, something rare is asked in return. No one had to tell me this. As a child, I shared my toys; I gave them away. In games I always chose the short stick; I was free with money and candy. I took the blame for "accidents," fights, messes, mishaps. Fat, with eyes like slits and hands like hams, I was the most popular boy in school and in town. Everybody wanted to be my friend.

My mother died when I was fifteen and in boarding school. My father died the next year. Summers I spent in camp or in Europe, winters in Vermont. At Christmas I went to an aunt or an uncle, to cousins in Colorado, once to a distant relative of my father, who owned a race track and stud farm. Naturally, I didn't ride, but the horses liked me, and, once I'd learned from the trainers, I was entrusted with the overbred, the skittish, the "mules" to break and saddle. Two of them I turned around: one became Sun Boy, who placed two years consecutively in Kentucky and won the third.

It was different with women. That's when I began to feel the strain. I had no girls in high school. Girls that age invest too much in their eyes and in convention. I was a stag at many parties, but I never stood in line for a popular deb, much less broke up a couple already dancing. I was there for the mothers and fathers, who laughed at my jokes and relished my jabs. Like most boys my age, I was ruthless, literal-minded, and petty.

This passed, and by freshman year—softened by my reading, by summers spent in France and Italy, and, most of all, by my first mistress, a married woman who saw in me what I am today, a man—I kept an eye peeled in classes and my arms open at dances, and in them a dozen wounded creatures rested, huddled, fluffed up their feathers.

My beer had puddled, soaking the linen coaster on the inlaid table. I mopped up and polished with my handkerchief, placing both glasses on the steward's tray. With the handkerchief, the paper with the phone number had popped out of my pocket. I ordered black coffee, lit a cigarette, and opened the folded blue sheet. Written on it, in a loopy, backward-slanting hand, was my mother's (and her mother's) name, Louisa. An address, "10 Rod Road, " and a message: "LaSalle," it read, "when you've finished your work, I'll be eager to hear from you."

I had finished. My coffee arrived and, with it, the battery phone I had requested. The steward showed me where to switch the connection.

"Louisa," I said, when a wispy voice touched my ear, and heat flushed my body and soaked my shirt.

"Yes?" I heard.

The voice was reedy and weak. I thought of the time that had elapsed with its unknown threats and miseries.

"Louisa," I said, "you don't sound strong. LaSalle here. I'm calling from the city."

There was a pause.

"LaSalle," I heard. "I thought it might be you when the phone rang. I thought you might call today."

"Today's my birthday."

"I know." The voice in my ear was smoother, deeper.

"You are all right?"

"I'm fine. Where are you, LaSalle?"

"At the club."

"Could you drive up here tonight? What would it take—two hours? Less?"

"Not tonight, Louisa."

"I see."

"But soon," I added, breaking the connection and laying the slim phone, ear- and mouthpiece down, on the card table.

I ate my lean dinner, drank my single glass of wine, and took a cab to my apartment. My rooms were filled with the scent of hyacinths and roses. I stripped and approached the three-way mirror, whose faces had been folded up and locked for several decades. I unhooked the latch, resting my head for a minute on the beautiful mahogany frame. The mirror had been my father's. It came to me at sixteen, when he died, but then I had no use for it and left it, with his other furnishings and effects, in storage.

When I moved upstairs, I had the mirror, the valet, the boot polisher, dressers, benches, chiffonier, and pant-press delivered, with everything that they contained. These items I installed in my own dressing room. A week ago they had arrived.

And now I had survived forty years of life with three times as much meat as what my father carried when he died. Today I was his weight. Today I had worn his yellow linen shirt, his charcoal gray pants, the socks with clocks, and his silk boxer shorts and undershirt. My life had been stripped down to this—to him in the clothes he wore in the 1930s, when calling in Topsfield on Miss Louisa Leverett Pingree, a spinster of thirty. I opened the mirror's outer faces first: the left, then the right. In that tarnished, sooty glass, I saw a man I'd never known: my collegiate father. I stepped closer. Here were his hairless hands, the tapered fingers and double-jointed thumbs, his straight thin shoulders. I was too excited to look at the face and head. I gazed instead at the tops of the light-brown shoes with, on each, a strip of woven leather over the arch. My feet lay in these shoes, stiff with age, but seasoned a bit by my winter's walk. I felt through the stockings the imprint of my father's lean feet: the deep depressions at the heels and at the root of the big toe, the smooth ovals in a descending line for where the balls of his toes—and mine—rested in the toe box. My feet had been cold and stiff all day, but now, in the warmth of this reflection, they relaxed and filled their places.

And then I looked straight from the shoulders and there, on the mirror's inner panel and just under the frame, was his sandy hair, parted and combed smooth across the crown. A smile—his smile, with the long, narrow, crooked teeth. And his eyes, deep-sunk, large and hazel, ringed by shadows. The high-bridged nose and large ears slightly tipped from the head. Francis Charles, Charles Francis.

I felt light-headed and staggered away from the tripart glass to the sofa, and then folded, head in hands.

When the dizziness passed, I recollected and reached for the phone.

"Thank you, " I said, when the first friend answered. "I am so grateful for the remembrance."

I called all ten—the ten who'd attended the party. Some had already retired: it was after midnight.

My father would have penned notes on his letterhead. I had a ream of it, with my name, which was his name, and his address, which was mine.

Then I played back the messages stored that day on my recorder.

"LaSalle, this is Aunt Catherine. Happy birthday, dear. Many happy returns of the day. And from Uncle Tom, dear LaSalle. We're thinking of you."

Next: "I know it was you. I saw you on Central Park West. It was you, wasn't it? You seemed so strange. I didn't even recognize you. You looked so young. Please call me, LaSalle. I'm leaving my number. Please call. I've never stopped thinking of you."

Second to the last: "LaSalle, or should I say, Francis? My darling Francis. I will always love you. Mother."

The last, I knew, was just Louisa, my cousin—second-cousin Louisa, named after my mother. Twenty years my senior, maybe more. After so many years, I'd found her. First I'd found her name—by chance—in an alumni magazine still being delivered. By then I had begun this. I began it, and now I've finished.

I raised my head. The room was lit by a single lamp—a brass lamp, my charioteer. It shed the light of a bare bulb.

In the mirror's heart, my father was smiling, tooth reflecting tooth, eye on eye, in that lean and hungry head.

With Her

It was only quarter to ten, but Green had been to the men's room twice, slipped a mint between his lips, and examined his neck for rough spots the razor had missed. Both times he had (in an interval of clapping) climbed over the legs of his row, and then he would wait (behind the balcony bar) for the next aria with its spatter of clapping, and back he would go. This wasn't a good section of the house; there was no more room than the cheapest airline seat, the stage with its bawling singers no bigger than a stamp. The orchestra pit looked like an ant colony, and in front of that, a double square of mostly white heads. The ceiling was coffered and perforated, with disks that seemed to float on air. Around the rim, of course, were the comfortable boxes, some with red-plush easy chairs. It wouldn't be any better to sit there. He'd prefer to have the hall in front of his eyes; it gave him something to do, while his wife, whom he still—after fifteen years—didn't understand, occupied her time (this was clear from the look on her face) differently.

Green had just turned fifty. He didn't feel old, and Betsy was forty-eight but looked thirty-eight, so together, they looked even younger. How old did he look? It depended on the time of day and the number of hours he'd been boxed in an office. It depended on his haircut, his weight (even the fluctuation of a few pounds), and how many days of tennis he had logged that week or that month. Did it depend on his bank account? A little, and on whether he had paid his bills and forgotten them.

How old did he look that very moment, settling in his seat in the middle of act two? Hard to tell because the stage had just gone black.

Green, in his light-weight suit, felt the nearness of his wife, the silk of her sleeve. The piercing scent she liked to wear on big nights out had dulled, and she was enveloped in a cloud of nothing more jarring than salt air. She was thin and her dress fit her slim frame with nothing left over. She had long, thick hair, but it was confined now in a jeweled barrette, pulled tight flat against the small head. Betsy had been a beauty in the Dresden-doll mode, and age had only refined this delicacy. Her eyes were a paler blue, her nose thinner, and the threads of silver in her hair—especially when pulled back like this—gave her the look of an eighteenth-century miniature without the powder. Betsy was a twin, and Caroline, who lived in Paris, had resembled her in every detail except for the fiery red hair. Green had liked them both, had actually dated Caro first, when they were all in college. The sisters got along but were not close, and now people scarcely guessed they were related, let alone twins, although the resemblance—when they were together, however differently dressed and coiffed—was staring you in the face. Just thinking of it made Green smile. Just then his wife's eyes met his, and the smile betrayed; he hadn't, as she'd feared, heard a note. George Green was the most impervious man; you couldn't teach him anything: he had closed up shop at age twenty, in 1972 (music was Bach and Beethoven, pleasure reading was the classics he'd sampled in the core curriculum, film was German silents and *nouvelle vague*; he also listened to Cole Porter and the Beatles). He had been finished at and by Harvard, as had Betsy. They had that in common.

Settling in, and ignoring the spasm of irritation that compressed Betsy's fine features, Green focused on the lines of dialogue rolled out over the stage. They were so short, so senseless. Cartoon captions had more tonal variation. To distract himself, he allowed his eyes to fan first over one side of the balcony (blank faces, glasses, makeup, and ties), and then the other, and that was when he spotted, two tiers away, several rows forward, a patient he had treated last year, year before, for headache. An actress, he recalled, playing here and in Washington and teaching at the conservatory. She suffered from migraine and cluster pain, once so intense she had been rushed to the emergency room and was wheeled onto the psych ward, raving—but that was just a phase of the aura, and by next day they'd removed the restraints. That was before she came to him and he had so managed her care—at least for a while—that acute episodes were averted. She was grateful and, being theatrical, had brought him a bouquet of stalky orange and blue flowers. They had no vases in the suite, so they set them in a janitor's bucket, but even that wasn't quite big enough for the flowers, each of which was like a little tree. Managing her pain had been a delicate business—different drugs were involved and she was already being medicated for depression—but for a while (thanks to extra legwork, trips to the medical library downtown, conference calls, and her willingness to try experimental protocols) she was—not pain free—but less liable to full-blown attacks. They were still juggling her drug load and monitoring diet, sleep and stress, when she missed an appointment, canceled the next, then sent his office a card saying she had moved out of state and would ask for a referral when she got settled.

His specialty—more an art than a science, people liked to say—was noted for failure, imprecision, dead ends, patient bail-outs. Neurology was in its infancy; it had been in its infancy for over a hundred years, and it would continue, even in its advances, to be no better than a medieval science. The brain was a house with a plumber but no electrician.

*A*t the intermission, Dr. and Mrs. Green strolled through the lobby holding glasses of complementary champagne. They were opera angels, on a modest scale, as they were angels for the symphony, choral arts and the art museums. Betsy had said often enough that it would be better for opera to buy a block of season's tickets and bring their friends to the concerts, but their friends were mostly doctors and lawyers, whose grueling work and active families left them little energy or spirit for spending the rare, free Saturday night in an opera house. And even if they had the time, opera (he knew) would not be their relaxation of choice.

Walking beside her, he never failed to feel their incongruity: he was almost 6-foot-3, built like a linebacker, and had played college ball, although not varsity, and by now some of that beef had softened, but she, at just 5-foot-5, was "tiny," as they liked to tell her in dress shops, and birdlike—and not a very large bird. But that made him laugh (he was such a talker in his head, where no one could hear the talk), and she turned and said, "What, George?" Nothing, of course, is what he might have said, but instead he pointed ahead (his eyes were forever sweeping a scene and he missed nothing, even daydreaming) at a youngish man with dyed red hair who had a tuxedo jacket matched with shorts and sandals on his feet. "Oh," said Betsy, in a thoughtful tone, which meant she was scanning her mental files to place him. Betsy was a fixture in the city's social life (cultural life made social to raise money); she also practiced law in a downtown firm and was active in their daughters' schools. The Greens heard Mass at the cathedral, but also attended service at Second Presbyterian, so Betsy did have a wide circle, but why would she think she knew this kind of a fellow, a kid really, art student probably? Oddly, the tuxedo-shorts was walking toward them with his arms out to grasp Betsy's hands and then to kiss her on both cheeks. So glad to see each other that, after a quick introduction—and Green was already excusing himself to hit the men's room—he saw them retreat to a bench; the artist held his wife's hand, and she was laughing at something he said, and flushed a color Green hadn't seen since before their children were born.

In the john, enumerating the signs—not of whether this man was gay, but how gay—Green saw someone he recognized, the man who did their taxes, and then, leaving the gents' without fully drying his hands, he found himself chest to head with his former patient, and he offered a damp hand, instantly forgetting her name. Or maybe he never knew it. "Dr. Green," she said, "Holly Davies." Now they were blocking the line to the water fountain. A place was found near the windows, behind a thick wall of people lined up for drinks and dessert. Once there, he wondered what he had to say and felt the absence of his partner, who could keep things going for the five–ten minutes before the bells began to ring for act three. "I have something to say to you," was what he heard. "Should I make an appointment?" "Yes, fine," he said. "We wondered where you had gone." "It's not medical," she said. "May I still come?"

She had an actress's throaty voice, penetrating even in this crowd. "Of course," he said, "but you'll have to call for a time. How are you feeling?" he said. "How's the pain?" And he could feel his face readying itself, checking boredom or vacancy, to receive the dry, physicianly history. "Fine," she said. "I have no pain at all."

And before the bell began to chime, his wife (who could find anyone anywhere) was standing before them, and introductions were pouring from these women's mouths. "A cure," he said to Betsy. "But not by us." And then the two women walked ahead to exchange notes on sickness, pain, and cures. But before separating to file into their separate tiers, Holly looked back, walked past Mrs. Green to Dr. Green, and handed him a card.

"What did she give you?" his wife asked, in the seats, with her coat all piled up on her lap, but "never mind," she added, waving at the air. "It's none of my business." She turned her eyes to the stage, black, but the orchestra now tuning up below. It is your business, he wanted to say, but he hadn't yet looked at the card, just a business card.

In a few minutes, the curtain rose, and lines of speech

started to unroll above the stage, which was tilted at 15 or even
20 degrees, to suggest the disorder on this Wagnerian ship. He
liked the set. His own eyes were perfect—for distance—and
he had never had a headache in his life. Holly Davies was one
of these women (so odd for an actress) for whom everything
was personal. No matter what Betsy might say, he was no fool
and could always detect this in a patient. And it wasn't just
women; old men, too, would refuse to be just patients, and
everything you did for them (or didn't do) touched off some
deeper feeling, something that had no place in the office. And
if they were strong enough, these patients could create of the
medical scene something different, that could never afterward
be corrected. The balance was off, although the clinical work
might still be flawless. He had really hated seeing such patients
when he was younger, when his own marriage and later his
girls gave him more than he needed of the personal, a hot, vis-
cous daily bath from which he barely emerged—and a bit later
every day—with his face alert and dry. He managed (just) to
knife himself out those early mornings. Medicine clarified; the
office hours, the pain histories rewrapped him in an element
just as enticing, but clear, where his mind and hands, his rout-
ings through the network of textbook cases, the intricacies of
drug biochemistry, the film images and sheets of data, and the
play of pure hunches, could produce for them—the patients—
treatment plans, and nothing else. Returning home at night to
the hive, all these plans were filed away, the patients sent
home, or to surgeries or pharmacies, to begin their own work.
The two lives (and the two Greens) were cut clean, one from
the other. Unless a patient, like Davies or others just as gluey,
did their best to merge them again.

Somehow, paying less attention to the stage and the shrilling,
he saw more. It gripped him in a way that music rarely (and
opera never) did. He was not distracted, although his hand was
in his pocket cupping the card. It was in the pocket opposite

his wife. Somehow she sensed his absorption and left him alone, no taps or sidewise glances. After the finale and storm of applause, he offered his thoughts on the singing and staging as they walked down the grand stairway with the other streaming hundreds.

"Can you hear me?" he said, and she nodded. She agreed with him (for once): the set was perfect, as were the lighting and costumes; the translation of the piece into an eighteenth-century spinning mill—with the Dutchman's ship—was ingenious, but the raucous beerhall party, in the style of Georg Grosz, was absurd.

"How fast you've caught on," she said, "for someone with no background." Her eyes were sparkling; she meant it.

But he did have some background. He had taken a music course and done the assignments; he had a good ear and remembered what he heard. Unlike his suite mates, he didn't use the time in the listening room to memorize orgo molecules. He listened and even read scores. It was wrong of her—a desperate measure—to undermine him. When he paid attention, he was fully there, and his intelligence wrapped itself tight around whatever it was, and so much faster than hers.

She was holding his arm now, and they made their way across the street to Grimaldi's. The musicians often descended on Grimaldi's, stripped of their costumes and makeup, and infused the place (he liked this) with their surging, near-hysterical energy.

"So who was that? I liked her," his wife said, accepting her menu and laying it down on her plate.

"A patient," he said.

"I know that," she said, picking up the menu and opening it. "I spoke to her about headaches."

"So why do you ask?" he said, and even while he said it, he realized he was taking a tone with Betsy—a first.

"Because," she said, slipping on her reading glasses, "she's more than a patient. She knows you." She took the glasses off.

"No patient comes up and talks to a doctor at the opera. That's against the rules."

He laughed. She did know the rules. But now, even she was breaking them. "I don't know her outside the office, if that's what you're implying."

"Do you want to pick the wine, or should I?" she said, holding up the separate sheet. "I trust you, you know," she said.

He was enjoying this. He took the wine list and picked a decent red, spending a little more than he usually spent. When the wine arrived, he tasted it and offered it to her to taste.

"Pretty good," she said. She knew nothing about wine, and very little about people, too, for all her self certainty.

"Who was that little man?" he asked.

She sipped her wine. "A choreographer," she said. "You've seen one of his dances. You might not remember. It was the Washington Ballet last spring. We brought the girls."

"Did we?" The appetizers arrived, and Betsy watched the first wave of singers, in evening dress, flounce in behind the maître d', who had a special table reserved (Green had been watching them set this table with gift boxes, flowers, and tapers) on a raised platform in the rear. The table was half concealed by a linen drape hung from the ceiling on an oval wire. They never completely closed this drape; it was more enticing, he figured, to have this group half concealed.

Taking a minute to examine his plate, to take a hard roll from the basket that was circulating, and to butter it, he missed seeing the clump of singers and musicians passing through, raising the temperature of the room and now noise bounding off each hard surface. They were arranging themselves around the raised table, when he saw Holly Davies (it had to be her in the white satin suit) seated among them. Now they were drinking a toast, but almost hidden behind the four waiters who'd flocked to their table with trays of hors d'oeuvres.

"Don't stare," Betsy said, but she turned to look too. "Oh, there's your friend. Do you see her?"

She was in his line of sight; all the artists were, but so were his wife's eyes. Now they were opening their gold-wrapped packages—favors, or whatever they were—but something would have to be done (or said) at his table. The air was getting thin. "Talk to me," he said. "Tell me about your day."

"Today is Saturday, George. We had the same day," she said, but smiled to lighten it.

"Well, yesterday," he went on, undaunted, "was Friday, and we didn't have the same day. What about yesterday?"

Betsy liked to talk, and even a half-hearted, transparent invitation like this was irresistible. During the interval in which she lined up her appointments, lunch date, chats with this and that office mate—then, the discoveries made about the latest habits and interests of their two teenage daughters—he studied the raised table over the lip of his wine glass.

Talk away, he said to himself, wrapping himself tightly in two lines of thought, the future and the past, but keeping his eyes fixed on Betsy's oval face and flexing lips. *Three* lines of thought: those lips, so elastic, firm and smooth, opened now not just one, but two further lines of thought. His tongue went through them, tasting their clear shape. The banalities of life in her office and at home, sitting at the kitchen table and loafing on the deck, washed over him. He saw their three cars, two in the garage and one (the kids') parked on the street. But peace came, at last, thinking about the clammy, pre-dawn hour when, at 5:30, without so much as a sip of coffee, he exited the warm, overfurnished house (there were so many rugs, some were piled on others) and slipped himself into his cold car with the night turning blue over his head. In the middle of this thought was Holly Davies (over there and in here at the same time, here now and there then) sitting on the examination table, one leg crossed over the other. When he leaned in with his ophthalmoscope, her knee bumped the metal of his belt buckle, and all the life went out of his body.

The lips were still talking and forking something of pastry

and cream within their small opening. Now it was his turn to talk, and he wanted to speak of the music, a little bit about the trumpet pumping jazz into the restaurant, but also Wagner's tilted ship across the street and how different the two were, and separated only by an hour, to speak the way they did in college when the roof over their heads was just shelter and their ideas could expand to fill all available space. That kind of talk would save him. He wondered if he could communicate this necessity to his wife of fifteen years without having to open his mouth.

He tried, then he talked to buttress the effect. At first she looked puzzled, then grim, then her features froze in place. He could see the cracks in the china even before saying, "You're a beautiful china doll," which he did say to explain why he was here with her and not up high on that platform with the artists, unwrapping his own gold present.

Landing

John took Abigail to the pharmacy to buy Christmas cards. Row upon dusty row. It was surprising that the place, first on their list of errands, was such a mess. What was wrong with the store? No time to think or gaze behind the demi-wall to see the papery face of the eighty-year-old "senior" druggist, picking up pills with the pad of his thumb, flicking them into an orange plastic bottle. The cashier standing under the pint bottles was even older, waiting so patiently for custom.

"How many do you need?" John asked his new girlfriend, a beautiful redhead just out of the army. How straight her back was, and all the fluffy hair had grown out lapping around her milk-white face, racing over her shoulders. You beautiful queen, he thought, touching one of those slightly sticky ringlets.

"Cards?" she said. She'd been looking around, caught the eyes of the elderly druggist and ancient cashier. There was also a customer buying a newspaper and cigarettes; he didn't see her, but when she gazed at his back, his head swiveled around, and who could ignore a look like that, and she such a dish! There were no dishes anymore: dishes were over. Women like this with the tight, stretchy pants and loose t-shirt and that straight gaze—they weren't cutlery, or flowers or jewels, Olympians or celestials, sleek beasts or vegetables. What were they? This one, the customer was thinking, was taken. At least for now.

"I don't know," she finally said to John. "A boxful, enough for everybody."

"I never sent Christmas cards," he said, still looking at the customer, who'd finally turned away.

"No? Do you get any?"

"A few. My mother, my mother's friends. Some of my friends who're married. The funeral home, the church—that kind of thing."

"Oh."

"And you?"

"I have a list I keep from year to year."

"And everybody who's on it stays on it?"

"Not necessarily. If they don't reciprocate, say, two consecutive years, I cross them off."

"What if they come back?"

"If they come back, I add them for the next year. But I put a question mark which says something to me about them."

"Oh."

John didn't know this woman very well. Everything she said hurt him a little, as if another of her many sharp, army-trained quills had punctured his fine skin. He hadn't had a girlfriend since Sally, his coworker, had been transferred to San Diego. Sad—but what can you do?—was what people said to him. Act of God, others said. One (his mother) said: I didn't much like her anyway.

"Do you see any you like?" he asked, touching the back of Abigail's rich vermilion mane. She flinched.

"Should I not touch you in public?"

"It's not that," she said. "I don't like my hair touched. I don't know why. Touch me anywhere else."

He waited.

"Not my face. Don't touch my face."

He waited.

"It's because my skin is sensitive. It still breaks out, say, if your hand is oily or there's dirt on it."

John fisted his hand against his thigh. "I see."

"Is it okay?"

"Sure. It's *your* skin."

She laughed. "*Now* it is," she said, showing a plastic-lidded box with a still life of flowers and fruit—a beautiful thing, but what was Christmas-y about it?

As if reading his mind, she said: "I like to think of it as a holiday, winter holiday, solstice. The religion stuff bores me."

"Fair enough," he said. "Should I buy some?"

"Only if you want to send them."

John hesitated. Did he? Not really. "I like Christmas, but I don't do anything but feed off the fat of the land. If someone throws a party, I go. My mother puts up a tree. She sang Christmas carols in bed. It was touching, but I don't sing."

Beautiful Abigail was staring at him. What was she thinking?

"Pay for them," he said. "Or do you want me to? And let's go."

She grinned, blushed. "Why would you pay for them? You're strange."

He waited till she pivoted, faced the cashier, then he flinched. Every time, no matter how trivial, she got him. Why was he suddenly so thin-skinned? He looked at his hands and forearms. The skin looked normal, though there were ropey blue veins on the backs of the hands and up the inner arms. Abigail's nearness, he learned, caused these veins—or arteries, whatever they were—to open. He felt warm and full of blood, sometimes too full. Even his feet were throbbing.

But he had let a gap open up between his blood-logged self and the handsome, straight-shouldered redhead, the glory of her sex, he whispered, and where did a flitty phrase like that come from?

And they were on her. He could see. Druggist, cashier, customer ringed his redhead. He could see the air between them darken and flash, and, of course, he knew she could feel it too. How? When she turned to find him, her face was red as the mane. What he was noticing in these two months he'd known her was she was getting better at it.

Carrying the white paper bag, she let him open the door, and exited a little sideways because once, at thirteen or so, she was a fatty and still feared to brush a doorway, especially when— as they always do—men lined that door jamb with their own bodies, dorsal side out, just in case something of yours might brush theirs.

The outside—street, sky, shops, trees, pedestrians, and cars—was still new to her without the uniform. First she was different, and then it was because she was. She wasn't even sure which self was on top today—and hadn't been sure since the day Sgt. Maj. Abigail M. Coach had been discharged. The uniforms weren't that bad really; the fit was good, and a big shapely thing like Ab looked trim in starched, tailored cotton, belted, jacketed, and hatted. It was good.

Now she had to find other uniforms, for day, some for night. At first the new uniforms looked like the old ones—fitted, starchy, hard-edged; then slowly, with the help of her sister, Emily, mother of two, and the help of John, she found second and third uniform types. She learned from the looks of the salesgirls. At first she expected respect and deference, but after a while, when they knocked and entered her dressing room while she was stepping into skirts or trousers and slipping on a dress shirt, she saw them take her measure, scoot out, and bring in a different kind of clothing—velvet pants, stretch pants, and lovely blouson tops of sheer material. They all picked solid black and white because the flame hair, so curly, seemed to have a strong pattern of its own. So, she learned from them, although Emily and John had said: that's going to attract the wrong kind of attention (Emily) and are you sure you want to wear that to the ball game? (John). But assessing for herself the effect of these foreign clothes, Abigail decided to give the new uniform a month or two.

In a way, it was like showing rank. Eyes swiveled, heads turned, faces flushed, and awkwardness jerked the bodies of onlookers—embarrassed by Abby's gaze, which could shoot a hole right through your head—before they flexed and went their way. She loved to call them to attention, even if attention were cut with other attitudes.

And here was John bringing up the rear. They walked on. "I wouldn't have minded," John started up, "if you were half as pretty and a fraction as—"

"As what?" but she didn't stop, kept treading, matching her strides to his.

"Attractive."

"That wasn't what you were going to say."

"Well, I'll say it then, but don't fly off the handle. Sexy! There, even if you were a tenth as sexy."

She smiled. "So I'm—is this what you're saying—nine times more sexy than necessary? Is "necessary" the word you meant, or "desired"? There's a difference."

"Yes."

"If I were nine times *less* sexy, as you put it," she said, walking faster (she was creating a little wind in this brisk pace; John felt it fan his face), "what would be different? Think of it; it's an interesting question. Starting at the top, my hair would be maybe gray or that ugly blood color I've seen when a dye job goes wrong."

"This isn't important. I don't want to listen."

"The weight that's here," she pointed to full shoulders, deep chest, and a full set of fatless hips and thighs, "would disappear; my tallness would shrink, so the middle would puddle. And—"

"Enough." They were standing now in front of Anthony's, the ice cream shop.

"And my facial features. Look at them," she said, grabbing him by the arm, because the idea was sundaes, or at least cones, at Anthony's, even though the temperature hovered in the low 40s and not a leaf on the trees.

He looked. He looked and, worse, he saw. For a minute he saw, but he listened anyway.

"Extra fat here," she said, pointing to her underchin, "and none here," indexing upward to the rich rosy cheeks. "Then there's coloring, but that's guesswork. So what do you think?"

"I don't know," he said. "You're a totality, Abigail. Everything is part of it."

"You said I could be so much less and you'd still go for me, but this is never true. Even if I were nine times more sexy, it wouldn't be true."

"You wouldn't be real."

"Let's eat," she said. So in they went and split an extra-fudge sundae, eating it out of the bowl with two spoons. Twice the spoons touched, rang, and a current ran from John's hip to his foot. Second time it ran down the other leg.

She didn't notice. "I'm not as happy now—you don't know this, so I'm telling you—as I was before."

"In the service?"

"That was the best part of my life. So far. I compare everything to those five years."

"The real question is," he said, sidestepping what could be a jab, "are you getting used to civilian life?"

"I'm an adapter," she said. "That's what they teach you, in so many different ways. It's the lesson of a lifetime."

"I envy you," he said, scraping the bottom of the thick glass bowl. He removed his spoon. She could have the milky pool veined with brown and a little red from the artificial cherry, but she removed her spoon and lay it across the bowl. Did he or did he not like her air of authority? He liked it. It added to the other. Everything added, nothing took away from this "living doll." (This was an expression from childhood; he knew it, but it applied to an earlier generation, painting Betty Boop and Betty Grable on the nose cones of their bombers.) Everything about her was novel. In college he'd been against the war, against the cancerous growth of the military-industrial complex, as Ike called it. He had let his hair grow long and tried to learn the guitar. He marched in Washington, he chanted, he loved the Beatles. The war came to an end not long after the march when Tricky Dick circled the White House with buses and not one inch between the nose of this jitney and the ass of that. It was something to see.

And here she was fifteen years younger and a military pro. No combat duty maybe, but based in exotic outposts—Iran, Iceland, Panama. She hadn't seen action, but she'd been trained to coordinate tank battles. She was in the canebrake and on the barren beaches, mudfield and rock island, and on the mist-blown flats. She didn't see anything funny about "Uncle" or the Joint Chiefs, or know that the days of American imperialism were over, at least for a while. Her army was new, strange, and so was her planet.

He never mentioned 'Nam, draft dodging, the lottery, My Lai, or any of that. They couldn't even talk about Watergate (she was a child!) without flashes of anger. She was ignorant— yes, sometimes he thought that—but her will was fifty times stronger than his, and his love. . . . That was too sad. He put his spoon next to hers, but there wasn't room and hers dropped off, catapulting a milky glob to the neck of her t-shirt and slopping onto the skin, color of swansdown and just as soft.

"John!" she rang out.

"Sorry," he said. "Clumsy."

"Clumsy?" she repeated. "Stupid!"

He got up to request of Anthony or his minions a cloth or paper towel soaked in water. Returning with a wet sponge: "I'm sorry," he heard, "you're not stupid." She dabbed her shirt and patted her neck. He was up to get a towel, and back, hovering behind her chair to stroke her lustrous skin.

"Ab," he sighed, after a minute. "Please, can we go back to my place?"

"As you wish," she said, standing, hanging her purse on her

shoulder, smoothing her black and white uniform, throwing her chest out. John looked, but Anthony was busy with his ice cream tubs. And there were no customers.

John sighed, picked up the bag of cards, and followed her out. The day was just beginning, but he had made his first mistake, and, fifteen minutes later, as he wrapped the nude Abigail round, using arms and legs, he saw it. Instead of dragging her home for boff number three or four of the day, he should have helped her (he could kill himself for the thoughtlessness) to finish her errands.

He kissed at his Venus, first only down the flanks, although to her mind, the center strip—face downward, over the bumps and into the hollows—was the strike zone.

Down the flanks he went, loving Abigail's every inch, lifting up an arm to run his face along the bump of each rib, touching the soup plates of the hips, all the way down to the long feet, smooth as glass on the arch and sandy at the heels, scaly at the toes. Sometimes he became distracted by the terrain, and she pulled him up. When he was ready, arrow sharp, eyes clamped shut, she flipped him on his back and pocketed him.

As they both lay, on their backs, replete, breathless, his leg twitching a little, he asked himself the question: how did this Venus survive in that man's army? How did she have an inch of skin left? He had already asked this question, and her answer? Fraternization was a no-no; they were busy; they were tired. And in the outposts? he asked.

"Hate Americans there."

"In Iceland?" he asked.

"In Iceland more than anywhere. We're aborigines to them. This, " she said, grabbing hanks of the heavy, glistening hair, "its color and curliness, put me off limits."

"But why?"

"I was another race to them. I was a mongrel, human trash. Those were just some of the things I heard."

"You learned Icelandic?"

"They all spoke English. I had a boyfriend," she added.

"I knew it," he said.

"But he was American, Navy Seal. It didn't last. He was shipped to the Gulf. I never heard from him again."

"Are you mad at me?"

"Why should I be? she said. "What have you done?"

"I distracted you," he said, warming from his lower trunk to his limbs, "from your day," and so they made love again, although this time he had nothing left in him, although she tried to help in every way that she could think of.

"No problem," she said. "It happens to every man some time."

"It never happens to me," he groaned.

"No big deal. Let's hit the stalls," she said, and he saw the bronze goddess vanish and, not long after, wreaths of smoke roll out and cloud the mirror over his dresser. How lovely it was. He could see his feet in the mirror, and he propped up his head. He looked a little like Robert Redford, people said, and he could see it, but since Abigail, in six weeks, two days and—he looked at his watch—six and a half hours—he was fifteen pounds lighter. He lifted a leg, twiggy-looking, although hard muscled. He raised an arm. You could see the tendons. That was bad. But there was never time to eat, and he was in no mood to really stoke. He had an appetite for one thing: the sergeant-major. That he couldn't get enough of.

*I*t rained on Friday, a week later, the day they planned to go to the beach, a winter holiday—alone, he hoped, in a vacated hotel. Restaurants, yes, but nothing else to do but . . . well, some shopping. He'd promised her the delicate shopping of a seaside resort devoted almost exclusively to gay vacationers, mostly men.

Along the flat roads, riding in his white car, they could see miles of dead farmland—not dead, just mowed and dug under, muddy-looking with bits of straw-like tillage. For miles nothing but mud with those stunted pine trees in the distance, sometimes fogged out. The road was empty and most of the eateries closed, boarded up. Even a lone HoJo's, faded paint, was closed for the season.

Ab had to go to the head, and John was ravenous, thirsty too, but nothing in sight until, almost a full hour later, they took the turn-off for Opakawam Island and its twin, Dekatawam-on-the-Sea. A dark fog lapped at the edges of their vehicle, night was falling too, and the little town of Dekata closed on Fridays a little after four. Luck found the hotel. To THE BEACH, signs said. That helped too. As they approached the sea, the rain drove into their windshield, turning the road and its colorful borders into a rippled sheet of gray. They halted. Rain pounded on the roof. What was dark grew darker, chilly too. John offered to put the heater on, but the long silent drive had stupefied them both, and Abigail didn't even respond. They sat quiet, engulfed in water. John, who felt more alone than ever, enjoyed the sensation, especially the sound. It was the sound of being inside a waterfall.

"It's let up," he heard.

"What?"

"Drive, before we're stuck here all night."

He looked out his side window. It was already night, still raining, but not so driving a rain. "Are you mad at me?"

"For what?"

"For bringing you here."

"You didn't expect this!" Abigail sighed, adding, "You apologize too much. That alone is wearying."

"That alone," he repeated; her words were sometimes a lash, but this time no. The rain had buffered him, the waterfall too. The long, mute drive, even the sight of those mucky fields.

So he shoved the gearshift into first and soon they were moving through fluid and now fog, as the cooling night vaporized. They found the hotel, Ocean Rest, and the parking lot next to it, like a desolate skating rink with pink lamps that balled the fog but shed no glow beyond. John stopped where he hoped there was a parking space.

The lobby, too, low-slung, cool and musty, was empty. There was no bell at the desk, but Abigail could hear a TV going somewhere, and she rapped on the desk, then whistled—without fingers. Good, thought John, that finger-whistle could wake the very dead.

Out came a college boy. Was this the right hotel? Yes, the kid said, reservation for the lady and gentleman. I'll need your driver's license and a credit card.

"Water view," the kid said, when he unlocked their door. And sure enough, judging from the absolute black outside the picture window, they were not facing the town. There were odd breezes and drafts, one rushing along the carpet, others angling from the window sill, and an occasional scream from the room or from the ocean—it was impossible to tell.

"Gee, it's cold in here," John said, tipping the kid, who'd flung the suitcases on the bed and turned on the bathroom light.

"Is it?" the boy said. "You've got a room heater somewhere. Or, if you need one, just call."

"Off-season," John said in a quiet voice, almost to himself.

"It's not too bad," she said, "as long as there's food somewhere."

"Oh, there's bound to be," said John, and he was right. Food and nice conditions to eat it in and to drink a fine wine—this was never a problem throughout the stormy weekend, with such a driving rain from Friday to Sunday that, even with the slickers they bought, pant legs were soaked to the knee and hands and faces, sometimes even hair, drenched.

"This motel," said Abigail, that first night, before the first restaurant was found, or even believed to exist, "isn't on the water; it's *in* the water."

"Sure," said John. He was looking seaward where nothing, at first, could be seen; but after five, ten minutes, threads of light—something from the moonless, starless sky—played out upon the waves. And Wagnerian (that's what he'd call it) or Beethovenian sound. It was completely distracting. Only an act of will allowed him to swivel and see, in the blinding bathroom window, a "negative" of Abigail's form in tube top and bikinis, applying make-up, or whatever she was doing, but John's head swiveled right back, so he could feed at this square of the absolute—the first since his drug days, the few "trips" taken on mescaline or acid, and never at night.

At dinner, Abigail chattered from appetizer to cheese and fruit course. Something—the ravaging night, maybe—had jogged her out of her sullen reserve. She was not anti-John; that he always knew. She was one whom nature and the army had driven deep inside, who seldom felt the need to rise to the surface, climb out the hatch. It was not a pretty sight. The face, beautiful in its marble rigor, creased and puckered. She didn't speak well, her talk had no logic or fluency, she didn't look you in the eye. Instead her eyeballs lolled or flicked side-to-side, where other diners soaked up the darkness. With the nail of her little finger, she cleaned around her left eyetooth. They had had crab, cole slaw, and a coconut dessert, and slivers of any of these could be wedged in there. She inspected a filament, flicked it on the floor.

"Are you grossed out?" she said, catching the look he was giving her.

"'Grossed out'? Did you get that one from me?"

"What one?"

"No one uses that expression anymore, but we used to like it."

"Don't you think I've read any magazines? The world knows all your expressions and is free to use them, too."

Where was the sharpness coming from? It wasn't the first time he'd noticed that she could read his mind when it contained a criticism of her.

He flagged the waiter, asked for the check, paid it with cash.

"I'm finished," she said, looking down at the bowl where the coconut cake and ice cream, a generous portion, had left a curdy, white mess, although she'd eaten everything she could spoon up. The bowl bottom, she'd explained to him, was hobnailed so the dessert milk had pooled, inaccessible, among the hobs.

"Food means a lot to you," he'd said.

"To whom doesn't it?"

It took John, an educated man, a few seconds to parse that sentence, but she answered herself. "To you it doesn't. Not as much."

And he waited and soon heard what he waited for.

"If you'd seen army fodder, food would mean everything. Food *does* mean everything. That's the natural order. After that it's all training—or socialization, as you'd call it."

"You could be right," he said, tentatively,

"Fuckin' A," she said, but grinned, because this was not the way they talked.

$\mathcal{B}$ack in the dank motel room, she stripped, peeled off the blanket and top sheet, as she often did, to lie on the sheet and mattress pad, and offered him her body. He was chilled from the walk; his feet were soaked. Even the rug felt wet. There must be a crack, he thought, between the balcony door and the tin walls. They weren't tin, he knew, but the water drummed against them as if they were.

"I'm freezing," he said.

"Come in and warm yourself up," she said.

He was struck by what had to be the first invitation he'd ever gotten from Abigail. Usually he leapt or sidled, but the impulse always came from him.

But instead of landing on that exposed flesh, its outline picked out by the lamps now spotlighting the beach, he closed the shade. He swore under his breath. The beach, especially in this weather, was supposed to be dark, empty, pure.

"John?" he heard, but he padded into the bathroom, closing

the door behind him. If you put the ceiling heater on, this little room—so clammy—might become a steam bath. He spun the dial, and as the lamp reddened, a fan started up behind it. Heat flooded down, dry and hellish. He stood shivering in the hot current. Tears were rising from a place behind his nose, but he held them back. I'm cracking, he thought, and why? Maybe it was the sex—four, five, once ten times in one day—with no love, no tenderness, not even a sense of familiarity. His body had become one stinging nerve. But now, that nerve was slack, and other things were surfacing.

He moaned to the tune of the whirling fan.

"Hey?" he heard, and then a knock. "What's the matter?" Her mouth must have been pressed to the door, because he could hear every word.

"I've got a splitting headache." The room was red hot.

"Take an aspirin," she said. "Come to bed."

"I'm going to soak in the tub a minute, okay? I might be sick. It's a migraine, not a normal headache."

"Okay," he heard. "I'll read. There's always a bible here somewhere, right? The bible used to be my favorite reading."

He had no headache. His head was clear as a bell on a scorching winter day. He was approaching, he felt, a new frontier, where love and revulsion coincided. He'd never wanted to go this far. What good would it do him to know that they united in him?

But he had only closed, not locked (as he'd imagined), the door, and after a while—twenty minutes, half an day—a darkish form appeared. Next, the fanned heat stopped whirling, and now clear water was flowing in the bathtub; he could see it, and the tub was spotless. She was pulling off his sweater vest and the shirt that peeled off his skin; now the belt was sucked out through the loops, and his jeans were pulled down. Soon he was sitting, half lying, in the tub of fresh water foaming around his roasted flesh. Had he been torched? His face was raw, his hair was singed.

She bathed him, starting with his back. She shampooed his burnt hair, she toweled him, using every cloth in the bathroom, until he was dry. She combed his hair, first with her fingers to loosen the snarls, then with a brush she found in her suitcase. Now he was powdered and wrapped in a bathrobe.

He filed himself into the opened bed, and she beside him, drawing up the sheet and blanket. All that was left now was the sound of the ocean and the wind.

When he woke up hours later in the after-storm light, she was gone. He pulled the window shade, and first he saw the deserted beach, scoured by the wind, then the figure, wrapped in a blanket, sitting on the sand.

It was late for happiness, but happiness was here.

The Secret of His Sleep

George McCoy spent the first forty years of his life in a deep sleep. He woke up on a Friday in the month of March. Here were the facts: he was married but his wife was at work, he had one child, a genius, his mother was dead five years, but his father was alive. He learned all this that March morning just looking at pictures and raking through the most superficial layer of memory.

Look in the mirror, he told himself, and sure enough, there he was. How can I be tired, he asked himself, after all this sleep? He had been born tired. Even now, he had rings under his eyes and his skin looked parched. He was handsome the way his father had been—strong, bony, with no color contrast anywhere: his eyes, skin, and hair were only a few tones apart. His eyes were huge and deep-set; they liked to be closed. However, he did not go back to bed or slump on the couch.

The house was quiet, although if you lay your head on the lid of the piano, you could hear music of a sort. The clock ticked and sometimes a loosely framed window rattled in the unseasonably windy day. George liked wind, it kept him awake with something that didn't tax him with thought. All the time he had been asleep he'd been troubled by thought. He'd produced a tremendous amount of it—layers, knots and thin curtains, stews, blizzards and heaps of wonderfully fine sand. It was worthwhile but it kept him asleep, with ears and eyes tuned inward.

He put on his shoes. He'd always liked nice shoes and, in a dreamy way, kept them up: polished, oiled, heeled and soled, shoe-treed. He found the keys to the car, took a sip of water, and exited through the breezeway. In the car, a big white one, he put on sunglasses. It was his first day out and he didn't want to be blinded.

Out was wonderful: clean, empty streets, stoplights evenly dispersed, donut shop looked inviting and there was an old barbershop. He didn't need a haircut but stopped anyway and said: just a little off the sides.

"Hi, George," the barber said. "How are things?"

George was surprised the barber knew him, but he made a polite reply and waited. In the mirror George saw the barber at work. He was Italian, a little round in the middle, and walked on the toes of his highly polished shoes.

"How did you happen to get into this business?" George thought to ask the barber and that spared them the agony of a search for common matter.

The barber had a good story. He wasn't world-weary; he was enjoying his first wind. There was enough in the simple act of trimming different colors of hair on different sized heads to bring him the pleasure that we all look for in life—if not every day, at least one in seven. He seemed glad to be awake. The haircut seemed cheap. George paid and tipped. The barber swung open his door, goodbye for now.

Outside the day was less bright, or maybe George was getting used to daylight. Still marvelous, though; you could wring it out, there was so much of it. George walked a little, accepting the sunlight's kiss, mostly on the face, but he extended his hands, too, to feel it there. He was about to sift through the barber's words and odd facial expressions, but diverted himself by watching what was happening just ahead. In a tall tree, just in the one fork, was a box kite. Underneath, at the roots, was a child. George wanted to walk past, but the child turned, pointed to the string halfway up the trunk of the tree. It was

68

out of George's reach, too, so he took the boy by the waist, slung him up to his shoulders, and jumped a little, until the boy had the string in hand and yanked the box kite to the ground. The boy gathered up kite and string and was making off. "Thanks, Mr. McCoy," the kid said, turning back, then raced off.

I'm known to my neighbors, George concluded. He liked the neighborhood, all flat, clean sidewalks and evenly spaced trees—except for that ugly thing that snagged the kite. Except for that one, they were all fine. George looked back; it was a miserable, leafless pike. Down the street, he could still see the kid with his large bundle making his way like a dog on an outing, with no real place to go. Maybe he was an orphan. George put that thought aside, with the others piling up, for later.

I must have a job, or something, he did think, and yes, inside his pants pocket was a daybook, a portable calendar, but what was the date? Inside the pages was a variety of notes, nothing clear. But it was spring, wasn't it March? What made him think it was March and not a day in a warmish February or the face of September turning inward? There was a way to tell; it was the air and the freshness of the leaves—except for that one. So he looked into the early parts of the daybook: January, February, March and April. Names and times and a reminder or two, but here was March and not a scratch. The daybook was pristine, clean leaves golden-edged from February 29th onward. Life had stopped here, or at least occupation had. So he was unoccupied, and the year was? All the calendar cover said, in embossed gold letters on black leather, was "GRMcC."

He had seen mail and circulars in a basket on the dining room table and envelopes addressed to George or Mr. George McCoy, but nowhere had he seen an R. His wife's name was Carol, and she used her maiden name (unless he wasn't married?): Askins. The child—his own child, he suspected—was called Aaron. He was enrolled in the Speed Street Elementary, grade four, with all As and an I.Q. of 160. Many times he had been late this year, but never absent. His behavior was exemplary.

George felt worn out. There was a café on the corner, coming up on the right-hand side. Large coffee, he said, sitting at the counter, and a pastry. The waitress in a pink dress and apron lifted the lid from a cake dish, and George pointed to a Danish covered with liquid cherries. It was a delicious thing. With all this buttery sweetness in his mouth and the smoking coffee warming his hands, he considered. The life half-asleep had been painless; everything was wrapped in clouds, but never had anything tasted so good. And the look that orphan had given him, with his simple, grateful formula, had pierced like a needle. Even sitting here at the counter looking at a stainless steel wall waxed with grease—even this was something.

George had been born into a family of three, and first day home from the hospital, he turned his face, which his mother had been attracting with hers, inward toward her sleeve. He closed his eyes. His first thought wormed its way in when he was two-and-a-half and playing with a dog that bit him. It wasn't his first pain; birth and infancy were a well of nauseating pain. But it had caused a splash. With lightning speed, the dog was caught and expelled, little George wrapped in a blanket and brought to the hospital for the first time since the beginning. Something about that smell reminded him of before. The thought was that life could always flip back to an earlier point, that what had happened in between could be squeezed out. That one equaled one and would always be so (no matter many equilibrated minuses and pluses were inserted between). No idea had ever dislodged this one.

Two dollars and twenty-five cents was the figure on his bill. High for something so modest—although, by now, maybe it wasn't modest. Looking at his plate, he saw the pastry was gone: the thought had eaten it, although he could also feel it under the sternum. He had eaten too fast. Looking in his wallet, he saw a stack of ones, five fives, two tens, and a fifty-dol-lar bill. He paid his bill and left the change on the counter. The waitress waited until he had his topcoat on. "So, how's the family?" she said. He looked at her face, round, flushed and two blueberry eyes under the crinkly hair. "Fine," he said. "Last time I checked." She laughed, although it wasn't much of a wit-ticism. "Give my best to your dad."

Walking out, he noted that he had two families; people had two families, and sometimes more.

Later, George stopped for a drink at Kennedy's City Tavern, all blue lights on the inside, the kind of bar his father would go to, although his father he barely remembered. The bartender set an old-fashioned on a coaster. It was dark out now and he noticed a couple of single women having drinks together in a booth.

They had noticed him, too, and soon a fresh old-fashioned came his way with their compliments. He hadn't finished his first one, but he toasted them in the air and drank from the new glass. Soon the blonde—she looked like a doctor's assis-tant in her white dress and sensible shoes—strolled up to his barstool and invited him—his name was McCoy, wasn't it?—to join them. She extended a slim hand with no rings. He took the hand and slowed his clock so that each instant with it would be stretched to the limit. It was a nice hand, smooth and warm. "Come back with us. Join the fun." George looked at the bartender, who gave a quick nod toward their table. As far as George knew, the bartender didn't know him but thought the transfer okay. Maybe because there were two women.

One was a doctor's assistant—Mary. The other worked part-time at the florist's. Jobs obviously were where you started. George didn't know what he did, and luckily, the women seemed shy of the direct question. They had had a few and, after a long day, were feeling no pain, as they put it. George was not sure how well he knew them, or if he knew them equally well. One was a talker and the other shy. It was the shy one, Rose, who kept meeting George's eye. She had a sweet face and a headful of black curls; one eyelid drooped a little more than the other. That could be the source of her appeal. The blonde was drinking a gin rickey, and the other one a vodka tonic. Somehow those didn't seem from the same world. And then his old-fashioned didn't either. Wine was big now—that's what blondie was saying; people hardly drank cocktails, and no one used that word. The other girl laughed. Her teeth were higgledy-piggledy. George felt a stitch in his lower abdomen; now the stomach tightened and there was fresh new space down there where the crinkle was. The space was warm and something was fizzing in there, so pleasant.

After the two old-fashioneds, and when the girls had fed the juke machine with quarters so each could hear her favorite at least twice, George felt the urge to go home, if home was the right name for it. Days were ruled—he could see this much— by certain definite pulls, and this one, although not the strongest, had persisted for an hour. Goodnight, girls, he said to the two friends. "Why not a bite of supper?" the blonde said. "Don't we deserve that much after a hard day?" George said he hadn't done anything hard. What had they done? The two women looked at each other. If you had to ask! their eyes said, although the shy one wanted to include George's eyes in the exchange. How could such a nice person, he wondered, survive the wear and tear of being awake? Maybe she hadn't been, or no more than he. She spoke. "I don't really have time, Mary. I pick up Charlie at Cub Scouts and Isabel needs help with her homework."

Mary lit a cigarette. (How did these two get to be friends? George wondered.)

"I have to go. What do I owe?" the shy mother said. She opened her purse and out of a red wallet took a ten.

"Put your money away," George said.

"I like him," the brash one said. "He's my kind of guy." Then, she took out her own wallet. "What do we owe you, Jim?" she hollered to the bartender, who strolled over to present the tab: $22.50. "If you divide that by three, with tip, let's chip in ten and show Jim our appreciation." They did it, and the shy one carried the cash on its little tray to the bar.

"Can I drive you anywhere?" George said, wondering if he had brought the car.

*I*t was dark outside, and through the windows, the bar shone blue. "Goodnight all," he said. Awake, things began and they ended. What a difference. But tension was building in his gut as he wondered, not for the first time, what would be going on at home? What would he find there? Was it what he thought? Was all his feeling to be topped off there?

He raised his eyes to the sky: patterns of stars were clear along the curve; it was true the sky was rounded and even in appearance didn't seem flat. His car was parked somewhere. He remembered walking along these streets. It was dark and the streets were still pleasant but where was the car? He retraced his steps to Kennedy's and the lights were still on; through the window he could see the barkeep dusting bottles with a feather stick. There he had met the two friends, Mary and Rose, but they were home by now, or maybe Mary had dragged herself solo to a hamburger joint to finish off the night. Rose was probably setting the table for supper. Was there a husband? Nothing mentioned. George pictured a family of three sitting under a wagon wheel of light bulbs with a modest dinner spread over a round table. Maybe they were having tube steak, and frozen onion rings, a salad and the carton of milk was there on the table, although only for the children. Rose had her glass of iced tea and cigarettes for later. If George joined them, did they have the extra chair? Was there enough? Would the children be too startled to settle down quietly to their work and sleep? Did he and Rose have enough time to get to know each other before they had to climb into the same bed?

It was awfully dark now, just the dimness of streetlights. Around the corner was the café, the silver of the counter shone in the streetlight. Menus were stacked in one corner, a pyramid of juice cans caught the eye and the grill, cool now, was clean and smooth. This was the end of the day and George could feel both its necessity and the nice break from work and daylight.

Farther on was the pike. How did that tree lose everything, and why was it still standing? Did no one have the duty or the tact to pull it down? George touched its bark; it was still warm from sun or maybe its sap was running. Would it still have sap if it were that dead? The tree did have some life; the bark even had a springy feel and a wonderful network of wrinkles and troughs. It smelled good, meaning there was activity inside it, or the dry rot was sweet. George put his nose up against it, but someone was coming along the street and he pulled his face away. Started up again, passed the barber shop; the barber left a night light on, just a bulb plugged straight into the wall. Everything glowed red, even the black barber chair. Looking at the way darkness and small light created a small world, George knew this was the part of life he must have spent his time in.

He found the car. It was unlocked and the keys in his pocket with the date book. He drove home and inserted his car in the space left him next to the blue compact. His front door was unlocked and the minute he walked in, before he even spotted the woman placing a TV dinner on a tray set with a paper napkin and pink lemonade, his eyes closed. But he forced them open. The woman had dark hair, but he had not seen her face in the instant she looked up, then retraced her steps to the kitchen. She had a straight skirt on, and slippers, a black sweater with pearls or something around the neck. She came back with two glasses of wine and set them on the coffee table. He needed time to study her and the room, too, but he accepted the drink, after he had folded his coat on a chair. She picked it up and hung it in the front closet, but closed the door before he could see what else was in there. "Where's . . . ?" he said, hoping she'd fill in the name, but she just looked up. Blue eyes, nice straight nose, sad face. She must be thirty-five, thirty-six. He wondered what she did for a living. Maybe work wasn't that important to her. He was sure it wasn't. Nothing was. Otherwise why would that face be so sad, as if nothing had pleased it in long memory. No expectation, either, of anything better.

"Did you have a nice day?" she said, and he got to hear her voice: there wasn't much body to it, although it was low-pitched.

"Interesting," he said.

"Oh, your days are always interesting. Will you excuse me? I have to see to the boy."

"Isn't he eating with us? Aren't we eating together?" George asked his wife, if this woman was his wife. If he had, in fact, opened the right door, if he had, in fact, driven to the place where he had begun. He trusted that she would know, but maybe that was too trusting—especially with a woman this sad. She turned back.

"I didn't expect you," she said. "He ate already and now he's working on his model. Are you hungry?"

George sat on the couch, waiting for his wife (if she was) to do whatever she needed to do with that boy, then return. He certainly didn't want a TV dinner; he'd rather join Mary in a burger and fries, or eat by himself, if there was a restaurant in town still open. He got up, peeled back the foil and saw that it was a turkey dinner; even the cranberry sauce was steaming hot. He closed the foil and opened the closet, but instead of reaching for his own overcoat, he stood there and looked: a closetful of pale pastel coats, a shelf full of summer hats, a basket overflowing with silk scarves—paisleys and polka dots, and on the floor, white and black patent-leather boots—nothing that would keep out the rain or snow. The thinnest leather with the tall tops falling over to one side or the other.

He remembered falling in love. But before he could envelop himself in the paleness of the coats and the leathery pool of boots, Carol descended the staircase with little Aaron stepping before her. He was older than the kite kid and twice as thin. Carol had a hand on his shoulder. What was wrong with him?

Aaron ran to him, and wrapped his skinny arms around George's waist, laying his head against his father's breastbone. Now he pushed his face into his father's chest and George could feel the little nose bone. George wrapped his own arms around his child's reed-like back and they stood there like statues.

Dinner was a quiet affair. There was no thought of splitting that TV dinner in three. Fresh supplies were found, washed, cooked and laid on platters and in bowls. Wine and cider filled the glasses. There were cloth napkins and candles. They boy wasn't very hungry but ate anyway. George was "in life" now and he knew it. He stroked his boy's hand and received a look that pierced him in the throat. Carol excused herself to fetch the block of ice cream, tricolor, and presented it in oblong cakes. It was an Italian ice cream, smooth and perfect. With this richness on his tongue, George closed his eyes.

No one cried themselves to sleep that night, but next day, when George McCoy woke up, they went off again.

What kind of world was it? In all the thinking he had done, not much of the world had filtered in. George knew the world was laid out in concentric circles: first the self, then the family, then the neighborhood, the city, state, country. Beyond that was a dark blur, where wars, famines, chaos, different kinds of extreme weather, and conflicting gods, not like his—the one the barber, Mary and Rose, the kite kid and the George family could agree on—spoiled each day. The world was dying. It wasn't as far gone as the pike, but it had long passed its midpoint and even the midpoint of its second half. The built-up waste and exhaustion thickened the air and, although people seemed to be living longer, their lives were mere stumps, not unlike that of the pike. The older people remembered something different, but they kept it to themselves.

George's slim body had rested beside his wife's all that night. He didn't want to waste time sleeping, but he wanted to be with her and she seemed to need sleep. While they sat in the living room, they had tried talking, but each subject tendered was lost in the strangeness of being together. Even Aaron couldn't reach them with the undemanding subjects of childhood: games, schoolwork, the pets he wanted, the decals on the new model and what part of the space war they referred to. Sometimes the strangeness emanated from him. They stayed up as long as they could, then Carol took the boy to his bed and apologized to George for retiring to hers. At first he was left downstairs alone, but not fifteen minutes passed before he, too, climbed the stairs, undressed, unpeeled the bedcovers and entered.

"Are you too tired to talk?" he asked his wife.

"I'm not too tired to listen," she said.

"What have we been doing all these years, Carol? What have you been doing?"

"A hard question," she said. "Should I turn on the light?"

"No need," he said.

"Well, you might like to look at some pictures I have here in this bedside drawer."

"What are the pictures of? Could you just tell me?"

She didn't answer, but George found her silences enriching, the way each phrase of music needs space between the notes and more at the end and the beginning of the next. Otherwise, he thought, cacophony.

"Just look at one?" she asked. Light on and into the drawer, she presented him with a snapshot. In a boat were three people: a young couple on one seat and an old man who was holding the oars. "That's my father," she said, "and us. That was taken just before we got married. My father's gone now. I don't suppose you remember him."

George pushed his skull into the pillow, covering his eyes with his hands. His wife, Carol, took one of the hands in hers, so George used the remaining hand to cover both eyes. Tears were coming forward. He couldn't stop them, but he wouldn't parade them either. "Do you miss your father?" he said, steadying his voice.

"Sometimes," she said.

"What was his name?"

"Edward Michael Askins," she said.

He didn't recall the name, or even that his wife had come to him with that same one. "He looks like a nice man," George offered.

"He could be," his wife said.

"Did I like him?"

"He liked you," she said.

"So he let us get married with no interference?"

"None."

"And your mother?"

"She died when I was ten."

"Did we have a nice wedding, Carol?"

"Simple," she said, adding, "if any wedding can be said to be simple."

George was fascinated by her tone, in talking of the wedding. Was she that detached? Or was it sarcasm? Things up close were so much richer than he would have dreamed. But mysterious, too. His wife breathed deeply; she turned from her back to her side, and now she was asleep.

All night long he lay like that. He was tempted to sneak away, first, check the boy in his bed, then leave by the door. George searched every corner of his mind for the logic of his disappearance—or the story. And that was only the first thing. The second thing was: why would anyone marry a person like that? The third was: why wake up now? The fourth: would he sleep again?

II.

Then, the light of the new day filled the window. Soon the boy scampered in, took his father by the hand and led him to the little bedroom to show him the models: planes, cars, robots, spaceships. George sat on the boy's rumpled bed. The child had a strange bald spot on the back of his head, where the fuzz of hair—cut right to the skull—had worn off. The curve of the head was slightly dented there.

"How old are you?"

"Nine-and-a-half," the kid answered. "I'm in fourth grade," he offered, gathering the papers and books stacked on his desk. "I have to get dressed," he said. "Are you going to get dressed?"

George ate breakfast with his family: juice, cold cereal and coffee. His wife had the radio tuned to weather and traffic reports. Aaron was bundled out the door to wait for the school bus. Soon after, Mrs. McCoy left in the blue compact for the city. What city? George wondered, as he cleared the dishes and washed them (there was a dishwasher, but he liked handling his family's things). He had dressed himself in yesterday's clothes with the change of underwear his wife had laid out for him. In the bathroom was an electric shaver and three toothbrushes. He touched all the bristles and picked the dry one. He didn't want to assail his wife with questions, but he did want to know if he had retired, or was someone waiting for him to do something that he was so skilled at he could do it in his sleep.

George opened the little drawer under the wall phone and, sure enough, there was a phone book. He looked under M: Uncle Bob McCoy, crossed out, and George McCoy Sr. George Senior lived at 2 Pequot Rd., Exeter, 02819. His phone number was only seven digits, so it couldn't be far.

"Is this Mr. McCoy senior?" he spoke into the phone.

"Speaking," said the voice.

"This is George," George said. "Are you free for lunch today, Dad?"

"'Dad'?"

"Did you have a child, Mr. McCoy, a namesake, about forty years ago?"

"Oh, that George," the voice said. "Hello, son."

"Carol's off to work, Dad, and Aaron to school."

"Good," said George senior. "So I suppose you're looking for someone to pass the time of day. Well, I have no objection to eating lunch with my son. Can you pick me up here, or do you want to meet somewhere?"

George only knew of two places and neither seemed right for this date. "Is there somewhere in between us," George asked, "where we could get a few fried clams and some chowder?" (It was the first food he thought of.)

"Well, Clam Shell isn't far from me. You take the old fire house road from where you are, then two or three stoplights and Clam Shell is up on your left. Past the old Cowesett Brewery."

"If I go out of my house and take . . . "

"Take a left on your street, George, until you hit Cowesett. Take a right and the firehouse'll be up on your right-hand side; go two or three stoplights, pass the brewery, and Clam Shell will be right after it. You got that?"

"Thanks."

"You never were good with directions," his father said.

George calculated how much time he needed to get to Clam Shell. It was 8:30. Lunch was at 12:00.

His desire was to repeat everything from the day before: barbershop, diner, bar, come home, wake up, eat breakfast, and see them off. But things, day to day, were supposed to be different—or just different enough. Otherwise it was too much like sleep. Still, he felt a need to relive yesterday, so he drove, parked, and walked to the barbershop. It was closed.

Death in the family, a sign said, and that light-stepping Italian, son of a barber and father to a barber, was probably home crying. George remembered that Italians liked to cry, men and women. George had not cried in a long time, so that last night's seepage made him stop short. Did he cry because he loved his wife and missed her? Or had he liked his wife's father? Yet not in the least did he remember Mr. Askins or his death. Maybe it was sudden. There was a mouse in the barbershop and George watched it race across the tile floor, get trapped in a corner, and turn itself around several times, then race back to the hole. George couldn't get the thought of his own old father out of his mind.

Farther on, George stopped in front of the pike. One of the ribs of the kite was still up there, just a stick and no different from the pike's own ribs. George remembered lifting the boy, or orphan, pushing him up there, his little body all loose, but tightening up to reach the string. Was his life already losing the little pungency it had had? That was unbearable, so George kept moving. It was 11:30; thinking was stealing life from life, and already this second day was faded. George retraced his steps to the car. Onto the road, following his father's instructions. Fifteen minutes later, he pulled into Clam Shell, a whitewashed box capped with a fish, a clam, a lobster and a shrimp in neon. It was daytime but the neon was lit.

George waited until the other car drove up, a white Chevy, and out popped a lanky old man, who puttered over to Clam Shell's storm door. He was wearing a seersucker jacket. His pants bagged on his thin bones, but his feet didn't drag along the blacktop; he made good time. George glanced in his visor mirror; the fresh haircut made his face raw-boned, but his eyes still looked half closed. When he opened them wide, they reminded him of the yellow agates he craved as a youth. He was his father's son.

Inside was dark, but glowing from fish tanks and a blue neon clam fixed over the bar. It was an old-fashioned restaurant in that no natural light was wanted. George's father was sitting on a curved banquette (for such a plain cement-block restaurant, the interior was sleek and leather padding everywhere.) His father's eye was caught by a pair of high-heeled shoes and graceful ankles belonging to the hostess, now seating a couple of businessmen. On her way to their table, she dropped two menus with Mr. McCoy, and George saw his father whisper something that made her laugh and pat him on the shoulder. Then she was off to seat the pair.

The sight of this made George review the scraps of his identity. His wife was sad, his boy a genius—a shy boy, devoted to his dad—his father was a ladies' man. Time spent awake was thickening.

George was at his father's table. His father stood and patted his shoulder. "Have a drink?"

The restaurant had a half dozen imported beers George had never heard of. He waited for his father to speak. "Dortmunder Union," he said to their waitress, and George said, "Make it two." "Dunkel," George senior said.

Were they German? If so, why the name McCoy and the broad, bony Irish faces? At least his father was alive. Poor Carol had no father, and for all these years, no husband either. Mr. McCoy Sr. was ordering raw shellfish, salads, and swordfish steaks. He even specified the type of cooking desired. The attention to detail soothed his son, and here were the beers in tall, clean glasses.

"Here's to us, Georgie," said his father.

They sipped and settled into the banquette. Halfway through the first beer, George junior was feeling at home.

Golf was discussed, and team sports (although to George, the names of players and the value of decimal scores meant nothing). When the raw clams and oysters arrived, silence tented them in easy, beery pleasure. The appetizer was delectable and only the sound of small forks scraping shell broke the wall of string music.

They were well into their greens when the father said, "Well, George, I missed your birthday this year. Happy birthday. Don't sweat the small stuff." Into his hand the father slipped an envelope. "No, don't open it now. For later," the father said, signaling the waitress for a fresh order of Dortmunders.

George took the envelope; there was no name on it. He hoped it was something personal, but it felt like money. "Thanks, Dad," he said anyway, and accepted the toast his father was offering of many more.

After the main part of the meal, when the table was cleared of all but the greasy glasses and a few crumbs, George junior opened the subject.

"Dad . . . ?" he said.

"Spit it out," his father said, his face crinkling into a monkey's grin. "Ask not what your father can do for you—remember that? That was Jack Kennedy."

George knew that the beers had hit, but why did his father not want to hear him out? Was this man his real father? He answered to that name over the phone, and his name was McCoy. George wanted to try again—who but his father could help? "Dad, listen," he said, and then out spilled the story. How he had awakened yesterday from a long sleep and had his first day: part of it spent on the street and part at home, where he lived with people he knew nothing about and couldn't lift a finger to help, except in the most trivial ways. His father listened; he even looked interested, but George could tell the story hadn't hit home.

"So," his father said, after George stopped. "And Carol and the boy are fine?" He waited for an answer, then said: "I'm just an old-timer, you know. Oh, I'm doing all right. No complaints." Here he stopped. "You never could come to either of us. Georgie, don't forget that. I never could help you, and neither could she. You were over our heads," he said.

The restaurant had emptied. It had never been filled. It was a sleepy place; maybe it did well at dinner and on weekends.

Suddenly his father said: "I'm going to go get myself a pack of Luckies. Haven't smoked in years, swear to God, not since the cancer. But since we're here, just us—and I have no secrets from you, son—I'm going to treat myself. You too. Let's move over to the bar, Georgie, and have ourselves a stiff one."

George senior located the machine. They placed their order for an Old-Fashioned and a Cutty Sark, and waited. Then, senior told junior that he'd never been much of a father. A good provider, yes, and no gambling, women or rough stuff. George listened, visualizing a 1952 Plymouth and two hats rising over the front seat. Thank God they'd only had the one kid, and you, good as gold, never asked for anything, never cried or acted up.

"Remember when that dog bit you? Jeez!" It was a dog from the next-door family. Kiwi—named for the polish. "Took a chunk out of your leg. It wasn't a bad dog, and they kept it chained up. I can remember it just like yesterday. Here, Kiwi, I'd say, if I had some slops or meat. Kiwi run right over. God, that was a long time ago."

Stop talking, George wanted to say. Instead he ordered fresh drinks. He was going to trick his father into spilling. His father knew. The hard part was knowing enough of the facts to tempt his father. Or just give him a straight lie and see if it made a difference. George gulped his whisky and said: "Isn't it true your father and his father and the father before that, way back when, living in great want somewhere up north, all killed themselves before they were fifty?"

His father's eyes grew big as moons. He pulled a handkerchief out of his pocket. It was only then George noticed how dry his lips were, chapped. Inside the teeth were false. His father smacked the chapped lips and replaced the cloth.

"Oh, Georgie boy," he said, head in hands, "you're a real winner."

So this much was right. "Why?" asked George, hardening himself up for what lay ahead, and not just today.

"Jesus, Mary and Joseph!" his father erupted. "Open your present," he said. "See what I bought you."

George fingered the envelope and dropped it on the bar. "Why don't *you* open it," he said to his old man.

Inside were ancient insurance policies, made out in the name of the first father, the second, and the third. They weren't big and the funds had long been exhausted.

"Where's yours?" said George.

"It's in there," his father said, but George looked no further.

"How old are you, Dad?" George asked.

"Sixty-nine last Christmas," his father said, pulling out the hankie to blow his nose.

"Are you insured?"

"Yessir."

George touched the edges of the last folded sheet. On it would be the value of his father's life in cash. "What do you know that you're not saying?" he asked his father.

"I'm offering. You taking?" his father said, signaling the waiter for the tab.

"You're not leaving here until you tell me something I want to know."

His father focused the moon eyes on George's. In the gaze was nothing but the reflection of the bar lights.

"No thanks," George said to his father, handing back the envelope with the claims stuffed back in. "It might have helped in your case, but it can only make things worse for me."

"Think about it, son. It could sharpen you up. I see what's wrong. You're asleep. When did you fall asleep? I don't know. So long ago, I barely remember you. Didn't you notice on the phone?"

"Are *you* asleep?" George snapped.

"No, sir," said Mr. McCoy, "and neither was she."

"Why'd you bring this?" George said, pointing to the envelope, brown, slightly wrinkled, cheap.

"I've been saving it. My father saved it for me, and his for him. That's the way we do things."

"Things fell off in your case," George said, then bit his tongue. He was glad his father was alive.

"I didn't conk out like you, but there was something. I remember."

"*Can* you remember?" George urged him.

George senior thought a minute, then gave up. "Nope."

"Isn't it time for you to be starting home?" the father said, rousing himself, tapping his watch face.

"It's only my second night," George reflected.

"It'll come back to you," his father said, "like riding a bike."

George wanted to trust his father. His wife Carol's tone shimmered in multiples, but his father's tone showed only its false side.

"Are you sorry for me?" George asked.

"Should I be? Are you sorry for me?"

"I don't know you. Maybe I would be if I did."

"That's a start, son. It'll get easier."

George and his father had run out of things to say. There was a dead spot in the middle of the afternoon and they drank through it.

"Okay, then," the father said, after a long, boozy silence. He snapped up the envelope. "I'll take these," he said, patting his jacket pocket. "Can you find your way home?"

"I'll read the directions backwards."

"Good, boy. Love to Carol and the baby. Go straight home now and don't forget your old dad. Call me!"

George ordered coffee, and when he lifted the clumsy mug from the bar top, he saw his hand shaking. He drank the hot fluid, which burnt his tongue. Had his father helped? No. Would his father help? Hard to say. Would he ask him again?

*I*nside the house things were different. They looked the same, but something was off. Carol was up in the bathroom using a hair product. Aaron was practicing on his child's piano, seven notes, then five, scale and arpeggio. A ham was resting on the stove top, cooling, and sweating a thick, sugary fluid. There was also a pot of potatoes, a casserole of green beans with something white over them and an oniony smell. The table was set for three.

George sat on his couch. A waft of hair dye irritated his nostrils, and now he could hear the hair dryer buzzing. Aaron was playing an extract from Bach. He played it through over and over.

What was the connection between these two here and that man at the bar? Had they ever seen each other? Was McCoy senior a "grandfather" to this kid, Aaron?

Carol and Aaron filed downstairs. Carol's black hair had a slick red coating; Aaron looked the same.

"Good day?" Carol asked her husband.

"About the same," he said.

After the ham dinner, the homework, and reading the paper, *The Plainfield Star* (so *that*'s where they lived), George agreed to read to his son. Aaron had been reading through the encyclopedia; he had gotten to "R," so George read an entry on the formation of religions.

"It's late," George said, after reading two, fine-print, and very absorbing pages.

"Are you going to be around now?" his child asked him.

George considered. Where have I been? he wanted to ask this young boy. Instead he said, "What did you do in school today?"

"I'm in fourth grade this year."

"I *know* that!" George almost shouted.

"Drawing," the child started to recite, "gym, composition, and spelling."

"Did you write something good?" George asked his son.

"I started on something."

"Bring it home."

"When I'm finished. I'm tired now, Dad," the boy said, flopping on his stomach.

"Good night, then," George said, noticing once again the odd growth of hair on the child's back skull.

Downstairs Carol was ironing something. He didn't like her, not the way he'd liked the girl he met at Kennedy's. Or the way his father liked the hostess at Clam Shell.

"Carol," he said, trying her name out, "what's wrong with our boy's head?"

She looked up, holding the iron horizontal. "He had a tumor."

"Hold on," George said. He found a bottle of wine, poured two glasses, and brought out the bottle. Reality could be suspended this way: by small bursts of activity and by drinking. This much he learned at Clam Shell.

Carol folded up the ironing board. The ironed blouse was on a hanger, cooling.

"He has cancer?" George asked. Cancer was in the family because his father had mentioned it. It was a crab shape, and George knew it could kill you.

"Had," his wife said. "He's well now. But to shrink the tumor, they gave him radiation. That's why he needs glasses."

"I never saw him once with glasses."

"He hates to wear them, but he can hardly see."

Carol sat on the couch and George took the wooden rocker. They drank their wine.

How come no one told me? he wanted to say, but maybe they had. He didn't feel connected to the boy, although he was starting to like him. His personality was pleasing. He liked him better than her. She didn't seem to mind, or maybe she was used to it.

"Would you like to hear something?" his wife asked.

"What do you have?"

"Classical, pop, cowboy music—that's what Aaron likes."

"Anything," George said, waiting to see what she'd pick, and if she knew what he liked. He didn't know what he liked, but he might know if he heard it.

Something very smooth came out of the stereo speakers: no voice, just a mass of instruments, a nice beat, subdued.

It was featureless, just like her, just like home. They listened to a few numbers, then she explained about Aaron. He had been well for two years, although that one spot on his head— the one, she said, he must have noticed—never grew hair in the same way. And he was small for his age, she added, but a nice boy, as he could see. And smart.

George wanted to say "I like him," but who would understand what he meant? He studied his wife. What part did she play? She had the reddish-black hair and a face with features crowded in the center: deep-set, light blue eyes and a small mouth. Had he ever loved her? Who was she?

And now what I'd really like to do, he thought, is sleep. I must have been doing fine. His wife gathered up the blouse on the hanger and went upstairs. She had no affect. George sat in place, rocking, pouring more wine. The music was finished and he didn't feel the need for more.

This second day satisfied no one.

III.

Storms had brewed all through the second night, inside and outside George's head. A cluster of thunderheads broke over their roof. By morning, a tree was down and electrical wiring draped to the ground. Power was out and candles were lit so that a cold breakfast could be fixed. But why go to work, George was thinking, if the lights are out? It was only Plainfield city, his wife Carol's portable radio said, where the worst of the storms were felt and power was still out. So work, for Carol, and school, for Aaron—both in Plainfield county, not as hard hit—were not, as such, ruled out. Soon they left together, mother and son.

When the kitchen was empty, cool and dark, George lay his

head on the table, pillowed on his arms. A wave of sleepiness (after two sleepless nights) was making the air heavy. But when George closed his eyes, he didn't find sleep. Not the sleep he was used to. Tiredness could make him unconscious, but the half-sleep he knew so intimately was no longer in there. Wakefulness or unconsciousness—those were the only choices. In this way, the two days and nights awake had made a difference.

More than ever, George wanted to redo the first day: barbershop, pike, coffee shop, and barroom. He wanted to do it and redo it. He did not want life in bed with this Carol of so many years; he did not want to see that bare spot on his son's head. He most certainly didn't want Clam Shell and the envelope full of dead men's policies. He had to find out what he did for a living. That could be the key to living awake in a world of unwants.

Outside the world had been transformed by storms. There were no lights and dirt had washed up the flat streets and over the clean windows and walls. Making sure his keys and date book were safe in his pocket, George found a man's raincoat in the closet and went out into the rain-sodden day. He decided to walk. The clouds were dense but high, and tatters of thin smoke were peeling off, clearing space for the more solid clouds. The sky was a sea of activity, lightening here, darkening there. Barbershop still closed, or so the sign said, but inside George spotted the Italian, in a black suit, sweeping his floor. How attached he was to the shop that, even on the day of a funeral, contact with it and with the labor of its upkeep could be so soothing! George watched until the barber looked up. He opened the barbershop door to a gust of rainy wind. Nothing to do but invite George to sit on a barber chair. "Gino" (read from the license on the wall) said he had lost a cousin, but more like a brother than a cousin; they had grown up under the same roof. No, not in Italy, but in the Italian section, where, when he was little, they spoke only Italian. His cousin was an orphan and raised with the six of them—

mother, father and three sisters. A glazier, he'd been cut in half by falling glass. The usual thing: a worker not broken in and drinking on the job. The barber started to cry; he put the broom away and sat in the other barber chair. George was electrified. His skin tingled; sadness pricked every pore of his skin. He sat with the barber until the barber sighed.

"Now I have to go. Mass is at 10:30, then my sister Mary Rose is having a time. She still lives in the old neighborhood."

The barber blew his nose and combed his hair, brushed the shoulders of his suit and plucked the trousers that were sticking to his small legs. George said goodbye, see you tomorrow, and the barber locked the door. He was on foot, too, but going in the opposite direction.

George checked in the first phone booth he saw, and sure enough, there were two Catholic churches in Plainfield: Martin de Porres and Rose of Lima. It had to be the Rose Church, so off he went with the torn page in hand. But where was it?

"Ma'am," he said to the waitress in the diner, "could you tell me how to find the Rose of Lima Church? I need to get there fast."

"St. Rose of Lima's? It's not walking distance. Well," she corrected herself, "you look like a fast walker." She named the streets and turns. "It's a big brick church with a tall tower, statue of St. Rose in the churchyard."

At full speed, George covered the distance in fifteen minutes. A forest of candles blazed on the altar; in front was a casket draped in black. The church was half filled, the front rows marked off with black bunting. George spotted Gino and his two sisters, among some old people, and one weeping woman, who must have been the wife.

The mass was short. In the middle, a priest and altar boys approached the casket. "Eternal rest grant unto him, O Lord," he said, and the people answered: "And may perpetual light shine upon him." Then, the casket was rolled out and hoisted down the steps. The widow was flanked on one side by Gino and on the other by an old woman—Gino's mother? You could tell the old woman spoke very little English; she didn't so much support the younger woman as hang on her arm.

Burial was in the church yard. Here the grief was extreme. Against a backdrop of wild, cloud-blown sky and fallen trees was the party of mourners, who one by one broke from their private thoughts to wail. The casket was lowered into a wet hole and each took a turn throwing a clod of earth. The priest, wearing a black coat and small, square hat with a feathery ball, read a prayer, then shook water from a silver baton over the casket. It was time to go.

George was invited by the team of men who'd been pall-bearers to come back to the house for refreshments. He said no. He wasn't part of it. The glazier was no relative of his; he hardly knew the cousin, Gino. Instead he took a walk.

As he walked—first in the light, then in the dark—George marveled at the day's richness. It was now his last few hours of day three, and he didn't want to go home and waste those hours knocking on the walls of his wife's isolation booth, where she kept hers and the boy's secrets. Still, they had a right to his attention, even though, if he had so much as an extra day left over, he'd rather spend it on the road, and with some other family—the lady who worked in the diner, or Rose, or even Mary, other people, maybe, he hadn't met yet.

*H*ome was home. Nothing changed. Carol's hair was greasy from how the sticky dye attracted dust and grime. She had combed it into a pony tail. What a face she had, now that he could see it: broad, almost Slavic with high cheekbones and hollow cheeks. The features seemed even more crowded, the eyes twinning over the high-bridged nose. She had something to say to him. He sensed that the minute he walked in. So something *had* changed. The boy wasn't there. He was at scouts, she said.

At first she busied herself, folding a magazine and punching up a cushion. She was still a silent woman, although this time a stronger mood was emanating.

"You'll never believe," he started to say, "what—"

He was stopped by a sigh. Now that he was sharper, he knew the sigh meant "Don't go on," so he didn't. The storms brewing all night were now in his house, or was that too self-centered to think? He still didn't know all his own characteristics, but she would be able to give him a sense of the wrong ones.

"Do you want to talk? I have a lot to tell you," he said to his wife, who laughed.

"After so many years?" she said, pulling the ribbon out of her hair and letting it drape around her face.

"Was I that quiet?" he asked her.

"A word a week, on average," she said. "In summer when direct sunlight brightened your mood."

"Was I moody?" George sat on the couch and patted the place next to him, but his wife stood.

"Your idea of conversation was, as it still is," she said, "to ask a question but never build on the answer."

So this was marriage. What was nice about his outside life since waking up was there was no background; everything was flat and simple, seen for the first time and acted upon. She sat down.

"Are you listening?" she said.

They eyed each other. Here was something he could feel. But would anyone want to feel it again? It was an experiment, he told himself. And he let himself test the deep, unconsoling waters of her eyes.

"I went to a funeral," he finally said.

"And you didn't even go to my father's. When he died."

"I went to one today," George said. "You might know these people. They run the barbershop."

"You go to a funeral for strangers, George, but you're a dead man to your own family."

"That seems to be right," he said.

"I've gotten to the point where I don't even care," she said. With that, Carol rose from the couch. "Except that I notice that I haven't felt like myself in so long that I forget what I was like." She turned toward the stairs. "But I know," turning back, "that I wasn't like this."

George couldn't help her. What she was like was also what he wanted to know. It now seemed they'd never know. George felt it—yes, this was it—like a hood drawing over his head, now pulled down and tied under the feet. But loosely tied; it was loosely tied.

IV.

Next morning, Aaron woke his father up, ate breakfast, and asked his father for a ride to school. Aaron's mother was taking a sick day to begin spring cleaning. She had a scarf tied around her head and had filled the basins upstairs and downstairs with hot ammonia water. The house would stink, even if every window were open, so Aaron suggested that his father take his (Aaron's) library card, and spend cleaning day there. For supper, they could go out to eat, and by then the fumes would have died down.

This was the first day in several that his father had been his old self: gloomy, snappish, gray triangles point-downward on his cheeks. The strange, vitalized father of the last two days was eclipsed by this more familiar one. After dropping him off at Speed Street Elementary, his father would normally be off to the ball-bearing factory. His father had been furloughed—that's the word his mother had used. He looked it up in the dictionary and drew his own conclusions. It was temporary, but ominous. The papers said that the factory was in chapter eleven but that an emergency plan had emerged, and a white knight. At home no one mentioned the fate of the plant, for fear of making things worse.

For two days, the family walked on eggs. First his father had gotten notice and then he had emerged—after so many years

Aaron couldn't remember what had come before—from the depths. They were playing it by ear, mother and son. He wasn't exactly a stranger, but close.

His father took the library card but Aaron wasn't sure, climbing out and slamming the door ("bye Dad," silence), that he'd use it. The sight of the boy's face as he offered the card, slamming the door and hoisting a backpack on a thin shoulder, woke George up for the second time in his life. But this time, he was only half out. The world through the windshield was dimmer, as if wrapped in wax. George drove to the barbershop.

Customers lounged on the mismatched chairs and a second barber, tall and stringy, worked the other station. George couldn't even catch Gino's eye. He had plucked a dripping comb from a glass of blue water and was smoothing the nape of a man's head. George didn't need a haircut, so after waiting his turn, he asked the second barber for a shave. Only then did Gino say: "Here, my man. Step up," opening his striped sheet for George to enter.

But it was all barber and customer. Even when George asked, "How's the family?" the barber said, "Fine." Had the death of the cousin been a dream? No, because when George said, "You weren't open yesterday," the barber said, "Oh yes, a family matter, and Eddie here had jury duty," pointing at Eddie with the shaving brush. George was no more to Gino than a customer.

The rest of the day went likewise: no kite, no boy, and the pike started growing a few leaves. It was spring and even this lifeless thing could pump a trickle of living sap to unfrizzle its fists. It was a maple, now George could see, and it was five percent alive. Its few leaves received the sun on waxy faces. George skipped the diner, no appetite, but he did chance upon the public library, killing time before Kennedy's opened. It was one story, with a low-slung roof. Inside, books dominated. They covered the walls in their leathery bindings, nearly all the same color. The glues and pastes exuded an odor like dead, salty pastries. George sat at a table. On it was a newspaper with its fold stiffened by a pale stick. If he was going to find things out, it wasn't going to be this way!

George went looking and came up with four books: a novel, a mystery, a book in a foreign language and one on origins—myths. He took his jacket off. So far, no sign of librarians. He opened the last book: there were five pages of nothing, then the title page, and then the bulk. First sentence: "After the Dark Ages, when the ancient man slept, although thought to be dead, a new mechanical man was born." He settled in for the story.

The mechanical man was just a few awkward folds compared to what came before. That much was clear. Still the mechanical man was the story's main character, and everything that happened happened to him. He was strong and he felt no pain. The ancient man had felt everything, hotter and more intense as life went on.

Soon a librarian hovered, arranging books, but he knew she was there to interfere. He had been reading too long. Something could be wrong and she was just a small woman in an isolated building. But George would not be taken from his book. Another librarian wheeled a cart across the wooden floor. Both women watched until they were sure he was reading and nothing more. He let them look: by the time they were sure, he was back in again.

The ancient man was big with a smooth, hairless skin. The mechanical man was a blood relative. The suspense was that they didn't know they were related, or that they shared the same space, but life had put the timer on and the difference between what was then and what was now would be closing up. The men would meet. Each would see his own deficiencies, but the ancient, soon to depart, would see most.

George closed the book and asked the younger librarian to reserve it. He would finish it tomorrow. When she offered to check it out for him, he felt in his pocket for his son's card, but changed his mind: he didn't want this book in the house.

Outside, the best part of the day was over. Color and light were draining from the streets, but the eyes of the few stragglers showed that night was welcome. George still liked seeing strangers. He found his car and drove it home.

The home was clean, spotless and damp. It gave off a sweet odor: the ammonia and pine had been rinsed and the surfaces painted with a candyish wax. A note on the kitchen table said: "Be back soon. Gone for groceries. A and C."

"A and C," he thought, taking the note. "And I could be B if I weren't G."

Although he felt weary enough for a nap, George decided it was time to do some snooping, see what was there of puzzle pieces. He noticed a jumble of papers on the table under the phone. In his wife's hand were messages. The first was an appointment: Dr. Applebaum, 4 P.M., Thursday. "Empty stomach," it said, "and bring two samples." There was a phone number jotted at the top, and George dialed it. When the message came, he knew he'd "reached the offices of Stanley Applebaum and Kristen Katz, Group Pediatrics," but there was no need to dial the emergency number.

They were keeping things from him. That was a painful knot and George touched it mentally. Sitting down at his kitchen table, George dropped his head into his hands. His brain material swelled so as to fill all available space.

Meanwhile, the two other family members entered and, having seen the car, made their way to the kitchen. Their appearance, even before he saw their faces, wrenched George from his burial place. The face he showed them was uncut anguish.

Mother and son went upstairs together and each changed out of day clothes: Carol put on a green, fitted dress, something that, years ago, George would have liked. She had washed the stickiness out of her hair and bathed off the sweat and cleaning powders. She had worn rubber gloves so her hands were smooth and no hangnails. You'd never know that she'd cleaned the entire house, scrubbed the floors and applied a powerful wax to all the wood. In fact, the hard labor had smoothed the wrinkle on her brow and relaxed the jaw muscle. She looked younger.

Carol opened the shades to let in the faint, evening light. The work day people were arriving home (nowadays that could mean men, women, and sometimes older children, too) and were meeting each other for the first time that day. The clash of home with the outside was the dramatic nexus of the day. They survived it—the three McCoys—or they had so far, Carol thought, because one of them was never home. It was different now. George had shown signs of coming back. She and Aaron hadn't discussed it yet. They were waiting to see how lasting the change would be.

Meantime family life had gone its sweet way. School, work and vigilance to the ever-changing menace of the disease. They lived their lives around it: that way, it never could fool them. They always included it in their routines; it was in the foreground and in the background. So today, when they got the news that it was back, that it had regrouped somewhere and had invaded another organ, they were ready. Dr. Applebaum and his team had what they needed, and Carol and her son were ready to march to his tune.

Carol left the window, with light shrinking and the houses losing their crispness. She could hear a burble of conversation from the kitchen. She went to the boy's room and folded the clothes he had tossed on the bed. She unpacked his schoolbag, pulling out a test and a paper. She pictured her child's fastidious hand shaping letters for the composition entitled: "Spring Flowers." There was a choice of two topics: Spring Training or Spring Flowers. Her boy chose the hard one: "The oldest flowers on earth were uncultivated grasses. In ancient days no flower had any color but green because man did not grow for color. Some think he was color blind." Like all the child's written work, the essay was pristine. Where he got his information—because Carol doubted its accuracy—she had no idea. Aaron could make up things as easily as see them, but the germ of these fabrications came from somewhere. The rest of the essay told the story of the coming of color: that man put aside his bodily needs, or satisfied them easily, and then sought to create in the world fodder for dreams.

Carol returned paper and test to the bag, zipped them in and joined her family. Aaron had started dinner: three potatoes were peeled, a pot of water was set to boil. Different fresh meats were in the meat bin. He was snapping beans. His father had his nose in the refrigerator.

When they turned, she saw they had the same large, stretchy mouths and stiff necks; their heads, turning in the same direction, made a scant arc. How natural it all seemed.

"Will you have a cocktail?" her husband said. Then Aaron waved them out of the room to mix and drink their cocktails, while he finished the beans and selected a meat for broiling. He didn't yet use the oven, so his mother would have to return. George filled a bowl with ice cubes; Carol covered a tray with a napkin and two glasses, bottles, jars of onions and olives and a couple of fresh citrus fruits.

"He's very grown up, isn't he?" was George's first offering.

"He's a genius."

"I know you know him a lot better than I do," said George, clinking his wife's full glass.

"I suppose it's easy enough to see."

"Do they see it at school?"

"Oh sure they do. It's not much prized, though." Carol sat on the couch and pointed to a chair for George.

"Are you a genius, Carol? It wouldn't surprise me." He got up from his chair to clink her glass again.

"No."

And then he sprung it, because everything seemed so normal. "What is it you do for a living, if you don't mind my asking? I know I should know."

"My life isn't organized around work. I can tell you, but it's not the keystone."

"*He* is."

In came the boy with a platter of meats. "Mum," he said, "I'll give this a try if you light the pilot."

"I'll light the pilot," George said, "if you'll tell me where the matches are."

"They're up high," Carol said, "where young fingers can't reach them."

But even George knew that nothing could be kept from the reach of genius. He would get there.

When Carol asked if Aaron wanted to read his composition, and the boy ran to fetch it, read it aloud, and bask in the glory of their united attention, George noticed—aside from the stylistic beauty of the writing—a likeness between it and the story about the ancient and mechanical. Aaron's was just another part of the same story, an earlier part. It was fine to think that disparate materials (dreams) could be so related, that nothing was wasted.

Carol sent the boy to his room to do problem sets. When he was safely gone, George asked his wife what Dr. Applebaum, or his colleague, had said that day.

"About what?" she said.

In a flash George knew that it was this infuriating vagueness that made him sleep. "Does," he said in plain English, "Aaron still have cancer?"

"You asked me that already," she said. Was she drunk?

"I'm asking again."

"Yes," she said, "if you really want to know."

If George had had a knife, or even a pencil handy, he would have plunged it down her throat. "Sit down," he said.

She did, and he heard. Now he knew. He'd wasted his time and the boy had no time to waste.

"Make me another," he said, after a time.

*I*n, in, in!—the world was driving him in—but he stayed out. The dinner was eaten—everything tasted sandy—but George ate what was dished on his plate. Dinner time was quiet; even clicks of silver on plate were muted. Mother and son, exchanging dozens of glances, could see that their man was still there with them. He was in the family, although his capability was low. Compared to them, he was an unarticulated blob.

After supper, Aaron returned to his math.

Dark night covered the house and before sleeping, Carol rocked her husband in her arms. George let himself be handled. He was not tired, but he would sleep.

V.

Real sleep, as he knew it next morning, when he awoke and his eyes were clear panes, was not thought. Thought was a buzzing relative to life; sleep was a smooth cone into which a head-first dive led to springs under the earth. The self was a diving suit and no more. There was real worth, and separation, in sleep. Now he knew.

When he was fully awake, and had separated the skins of sleep, not examining but laying them aside; when he had washed and dressed, filled his pockets with necessaries and patted them; when he was ready to begin a day, he noticed that the house was empty. Clean, bright, fresh-smelling (although lurking in the still air was a remnant of soaps and cleaning agents, just enough to sour the stomach), but vacant. A place was laid for him at the table and he could see where the other places were, although an attempt had been made to wipe glass rings and the skid marks the vinyl placemats had made. His family had given George a linen placemat (he must be fussy, or maybe from a different class) and a linen napkin. They had laid out a juice glass that was really a wineglass, three plates and a cup and saucer. In the middle of the table, on its own fresh mat, was a porcelain coffee pot, sugar bowl and creamer.

The phone rang. George reflected on his right to answer it, or even his obligation. (Perhaps the child was sick?) "Hello?"

"It's your father," he heard. "I called you yesterday. D'ya get the message, or what?"

"What do you want?" George said. It was simple, even brutally simple, but something George could pull from the air without a single encumbering thought.

His father laughed. A cascade of coughs. "You're getting it."

"So?" George said.

"Got plans for tonight?"

"As a matter of fact—" George started.

"Meet me at Kennedy's at five sharp. Do you remember how to get there?"

"Kennedy's Tavern?"

"Corner of Academy and Eddy."

George found a teabag and soaked it in hot water from the tap. He left his place setting on the table.

He drove to Aaron's school and continued to the library. His book was there, but the librarians were different women, although still two of them.

His table of yesterday was empty. Here's what he read: The mechanical man was only a little smaller than the antique, but the world knew him as superior. The older smoothed things out for him, gave so much in food and services that the mechanical was free to squander his time, sharpening his eye for opportunity. How he got ahead! And why did the old support him so? Was this a mystery that everyone but George understood? George looked up with glazed eyes.

Everyone knew a piece of the puzzle, but they were so tight-fisted! They would give up anything but that piece. Perhaps if he glued himself to the surface and watched them every minute? Then he would lock in his pieces with theirs, but everything he knew from sleeping would be lost.

George lost interest in the book. He knew the ancient would never entirely disappear, and the mechanical would attain only something approaching full growth. The mechanical would never reign or replicate without the older brother's steady, but never perfect, self-extinction.

He closed the book. The librarians were watching him, without even raising their heads from their desk work. He could create that kind of sensation just by entering someone else's world, no matter that it was a public space and his son's card gave him rights. It was their world, and he was a stranger. If he came back tomorrow, it might be different. He'd be that "strange man who spends the day reading the same book. He must be out of work or maybe just got out of the hospital?" As a grown man, George should not be seen during the day on the street or in a public place. In bars—that was different. Having a solitary snack at a diner—that was okay, occasionally. He was somewhere between "once" and a familiar. He had no patterns. That one day, that first day, he was accepted: barbershop, pike, coffee shop, bar, home. By the second day, he was different. Even his own life tried to pull him in—his father foisting those insurance policies; his wife and son making room for him at home. New lives beckoned (the orphan, the widow), but only in catastrophe. Gino had hardened up right after.

George looked up. Both librarians were staring. Had thought arisen, solid, from his head and made him even stranger? When spotted, they dove back into their work, but one looked down and there was no work, nothing on the desk, so she grabbed the key to the restroom and exited through the door marked OFFICE USE ONLY. The air cooled from this embarrassment. "Call the police," the head librarian had written, but in the john, she crushed the note in her hand and disposed of it. Pray to God he doesn't come back tomorrow. And when she returned to her desk, he was gone. The book, *Industrial Revolution: History of Our Time,* was back on reserve. The head librarian flipped through the pages. What was so important in here that he had to keep it for himself? It was just history and a lot of it replaced by newer models. She was tempted to put the book in deep freeze (acid-free bath, bindery)—good for two months, at least—but he'd only find another one. If that kind of man wanted to come back and read, he'd do it.

George was back out and had found a new street called Broadway. The thinking had rested him, or maybe the ruckus it caused had cleared his head. The skins of fatigue were less tight, less dry. Without even planning for it, or dreading it, he was walking to work. The ball bearing factory, Plainfield Rotary, was only a few steps from the library. It was an old building with a new building attached. Front was four-story brick with gingerbread; back was cement-block. That's where the balls were made. Shipping was behind that. George felt a wave of pride. He remembered coming out here to get his first job. Twenty-one years old, just out of college. His father had worked here his whole life, before the new part was built, when the balls were made on the ground floor of 54 Broadway, right here, main building. George, though, was white collar, and by the time he signed on, front office was where the factory used to be. His memories were fresh, as if carved for the first time from brain pulp. Here was pleasure.

Walk in. And he did (unlocking the door with one of the keys in his keycase), but no one was there. The factory—even the front office—was still shut down. George roamed through the empty offices, some still with papers on the desk. One of the doors said: GEORGE MCCOY, SENIOR BUYER. George walked in. There was a picture of a sailboat on the wall, a green-shaded lamp on the desk, and one easy chair facing the wide window. Outside that window was West Plainfield Street, a dumpy place—auto body, vacant lot, row of tenement houses—but George must have liked the view because here was a chair facing it. Manuals of various kinds were lined up in a single bookshelf. Books of prices and amortization charts, another book on the engineering of solid spheres. A second factory must have been in the works because here, folded up, was the blueprint. Underneath was a shelf devoted to photos of Plainfield Rotary in the old days. A group of workmen stood in front of the gate, each carrying a lunch pail and thermos. They were in overalls. A man in a black suit stood to one side, and two women a little in the background. George recognized his father—just a kid then, with a thatch of sandy hair and eyes half closed. The other men were older and looked baked into their clothes. His father's clothes (dungarees and a plain, open-throated shirt) looked new; his shirt and watch fit to a "T" and gave the figure flair. Maybe his dad had a date that night with his ma?

George could get lost in such a scene, so he moved his eyes to the next photo: Carol, a young wife, holding his baby boy, wrapped in a thick blanket. Just born? The little hand was grasping a teething ring. George caught the eyes of his wife, looking straight at his (now and in the picture, where he would have been the photographer). The eyes were smoothed out, clear blue orbs. The features were less congested. The hair was loose. Looking out with their boy in a blanket, Carol's eyes met his. She hadn't been hurt yet, but here was their wedding picture right beside it, and already that mother differed from this white bride holding his hand. This bride was untouched; her eyes were clear planets. George shut his own eyes in horror. He backed up and felt behind him, then folded himself into the easy chair but did not look out the window. Inside his head he saw the ruins of his life.

How had he done so much damage? Was his body a weapon? Or had it come from talk? Talk like water causing a slow but inexorable erosion: brains, beauty, youth, confidence, peace. It had started happening (judging from the photos) before she even ceased to love him. From her wedding day until that boy's fifth or sixth week, Carol had already begun to spoil. George wished he could see the baby's face better. It was hidden by the blanket, but he knew that babies' faces reflected very little beyond the empty draughts of sleep they took to return to an earlier peace. Still, the little boy's face might say something.

George roused himself. His desk clock—still running—said past five, almost five-thirty, the day had been eaten whole. He let himself out of his office, out of the building, locking the door behind him. Life in such an old-fashioned factory (even with the new part) was over. Even George, awake five days, could see this. Perhaps it was also with the help of the library book. Smallness was behind us, now that Plainfield city didn't contain all its people, all its business and pleasure. Life was leaving the city and going elsewhere. Who knew for what purpose.

George put his hands in his pockets and trudged over to Kennedy's, one of the last depots. He passed Gino's barbershop—empty—and for the first time noticed painted letters on the window: UNISEX. What did that mean? Nothing about Gino, or the shop, suggested that Gino would know either. But someone had had it painted on; maybe the second barber. George looked inside at the clean little place with the ruby nightlight burning—needlessly burning because daylight was adequate. Unisex was a special license for something, or a form of insurance. "Sex" would be the root of something else. Maybe it was misspelled. Or a set of initials: u.n.i.—s.e.x. Was the future one sex? Or did Gino and his partner belong to a new kind of union?

Another hour had passed. George steamed along the sidewalk. Kennedy's was a scant block away. The car from Clam Shell was parked in front, and there was Dad with his face reflected in the mirror. George could talk to him from the sidewalk. First, George senior tried a smile, but George junior wouldn't receive it, pleasant though it might seem. George cast his father another kind of look—penetrating—and

George senior shook his finger in the mirror. It was a warning. He redoubled the hardness of his gaze and concentrated it evenly between his father's eyes. His father shook his head, then let his head drop. The two Georges did not connect, not that way. The father had his own terms and would stick to them, so young George entered the bar and took the stool to the left of his father's.

"It's not that easy," the senior McCoy said.

"I'll have whatever you're having," his son replied.

"I can tell things are better with you," the father said. "I can see it on your face and the way you've straightened up. Tell you the truth, first time I saw you, I didn't think you could be my George, such a wreck you were. You let yourself go, George, but now you've pulled yourself together. A Tübingen," Mr. McCoy said to Kennedy, "for my son here, and I'll take another."

"My kid is sick, dying maybe, and my wife, Carol—well, I don't know where to begin."

"Everyone's got problems, George."

As this approach would never work with this hard nut of a father, George held out his hand. His father felt in his jacket pocket and laid the envelope on the bar top. He tapped it.

"They're canceled, except for one," he said. "That one is redeemable."

"Who collected?" George asked.

"Oh, we all did, each in his own time," answered his father. "When we needed something, we used it. No harm done."

"The harm was already done," George said.

"Don't be too quick," his father said, and here were two golden beers.

"I was at the plant today. That's over," said George.

"Course," his father replied, slurping the head off his beer.

"It's okay for you," George said. "You're out of it now."

"True."

"But for me, and for him—" George started.

"Ah—for him! He'll do better. What's his name? Abel?"

"Typical that you don't know," George said, shaking his head over the untasted beer.

"I care, but not in the ordinary way. It's not for you to say that it's not as good."

"Oh, I'm not comparing," George said. "Who am I?"

"Indeed," the father relied.

"And who are you? Where do you stand in all this life?"

"Right where I always did," the father answered, toasting himself in the mirror, then tapping the policy envelope for emphasis.

"That's too easy," George said. A shiver went through him as he spoke; he realized only with his words, and their intent to wound, that his father was dead. The policy *was* his. Now he would know his father's worth, and collect it. But who was this strangely solid man, sitting on a barstool in downtown Plainfield? And who had driven to Clam Shell?

"You get it now, don't you?" the father said, staring at the mirror, where George could see his own stunned face turned sideways. His mouth open, it looked like he was going to eat his father's head, swallow it whole.

"No, I don't really," said George, turning the head so he could look full at himself, tawny eyes and close-cropped hair. In them was the secret of his sleep, but his dead father knew the answer too.

"Why are you involved with me?" George asked, his voice thin and shrill.

"You called, didn't you?"

"I called, yes, but I didn't think I called that far. And your number was in the book."

"Whose book?"

"The home book."

"Oh," the father said—thoughtfully, for him. "I guess they failed to strike it out."

"When did you go?"

"Here?" said the father, looking around at Kennedy's, empty. "I died in September, a year or so ago. I don't keep track of the date."

George wanted to ask one more question, but he held it back. His father was dangerous, too quick, and had no thought for anyone but himself. Was he any different now from before?

"The policy here——" George said, taking a different tack.

"It's worth plenty," the father said, cutting George off. "Take a look."

George wanted to look but he was afraid to release his father's gaze—those two half-moon eyes—from his own. He felt the envelope, opened the lip and plucked the folded page between two fingers. His father was fading now, although the half-lidded eyes were still clear, and the last to go, vanishing only with a wink of the left eye. The eyes were still in the mirror, although the gaze was sadder there and the lids were drooping until they closed. George was reminded—and resisted it!—of the perished Christ pulled down from the cross, lying limp in his mother's arms.

And here was the bartender, Kennedy, asking "What'll it be?" and removing the father's empty glass. (He was dead and he drank! Wasn't that typical! George thought, feeling his chest bubble with laughter.)

George looked to see what he was drinking, but there was no glass before him, just a wiped space. He hadn't ordered yet. No beer—he knew that much—was called Tübingen. "I'll have whatever's on tap," George said and, out of the three brews, picked a pale ale. And here it was. "I need this," he told Kennedy.

"Nice to see you in here," the bartender replied. "We old-timers need to stick together."

"Was an old man just here in the bar, sitting about where I am? I know that guy, but I forgot his name."

"You're my first customer today, and it's only . . . , " Kennedy glanced over his shoulder at an alarm clock next to the cash register, "6 o'clock. I don't usually open till six, and business is thin, unless it's payday over there at Gyrodynamics."

George listened and knew enough not to ask if Gyrodynamics was the old Plainfield Rotary. Things were moving fast now and he could feel the motion, even if he didn't understand the sudden burst of speed.

"Gotta go home pretty soon," he told Kennedy, who was fussing with a tape that fed into the cash register, "but tap me another."

Kennedy tapped and placed the full glass next to the first one. "This one's on me," he said. "Happy hour, you know?"

George closed his eyes. He had one of the glasses in his fist. He was going to think very hard. It would all come out now, or bust.

But only a wind was in his head. What was it blowing? Something was ahead of it, tumbling in the gutter. Was it a license or was it a list? George went after it, coat tails floating behind. Something important was written on it. The note he needed, written in his own mother's hand. But the note, worried by a last violent gust, blew to the sewer.

"Drink up now, Dad, and let's go home," he heard, and here was the kid, with that heavy backpack, wedged in the chink between two stools.

"How did you find me?" George asked his son.

"I found you. Can I have an orangeade at the bar?"

Kennedy was already uncapping the bottle and pouring it into a glass. Setting the heavy pack on the floor, Aaron hoisted himself up.

The boy, even from the side—seeing just the curve of the nose and the dove-like cheeks—looked tired. Was a day of school so tiring? Or was it the anxieties of the illness, Aaron's face reflecting his mother's watchfulness.

The boy picked up his glass with a reddish paw. He sucked up the garishly colored soda, and a bit of natural tint bloomed in his cheeks. The soda was like a transfusion. Aaron drank to the lees, glancing at his father just at the point when the sucking among ice cubes became audible.

"Would you like another?" said George, pulling the wet glass out of his child's hands, although the child did not instantly release it. Kennedy's eyes were on them. He offered the child a happy-hour refill, mentioning that minors, strictly speaking, weren't normally allowed in a bar, especially sitting at it, but as no one else was here and he was in the company of his dad, he'd let it go. The second orange soda was uncapped. This one had more pep to it and father and son smiled when the head spilled over, down the sides, and over the wooden bar. Kennedy was there with a cloth to mop it, setting the fresh drink on a napkin.

"Have a toast?" Aaron said. And clinking glasses, he added, "To you."

"And to you," was his father's reply.

Kennedy had picked up a glass and filled it with spring water from the tap. "And to you," he said, tapping each glass and looking into each set of eyes. A cone of something like contentment settled on the three males.

"Mom is waiting," the child said, as he sucked out his second soda.

"Run ahead then," said George. "I'll be there shortly."

"Come with me," said the child, slipping off the seat and belting the pack on his back.

"I can't, but I'll be there later. Will you shake my hand?"

After the shake and the rustling departure of the boy, when Kennedy had retreated to a phone booth, closing the folded door behind him, George closed his eyes and tore after the note, still tumbling down the gutterway, stopped now from its dive to the sewer depths by sewer grate. He had the note in his hand now.

"Dear Son," it said. "Here are your instructions: how to wake up, or sleep unmolested. Part A or Part B.

"Let me start here, where I am no longer—on earth—

although it's not as specific a space as you might think, or not as distinctly different or separated from where I am. Death is quaint, my dear George, it's smaller than you think in territory, and with locals only. My cemetery, out there four miles west of Plainfield, holds just the four thousand souls, most from the old neighborhood, but I got in late, so, just as in life, most of the dead are much older and I am the junior member, which suits me fine.

"There's a logic to it, is what I'm saying; death's not nothing or just vagueness. Sleep is related, but rooms of death keep opening up and there's no need ever to surface. (I think you know what I'm referring to.)

"Sleep is the foyer and most dead ones wait until they're very close to finished to sleep the way you did. How you learned it, I don't know, but it might run in the family, as my own father and his and the one before that chose a lasting sleep well before their time. They reached out their hands to death, and death took 'em. It's not in a rush, but doesn't look in the mouth of a gift horse, either.

"Even your own son is flirting with it, although not with the same kind of gun to his head. Are you that surprised, Georgie, that Carol, your wife, is sickening, surrounded as she is by wintry sleep and infantile self-sacrifice?

"Now I lay me down to sleep, pray the Lord my soul to keep." And such like.

George folded the letter and opened his eyes. This was very shallow, all too worthy of a man who called himself father but who was no more than a tough rump steak. Kennedy was off the phone and now washing glasses. Although he tried not to look, George was soon watching and felt he could watch forever. How satisfying the motions were, how clean and wet the glasses looked when stacked on the counter, tall with tall, bowls with bowls. But eventually, Kennedy finished his work, wiped his hands on a rag, and came over to check George's progress with the beers.

"How's the squirt doing?" he asked.

George opened wide the moon eyes until the whole bar was in them, Kennedy at the center; he encompassed the scene and then said, "Do you have any children?"

Kennedy said no, wasn't even married, didn't even have a serious girlfriend. No, it wasn't for him. He would have gone on, but George's eyes, still flooded with vision, stabbed him.

"He looks better, stronger," the bartender said, subdued. He slapped the bar with the rag. "God damn it, George, I put my fat foot right in it, didn't I?"

"He looks okay," George said, after a minute or two, "but he isn't."

"I'm sorry to hear it," the bartender said. "Mind my own business from now on."

George was touched by the barkeep's remorse. Remorse was a new one. Who had shown any? People were too jaded for remorse. They rode over their mistakes as life's relentless wave smacked them in the back or drowned them in its salty suds. But Kennedy here, a single man with only his job, had offered it in the wake of a callous remark, and the remorse itself had wakened in George once more the sight of the wave curving over his own head, set on its own timetable. The stillness of the wave, as much as its size, had englobed George in half sleep.

But in the sleep—as dead as it made him, and worse than jaded—had clarified the shape of other things (the whereabouts of his late father, for instance; the delicate dailiness of the social surface; and more, all these like fish coming up on the line, one after another).

George, in this satisfied state, above the wave of sleep for once but still sheltered in a larger tide, paid the tab, shook Kennedy's detergent-softened hand and walked home.

Home was home. Out was out. Gyrodynamics had supplanted Rotary. Long days, short nights, and the reverse. George traveled along the lip of life.

One day, he set off on foot. It was the familiar season, spring; it was the familiar time, late morning; the sun was a bright knob in the pearly, humid sky. George was hobbling along, George McCoy, to meet his grandson, Georgie, at Tomato Aspic, a health bar in the new downtown mall. George had been awake now for thirty-five years. He'd laid his saintly wife, old Carol, to rest just last year, in the earth where he would join her, where old George was now lying. Aaron McCoy was a nuclear scientist, now in a wheelchair, frail but working every day in his home office. His only son, Georgie, had graduated from junior college and was waiting tables at Aspic. He had a part ownership now and was waiting for his grandfather to arrive so he could serve him a tasty lunch on the patio and—if it was slow—sit with him and shoot the breeze. It was almost summer and the days were balmy, Georgie had a met a girl and a smooth, deep quiet—something he'd never known before— was settling over him like a thick seabed over the eelgrass.

Hers

Body and Soul

I.

For tea Joann had invited four, but Sandy couldn't make it; she was visiting her father in Colorado. The other three—Melinda, Jake, and Andrea—got along fine. In fact, Joann suspected that Jake, who had lived with Sandy for three years, was now drifting toward Andrea. Joann hadn't seen any of them in a while, so she could easily be mistaken, although the signs were there.

Joann left her company to brew a pot of tea. What were the signs? An excess of touching—taps on the shoulder, pats on the arm, strokes and squeezes. She'd seen Andrea, in a burst of hilarity over Jake's inability to tell a green from a blue, grab his leg above the knee. Her fingers were imprinted on the fine trouser material; the marks remained there, until Jake, who also seemed aware of them, moved his leg under the table.

Joann measured out the tea. There were other signs—something in their voices and those steady glances. Jake could talk about his classes, his gallery sales, about the ancient roll of crumbly newsprint he'd scavenged, then spread out like carpeting in his studio. Whatever it was, his eyes were having a different conversation with Andrea's eyes, or sometimes with Andrea's hands, because when Andrea's eyes went blank, her hands, folding and refolding her napkin, were still responding.

"Joann, my love, don't die in there!" Jake shouted. And here was Melinda: "You okay?"

The tea was brewed. Joann removed the infuser and carried in the blue pot, returning for the sugar bowl and creamer, which she hooked onto the fingers of one hand, grabbing the plate of lemons with the other. As she pushed open the door, Jake jumped up to grab the dipping pitcher. A little cream had already spilled on the new rug. Suddenly the guests noticed the rug. Was it new?

Yes, gift from a friend, Joann said—someone they had met but maybe didn't remember. He'd been traveling in the Middle East. The rug was a rich ruby color with borders in black and dark green. It looked old, but it was new. How could it be old, Joann had said, with automatic weapons woven into the corners? And sure enough, Melinda—who knew everything about rugs—was able to identify the Afghan tribe and region it had come from. The stylized guns she couldn't identify, but she'd seen them before.

"I've never seen them," Andrea said. "Love *is* blind."

"What did you just say?" Melinda asked her.

"Nothing."

"It's good quality," Melinda went on.

"I don't care for guns," said Andrea.

Jake told a story about an Uzi trade he'd heard about with lamas in Tibet. He'd seen the beautiful hides they'd exchanged for the gun. His friend was still stretching them. What a surface! You could use either side.

"I like it, Jo—the rug," he said. "It's high-grade wool, and the weave is very fine. Congratulations."

"Who's the man who gave it to you?" Andrea asked.

"Let me get the pie," Joann said. "And I'll tell you."

"No, let *me* get the pie," said Jake, jumping up, and he kissed her cheek and walked her back to the table. "You sit."

"Okay." Joann raised her eyes from the silver spoons her own great-aunt had left her—a silver, as Melinda had pointed out, you couldn't buy any more—to meet the gaze of the two friends who, for all their politeness, had been staring since they'd arrived. Every time Joann got up she could feel their eyes raking her fleshless body. How could you describe the look she was getting now from Andrea? You couldn't describe it.

But here was Jake with the steaming cherry pie.

"*You* didn't make that?" was out of Melinda's mouth before she had time to think.

"I didn't," Joann cheerfully responded.

"God, it smells good," said Jake and Andrea together.

Joann picked up the cake knife, but Jake took it out of her hand, whirled the hot pie on its trivet, and started cutting slices, hot clouds pouring from the red-and-brown checkerboard.

It had been six weeks—little over—since Joann had had her operation. She was feeling well, a little tired, but no pain at all. She'd been back to work a week now, and although she had her groceries delivered and never lifted anything heavier than a dish, people still coddled her, bringing supper and goodies, cases of wine and bottled water. It was now early September, and Melinda had lugged up half a basket of apples and Seckel pears. Jake had brought cheeses, and Andrea had baked three loaves of bread. Joann's refrigerator was packed with the remains of cheese and paté baskets, boxes of chocolates, and biscuits, jellies, and fruit butters.

Joann's incisions were healing, her surgeon had said, although they still looked pretty raw. No actual stitches had been sewn, she'd told everyone at the hospital. They now tape up the openings with Scotch tape.

Her guests were incredulous. "It's not *Scotch* tape, is it?"

"Look," Joann had said, clutching at her hospital gown as if to show them what she couldn't look at herself. She had gotten a glimpse in the mirror when the nurse had lifted her under the arms so the dressing could be rewound. Even without her glasses, she could see the slices, inky, with blue-black flesh around them. It was only up near the ribs that the skin was still white. The pain of the sudden motion had soaked her skin. She closed her eyes, listening as the gauze strips unrolled onto the floor. The Scotch tape stayed on. It stayed on until it fell off.

"Lucky for you," Melinda had said, at least twice, "they don't just rip it off."

"Not funny," Joann had answered.

Joann was one week in the hospital, one week at home, and now, three weeks later, she was "entertaining" guests, even if it was just tea for three friends. They'd insisted on coming. If they hadn't insisted, said Melinda—the instigator—Joann would never have made the move on her own. Even before the operation, Joann didn't entertain much. Her job, delightful as it mostly was, took her out of the house from early morning till late in the evening, attending dinners, cocktail parties, openings, readings; there were frequent trips to the State House and to D.C., not to mention board meetings, banquets, and political dinners. Illness had given Joann the luxury of staying home whole days and nights all by herself.

There was that, and, as Melinda put it, there was Mr. Anonymous Concert Artist, whom the friends had met, but never at Joann's, where they knew he spent most of his spare time. He had sent the rug, but otherwise—as Melinda had told Andrea when Joann was out of earshot—there were no signs of him—not in the bathroom, where she had checked, nor in the bedroom, although the door was closed. ("I opened it," Melinda had said, when Jake asked.) What was going on? They all wanted to know, but no amount of tactful pressure could force a straight answer out of their always discreet (and now hermetically sealed!) Joann.

The pie was delicious: tart with a buttery crust. Joann had forgotten the ice cream. She had some. Would people have another slice? Should she reheat the pie? Get the ice cream,

Melinda said, excusing herself to make another swing through the bathroom. Jake and Andrea, touching feet under the table, were content to be left alone.

Joann reached into the freezer for a fresh box of ice cream. Most of the full containers were old, their contents crystallized and separated, light brown under the lid. The fresh ice cream was rock-hard. She put the carton on the stove, over the pilot light. Then she sat down, facing the window. The sun, low in the sky, flooded, red and warm, over her face and chest.

The wounds were healing faster now, and they were itchy, a constant distraction. Joann imagined a dozen ways—other than on the operating table with a sterile lancet—they had been etched. Each way involved an intricate series of events, before and after. Joann would review the stories—carefully, some of them, and rush through others. The speculations were as ready to hand as details from her own life, at least life before the operation.

Glass knives, seam-rippers, old-fashioned can openers like three-branched trees; blowtorches, lasers, paint brushes dipped in acid; feral teeth, hatchets, branding irons. The deep wounds silently drawing together had made any weapon—including those whose high-speed, explosive pellets would enter as round holes and exit as craters—as familiar as the silver flatware from Aunt Helen. The wounds brought these weapons in close; they were the skin's own hardware or cookware, its natural partner.

The post-surgery pain had been so absolute that it had left no clear memory. This was a loss. Pain would never again (or, not often) be heaped up in that impressive way. Joann could only serialize it: a string of days, hospital guests arriving or leaving, the hours before and the hours after. The mind could not separate itself from the assault. It was lost in sensation. Only in the night, suddenly awakening, would sleep release the mind, for a few seconds, from its hive of pain. From these instants came a view of life stripped of sentiment and cut to the bone. This discovery was catalogued; it was cased; it did not need to be hacked or pried open. There was no need for it yet, because the mundanities of the experience were by no means exhausted. Even the "stories" she'd elaborated on before and after had not grown tiresome, because they were never quite finished. Some element or interval was missing, or just outlined. More work was needed. Perhaps, then —

"Dr. Mackie! Calling Dr. Joann Mackie!" Here was Melinda. "Where's the ice cream? What are you doing out here?"

"It's on the stove. It was too hard."

"Well, it's not hard anymore," said Melinda, squeezing the carton. It's melting."

"Put it away, then."

"Are you all right?"

"Put it back, or scrap it!" There was strain in Joann's voice. She could hear it herself. She hoped Melinda and the others wouldn't feel unwelcome.

"You think there's something going on out there?" Melinda whispered to Joann, pointing to the closed door.

It was only then—tears flooding her eyes—that Joann realized she was still in a weakened state.

"We're tiring you," said Melinda, opening the swing door to signal to the others. "Aren't we? We should leave."

They all fluttered around her: Andrea cleared the dishes and loaded the dishwasher, Jake put on some music—Bach for solo guitar—and Melinda walked Joann to the bedroom, helped her pull off her sweater dress, leaving on the slip, careful not to touch any skin, and wrapped her in the silk bathrobe they had brought to the hospital. The robe was midnight-blue brocade, heavy silk, with padded shoulders and slim lines. "Show us," said Melinda. Joann slipped her arms in the sleeves, and the friends gathered at the bedroom door.

"Holman Hunt," Jake said.

"Burgundian school," said Andrea. "Master of the Hainault Madonna."

"Let's leave," said a weary-sounding Melinda. "It's not warm enough anyway, that robe. Put your other one on, Joann. At least you won't freeze."

But Melinda let Jake and Andrea go out alone. She poured herself a glass of water "for the road."

"So," she said, "you're all right?"

"Fine."

"It was nice of you to let us come over."

"I enjoyed it."

"I hope we didn't exhaust you."

"I'm always tired. I'm used to it."

Melinda hugged her friend, careful only to touch shoulders. Joann kissed her. "I've missed seeing you."

"Why haven't you called?"

"I don't know. I'm waiting for things to settle."

"Don't wait too long," said Melinda. "Sometimes you have to push a little."

Edward called that night. Melinda had lingered on. She wanted to cook some pasta sauce for later, but Joann said that the tea and pie would hold her for hours. You can freeze it, Melinda said, slicing garlic and dropping the crescent parings into the sizzling pan.

Joann watched Melinda's black car make a U-turn in the narrow street, with cars parked on both sides. Melinda refused to waste an extra second in transit. Re-oriented, the car rushed up the street. You could still see its brake lights as it turned right, when the phone rang.

"How *are* you?"

"Better."

"Are you going to the doctor this week?"

"Not this week."

"Why not?"

"I'm healing. It takes time, that's all."

"I know that."

"It was nice of you to send the rug."

"I wanted to *bring* the rug."

"That's why it was nice of you to send it."

Joann hung up after another minute. The phone rang again. "I'm tired now," she told Edward. "I've had people here all afternoon. I want to talk to you but I have no energy." Still she stayed on the line.

II.

When Joann was fifteen, she volunteered in a lab at the Veterans' Hospital. She did simple tests and screens on the blood and urine samples, but mostly washed test tubes, beakers, and pipettes. Joann hated dishwashing, but the thin glass vials and flasks were different; and you didn't use Duz or Joy. You worked in a lab coat with rubber gloves and a rubber apron. Once a lab tech—Mr. DelSesto, or just "Mr. Del"—cut a strand of Joann's hair, then threatened to analyze it for "microbes." Joann knew what a microbe was, but she also knew that the tech meant something else because the other lab workers—all men—had laughed.

"If I find any bacterial life here," Mr. Del said, "we'll know she's not the Miss Priss she thinks she is."

Joann wasn't flustered. "You won't find anything," she said.

"Everyone has something in their hair," said Mr. Rao, a younger tech.

"Not me," said Joann, but they weren't listening.

Mr. Del put the strand under the microscope after he'd stained it and locked it onto a slide with a clear-plastic slip. "It's clean," Mr. Rao said, leaning over the lab bench. "It's sterile!"

They all laughed. Joann laughed, too.

She started going out with the team on Sunday mornings to collect blood at VFW posts. They taught her to draw a bead from the fingertip and do a simple test for blood typing.

Joann got up early, went to the 6:45 mass, then walked up the street to the hospital. The team split up into two cars and drove to posts all over the state. They worked through the morning, then went out for lunch. Joann, the only girl aboard, loved to hear the talk about husbands trying to get their wives pregnant (Al, Ray and John), or to get their wives *not* to get pregnant (Vince and Mr. Del). Joann was content as long as they didn't talk to her or—worse—*about* her. They knew she didn't have a steady and her father wouldn't let her date, so it was just dances where a bunch of girls were dropped off at a Catholic boys' school, then picked up a few hours later. They still asked, every single week, about her love life. She said it was fine, not too bad, and they always found it funny.

One day, in the elevator, wheeling blood samples down from the wards, Mr. Del asked how old she was and when was her birthday.

In summer she'd be sixteen, she told him, and her mother had said that when she turned sixteen she'd have to go out and find a paying job.

"Is that what she said?" said Mr. Del, with a smile on his face.

"Yes. But I like volunteering."

"Why? If I didn't have to work, you wouldn't see me here."

"I like it." She thought a minute. "There's no pressure."

"What do you know about pressure?" he said. "You're only fifteen."

Then Mr. Del talked about what kind of pressures there were and what parts of life they came from. "You look older than fifteen," he said. "You know that? Some days you look late twenties, early thirties. You're mature-looking."

"Do you think I'm matronly?" Joann blurted out. Her father had mentioned this to her mother not long ago. Joann had overheard.

Mr. Del thought about it. They bounced the blood cart down to the basement. The doors were opening. "Who told you that?"

Joann was embarrassed to say, but did: "My father. He said —"

"Your father?"

Joann nodded, head down, cheeks flaming.

Mr. Del wheeled the clinking cart over the gap between the elevator and the floor. He steadied the cart, straightened a tilting tube, and looked at his volunteer. "Your father must be strange. Is he strange?"

"It happens," Mr. Del went on, without waiting for an answer, pushing the cart over the shining linoleum. Then he turned around again. "I could go for you," he said. "And so could the rest of them."

Which was more embarrassing, Joann spent that night, the next day, and even the next weekend wondering: to be matronly at fifteen, or to be a kid and attracting men twice your age? Either way something was wrong. Joann's father had made that clear. How did he see so well? She could read *him* like a book. Her sharp remarks about people—observations, asides —could throw him into a rage. But she wasn't really mature in manner or looks; she was still shapeless, with a thick waist and uneven teeth. At least she wasn't "wayward": she went to mass and communion and was still enrolled in a Catholic high school known to be strict. But she wasn't your average girl, either. She had never been a child, pure and simple. That's what he thought, even if he never quite spelled it out.

A year later, in another hospital, less congenial, Joann was working for money as a "tray girl," sorting patients' diets (liquid, soft, special, and solid) and assembling trays for the floor nurses on the tall, rolling cart, then stripping them, and loading and emptying the industrial-size dishwashers. Joann hated the backbreaking work and the stomach-turning smells of overcooked food, scalded water, detergent, and ammonia.

The other tray girls, just out of school, nineteen, twenty, were willing to do this work till something better came along—marriage or, at least, a higher-paying job. For them, the tedium was eased by contact with young orderlies and cooks, who found reasons to visit the floor kitchens and spice up the nights—or at least just the talk—of the bored, chunky tray girls in their tight uniforms. Joann, still in school, was cut out of this by-play, although jokes and puns seemed twice as ripe when they'd reddened the ears of the youngest tray girl, so shy and naive. Racy quips and lewd notions were bounced up the floors just to try them out on Joann Mackie. Her reaction would become part of the joke and spin it a second time. People wondered how anyone could be so out of it. Was she a virgin? This was a question they didn't even have to ask.

Joann quit the job at the end of July, although she'd been hired for the summer with a promise of continuing part-time in the school year. She stayed at home when the family went on its summer vacation. The family was disappointed. It was a bad sign to have to quit your first job, and with no good reason. Joann spent the hot days reading novels and eating bread and jelly. She gained ten pounds going into junior year, sixteen and free at last to date.

III.

The matronly look burned off in college. For those years, Joann looked like other girls, sometimes better, sometimes worse. She was smart in school, and an eminent teacher, near retirement, took an interest, directing her thesis, guiding her to a graduate school where his own professor, the "father of iconology" had trained the next generation, already luminaries! Joann did well, but chose not to teach or publish. She had no training in arts administration, but that's what she ended up doing. She had had three museum jobs in three cities when she accepted her present job, head of the State Council on the Arts. It was in the first years of that new job that some other things happened. First, a strange, erotic beauty emerged from the husk and pulp of youth. Her face thinned, and its delicate bones pressed against the fine skin. Her body hardened into a perfect shape. There was no excess, no boniness. This devel-

opment brought in its wake a stream of belated lovers and suit-
ors. That was the second thing; the third was coming down
with cancer.

Two months ago, they'd found the cancer, but Joann had
known for at least a year that something was different. When
the malignancy surfaced in a blood test, and then, more precisely, on a scan, the doctor had been startled by its size. Surely
the patient had felt the hardening lump and its pressure on
nerves. But no, the thirty-year-old female (non-smoker, zero
pregnancies) reported no history of abdominal pain, no vom-
iting or diarrhea.

There was sensation, yes, and it was strong. It had been
there a long time—but who was to say if this sharp shock was
a medical symptom or could be written off like anyone else's
pain?

That same year Joann had bought an old house, furnishing
it with pieces from antique shops and estate sales. She found
a vintage MG. She threw out a wardrobe of suits and tailored
dresses, and shopped at secondhand stores. She had no one
style but favored silky, dark dresses with long skirts, men's
wear, and close-fitting skirts and unisuits.

While fixing up the house and settling into her job, she'd accepted offers from artists, dealers, and writers, in their thirties and forties—the kind of men most women would be glad
to date. But good-looking "sharpies," as Melinda, a college
friend and now state senator, had put it, bored her after a few
dates. They talked about royalties and commissions, collecting, cooking and wine, and mostly getting in shape—distance
cycling, rowing, weights. They were always rereading the classics, although they'd never specify which ones.

She started canceling these dates and wasn't seeing anyone,
finally, but the friends. Then she met Edward, soloist in a
Boston Symphony "celebrity" concert. Edward was violist, tall
and lanky, built like Paganini, his publicity said, with the same
spidery hands.

Joann was given two tickets to the concert—Edward Michael Joffe was playing viola and violin—and an invitation to the reception. From her seat in the tenth row, Joann had a clear view to the soloist. The black cutaway draped a long, fluid body. The head, ringed by black and gray curls, was small, with a boy's—or a monkey's—face. When he played the cadenzas, his eyes rolled back in his head. But he was superb, a passionate soloist, alert and technically perfect. There were no lifeless or predictable lines. The orchestra rose as one to applaud their soloist.

The reception, in the green room, was mobbed and noisy. Waiters wove through the human clusters with trays of yellow champagne. There were delicate hot and cold nibbles.

As a high-level civil servant, Joann was introduced to the celebrity. Like most string players, Edward Joffe's handshake was quick and loose, mostly involving the fingers, although he didn't drop her hand.

Up close he wasn't quite so odd-looking, although he didn't look like Paganini. His squirrelly face was unlined and high-colored. He had terrible teeth.

Joffe was led away by the concertmaster but came back several times and again at the end of the party. Joann was collecting her coat. He invited her to have dinner with the conductor and special friends. She declined, but agreed to meet him the next day for lunch.

He was in the northeast for two weeks. There were concerts in New York, Boston, Hartford, Burlington, and Augusta. From there he was going to Israel, followed by eight weeks in Europe. Then he had a month's vacation. The fiddle would be in the shop, and the fiddler with the yard-long arms fishing in the Snake River, hiking, and camping.

At the first lunch, at Sensei in Back Bay, Edward invited Joann to come camping with him on the Snake. When she said no half a dozen times, he said, come to Paris, at least, or Rome. I'll show you the Rome . . . of the Romans!

She laughed. I can't leave my job, she told him, to go to Paris or Rome. But she did show up at concerts in New York and Hartford. And Edward returned to town whenever he had two consecutive days off—unless he was on another continent, where four days were necessary.

$f$or the first visit, Edward arrived at her door in a cloud of scent, a spiked leather jacket covering a shirt with studs, and a stand-up collar. Joann thought it might be a joke, but Edward made no reference to his outfit. Underneath the jacket, the sleeves of the ruffled shirt were rolled to show bright cloth bracelets on hairless arms.

The dinner talk was sparse and stilted. Joann wished she had invited at least another couple. But after the first bottle of wine, and when Joann had turned off the stereo with its re-volving plate of discs that Edward obviously didn't want to hear, the atmosphere changed. At first Edward talked nonstop, as if he'd never before had the chance to say what was on his mind. He had much to tell her—about his family, his teach-ers, the search for compatible pianists, and other string play-ers. How little childhood he had had, or adolescence, because, one: he was so tall and skinny; and, two: he practiced all the time. In high school and even in college, he'd had nothing in common with his classmates. Now he felt he had everything in common with *them,* but nothing in common with his fellow musicians. He didn't know who he was. He was fifty, he was fifteen, and sometimes—like now—his own age.

"What *is* your age?"

"Forty-two."

"Oh. You look much younger."

"That's what I'm saying!"

Joann was pondering this disparity when the musician rose, drew her out of the chair, and sat her down on his lap. He put his face close to hers, and she could feel his breath on her eyes.

He kept his face close, his eyes open. He took off his glasses. His eyes were a muddy blue. When he had studied her face, he took up her hands and felt the palms, kissed the fingers and then touched her fingers to his own face, his lips, tongue, teeth. Had an hour gone by? With his thumbs, he traced every line and hollow on her face, on her neck.

"I feel a little," she said, when she found her voice, "like your doll."

He was unzipping the velvet dress, but only after he'd stroked her shoulders, back, breasts and waist through the plush fabric.

"Nice dress," he said.

His hand ran along the zipper, and then inside the dress. The lining of the dress was silk. He turned the bodice back and pulled down the sleeves. He looked, touched. And then, the musician lifted his doll, half-clad, and carried her limp body to the freshly made bed. Before he'd even undressed himself, he said, "I love you. Do you believe me?"

For the second visit, one week later (although concerts in the meantime had sent Edward off to Europe), he brought his instruments with him. He had to practice for the Mozart double concerto coming up the next day. He put it off, though, until morning. That day Joann woke up to music. First there had been—and this had been folded back into the easeful scenes she had been dreaming—a series of languid scales, alternating major and minor, each scale slower than the one before. This was the way, Edward had already said, to achieve center-of-the-note tuning. Joann still hadn't opened her eyes when he'd notched the metronome from lento to presto, and was playing the same D-major scale, at 200mm; each note, however quick, was bell-clear and point-perfect. Joann rolled over and opened her eyes. Between metronome settings, Edward looked up. He lowered his instrument into its velvet shell and leapt onto the bed. Joann pushed him out again a half-hour later. She pointed to the clock. He had two hours. In two hours, he'd be in a taxi, and, in four hours, he'd be shaking the conductor's hand.

What Joann learned from the second visit was that, in order to listen to Edward's playing, she had to pretend not to hear. If she read, paid bills, if she dusted, knitted, or just sat in a chair facing away from him, she could listen and even react. What was it like? The heart beat fast, the skin, usually cool and waxy, warmed, and whatever stiffness was in the back melted away as the column of bone and nerve relaxed. But there were places of tension, too, where the lines of music drilled a pattern.

The playing would soon stop, and then Joann would feel the warm (sometimes hot) fingers on her neck, wrapped around her waist so that his fingers touched her fingers, his long arms coiled around her.

If Joann was cold to him, it was because the music was still rippling through her and she wanted to hear its last echo. Soon enough, though, as the musician's sensitive body burrowed into hers, and the lifelong hunger he'd described as his only existence up to now began, ever so slightly, to be satisfied, Joann could hear nothing but the breaths and pulses of his body.

Edward's departure left her in a floating state. He'd call en route to wherever he was going, but she didn't like to talk to the disembodied voice at the end of the line until she herself had lofted back to earth.

Edward liked to eat. The couple dined in every good restaurant within a hundred-mile radius of Mansfield. He loved especially to drive into Boston, a feeder's paradise. They were having a nightcap at the Ritz bar when Joann had her first attack.

Edward seemed tired (he'd been teaching master classes all day) and was drinking a beer instead of the usual cognac. Joann had pretended to sip wine with dinner, but was in too much pain to eat or drink. Edward hadn't seemed to notice. Problems were cropping up with a new quartet he'd formed. Contracts had been signed for recording and management, yet there were still battles about flexibility for the second violin. Second wanted to switch occasionally with First. It was unusual, but Second was a first-class talent, a fresh voice. He just needed the stage experience. He needed, Edward said, to be given a chance to "let his sound bell out."

Even fixing her eyes on Edward's agitated face, Joann found it hard to pay attention. She had always had stomach pain, worse lately, but this was different, impossible to ignore. It came in waves. First came a flaming streak, then the whole stomach just seized up. As the organ relaxed, it thumped the way any fresh wound will beat. She concentrated on this pulse and its return.

"You look terrible," he said, coming back from the men's room.

"I think I'm going to be sick," she said. "Excuse me."

Joann walked—so as not to jolt the stomach—slowly up the bar steps, past the scented elevator, down the carpeted stairs to the gilded bathroom. She closed the stall door. Her face was soaked with sweat and now with tears. She dug her nails deep into the roll of toilet paper. The room was empty—it was late—so she let out a watery sob, then, after a while, unlocked the stall door and sank into a chair. At last the stomach stopped its pounding.

When she returned, Edward was marking a score. "Why are you so white?" he asked.

"I'll be all right now."

"What's wrong? Should I call a doctor?"

Joann shook her head to keep from crying in front of him. "Hold my hand a minute."

He offered both hands. To distract herself from the expanding pain, she held the hands and straightened the fingers. She had never really studied them. Edward claimed that the left had grown larger and stronger. Joann closed her eyes and worked his hands. She started with the heels and all around the palm—his left hand in her right, his right in her left. They *were* different. The bowing hand was soft, loose-jointed. It was sleek and smooth. The left one was a different story—the fingers knotty, the palm meaty, and even the wrist was thicker, fed by arteries that rolled slightly under the fine skin and over the bundle of muscles.

Edward liked to touch, but—for "professional" reasons, as he put it—he didn't like to *be* touched. But that night at the Ritz, he lay back in his chair by the window and closed his eyes. After stroking his hands, each finger and joint, each muscle and fine bloodline, she massaged them. The violist's hands were insured for over a minion dollars, and, while Edward played baseball and cooked, he didn't write much or type; he had a gadget for opening caps, an array of expensive soaps and lotions, and fifty pairs of gloves. He did not gladly offer his hands. But that night he fell asleep in the chair with those hands in her lap.

Joann decided then that, if this love affair (that was the only name for it) lasted till his birthday in March, she'd arrange to have his hands modeled. Perhaps he'd already had a cast made, although he'd never mentioned it. She'd never seen his apartment—the one he shared with a hornist from the New York Philharmonic.

"I'm going to get my own place," he'd said that night. "Then, you can visit. Or I could move to Mansfield. Why couldn't I fly in and out of Boston just as easily?"

You could fly—she'd remembered saying into his ear—from Boston to anywhere.

And the love affair, she thought, with all that it implied, *would* have lasted if a visit to the doctor that next week, and the tests and scans that followed, hadn't prompted a medical siege that was still in force. One group of doctors, certain that the tumor and its pestilence had been rooted out, felt that the female patient was as clean as a "carcinoma" could be when they'd "gotten it all." The other group, relying less on signs than on death rates, recommended the full use of all modalities.

It was up to her. But after the surgery she was finished. If the signs looked good to three doctors—one of whom had been her pediatrician—that was good enough. Life had already been altered. If the body were insulted any more, what would be left to recover?

For Edward, the operation had coincided with a seventeen-day tour of the Far East. He hesitated, begging Joann to understand the pressure of commitments made years earlier. He cried one night—they cried together—but he left with his quartet two days before Joann was scheduled to appear at New England General, to be prepped, to spend the night, and be wheeled into "op" at 6 A.M., the exact moment when Edward would be taking his opening bow in Seoul.

The surgeons weren't sure what or how much they'd find. There was a chance of death, as there always is with invasive measures; there was even a chance that the growth had outstripped the surgeons' skills.

Of course, it turned out otherwise. It *was* a large tumor, but dense, compact, and encased in a sleeve of non-malignant cells. Joann's body had produced something finite and 100 percent operable. Her chances for an average life were as good as anyone's, exclusive of the incision healing and the digestive system adapting—slowly, over time—to its radical re-arrangement. The rest, the pediatrician had pointed out, was up to Joann. This was her part and she had to "perform"— that's the word he used—as never before.

And she did. She began, in the hospital, while the intravenous tubes were still attached, to sip water, then dilute juices, skimmed milk, and half-melted Jell-O, and advanced to baby food, pudding, and farina. She couldn't be discharged, the dietician said, until she'd proven able to ingest "nutrients" she could prepare for herself at home. It wasn't painful to eat the simple, macerated foods, but it didn't feel like eating. The material tended to bulk in her chest and then only slowly drop. The newly built stomach, a quarter of its original size, felt full all the time. Joann had been told by both professionals and amateurs not to rely upon hunger or a sense of emptiness, but to feed herself by the clock.

At first she wanted nothing more—when his tour was over and she'd been home recuperating one week—than to open her front door and see Edward standing on her porch. She dreamed about it. She would hear the doorbell, three notes descending, then would have to unlock her bedroom door and take the time to relock it, unlock the pantry door, relock it, then run downcellar to the oil burner, and still be able to hear the doorbell ringing, but when she reached the door, no one was there.

When can I come over? he had asked when his feet had touched ground in San Francisco. He gave her a countdown of planes and schedules and just how quickly he could be there. But Joann, surprising herself, asked him to wait. She wasn't up to it.

"Why can't you see me?" he'd asked after another week went by, and then another. After a while he was less frantic, but more heartsick.

"I can't explain it," she said. "Maybe I don't want you to see it."

"But we're so close," he said. "I *want* to see it."

"Maybe you do. But *I* don't want you to."

He seemed to understand better, but after a day or so the reasonableness of this excuse wore off. He was busy for a while after that. They both enjoyed talking but made no progress toward a visit.

Then, the night of the tea party, during the three-hour call from Los Angeles, Edward gave her his ultimatum. He would be performing in California and Washington State for one week. He'd booked a flight to Boston for September 11th.

(Here we go again, Joann thought, waiting for the countdown.)
If the plane were on time, he'd land at Logan at 7:05 A.M. He
would be in Mansfield as early as 8:30. He'd reach her door
at 8:45, at the latest. If he rang the doorbell then—between
8:45 and 10:00, say—and got no answer, he was flying back to
New York *that hour*. Joann could enjoy her peace. He had always known he was too much for her. He was too much for
everyone. There was a long silence.

"Do you know," he said, "how much I love you?"

Joann let the question ring. It was not so much a question as
a dare.

The tea party was on a Saturday, and it was Tuesday, September 7. Edward had called again, and they had talked cheerily
about his back-to-back concerts of late-Beethoven quartets
played first in Portland, Oregon, then in Seattle. He also mentioned the Brahms' G-major sextet, which he would play that
night with the new quartet and a couple of friends from Juil-
liard. As a rare treat, Edward was asked to play first violin. The
date was sold out, even standing room.

"I'll think of you," he said, "and how much you like . . ." and
here he sang the opening line of the Allegretto.

Edward wasn't much of a singer, but Joann could imagine
the suave phrase spiraling in the hall's space. Once Edward had
played it for her at home. It was morning, winter, and the old
house was cold. But the sun that day, bouncing off the icy snow,
had flooded the window, and the musician planted himself in
the trapezoid of its white and blinding light.

Edward's lower body—spiny legs and boyish hips—was
black in the glare, but he had twisted a little toward the window so the instrument was washed in silver and his head and
shoulders hatched in fire orange. To absorb the music's rich
script, Joann would need to block this flashing apparition. But
her eyes were too dazzled. And did they interfere with one another—sight and sound—or were they apprehended sepa-

rately, to be reheard and reseen, later, clear as water? If the flaring figure hadn't stopped playing when he did, Joann felt she might suffocate from the thin air. But he did stop.

So the Brahms was what he would be playing tomorrow? Yes, he'd already said that.

After a while, Joann hung up. She couldn't recall if she'd said good-bye to him. She was sitting at her kitchen table, looking at the pears and apples piled up in the bowl. The apples were soft, but the pears—she had bitten into one—were succulent. She couldn't remember what she'd said, but she was sure she'd offered no encouragement about Saturday. And he didn't need it. He would come: this was his part. His low notes had sounded, and, in the coming interval, so fraught with suspensions, something from inside herself would crack, fine as light, out of its ravaged skins.

The Maestro

Screaming along the avenue came the car with the dog's head poked out the window. It was the dog screaming. Just an ordinary dog—reddish yellow and thin face—howling. Now the car was stopped at the light, and the dog, thrown off its pins, was toppled into the space between the two front seats. It scrambled up, was shoved back, poked its nose through the driver's window, and yowled.

I was standing on the cross street, waiting for the light, then jerked along by Arthur's rude arm. He was going to the pen shop. Arthur's Maestro was broken in the barrel. First I had taken its gold ring off with a tiny screwdriver and pliers, then I had hacked the lustrous ebony back in two. It was the most innocent part of the Maestro, just an empty shell. The guts were in the head or, rather, stuck into the neck. So the thing sat busted, but only in its most basic part, on Arthur's desk, just the pieces spread out, no leather case or box. "The cat did it," I said, when Arthur came home from work.

Arthur was not paying good attention. His head ached, he had a paper cut on the pad of his finger, and he hadn't eaten all day. He did not understand at first.

After he had eaten enough to take his head pills and had bandaged his finger and gone to the bathroom, he said: "What were you saying about the Maestro? Were you talking about the Maestro when I first came in? Tell me, if you were."

He had sat on the corn-colored couch and eased off his

shoes. I sat next to him. "Healy was playing hockey, see?" I said, "and the ball flew up onto the flat of your desk. He scrambled up and, spotting the Maestro—which you shouldn't have left exposed the way you did, Arthur, uncapped and unscrewed—he gave it a kick and sent it clear across the room and smash against the strongbox. It must have been made of Asia plastic, Arthur, because it split right in half."

That was how today got started. Maestro was an old family piece. "Not that old," I said, "for made of plastic, as you see."

"Was *not* made of plastic."

"Why did it break?"

Arthur had gathered the morsels into his hands and carried them to the bathroom, where he wrapped them in cotton batting; then to the kitchen, where he bagged the parts in plastic. And off we went, twenty blocks north, to the pen shop.

On the nineteenth block, where we turn, I saw the hunting dog's slender face and heard, for the first time, its shattering scream.

Arthur wanted to keep going. The Maestro was screaming, too, I guess.

"Arthur," I said, midstreet, "Stop." We were directly in front of the dog's windshield, with a clear view of the driver hunched over the wheel, now scraping the gears and running that peanut car right up to, if not touching, our knees, in such a hurry he was. "Light's changed," I said to Arthur, but Arthur was glaring at the driver, who slammed on his brakes, just in the nick.

It was only then, as if in a dream cut short, that I noticed the car was Lat's, Lattimore Leece, a boyfriend from the days of my youth. He noticed me a split second later, and we both—the dog was screaming, too—screamed out. Lat pulled over and jumped out, slamming the dog back in.

"Hey," he said, "for heaven's sake!" He wrapped me then and

there in his famous bear hug. It hadn't changed and neither had he.

Arthur, a taller, stringier type, was breathing down my neck.

"That was a stupid-ass thing to do," he said, "whether you know Angela or not."

"Sorry, pal?" Lat said.

"Lat, Lattimore Leece, this is my husband, Arthur Woodberg. He's a geographer, Lat."

"Lat," I turned to Arthur to explain, "works for Jell-O. Do you still work for Jell-O, Lat? Yes or no?"

Well, this led to that and soon, forgetting the Maestro and the poor canine locked in the Ford Fistula—and on the sunny side of the street!—Arthur, Lat, and I went off to a sidewalk café we liked. Something was in the air. It seemed like friendliness, but it wasn't. I knew that much.

Lat had first entered my bedroom one hot summer afternoon nearly ten years ago. I was in the bedroom but not in the bed. His face had that sick look that cads get when their loins heat—lids half closed, eyes sunken and veiled. This meant business, I knew that much, but Jeremy, my new boyfriend, almost seven feet tall, was due any minute.

"Not now," I said, but Lat was beyond that point. Even as Jeremy was locking his car door and pacing up the path, Lat had burrowed in and was there to stay.

In the nature of things, my front door was unlocked, and after tapping, Jeremy walked in and plowed the front steps with his heavy feet. "Angie!" I heard. "Angie?"

"Yes," I said, a tangle of hair in my mouth. I spat it out. "Yes!"

"Let me in."

It was only then that Lat's head (his mouth suctioned onto my neck) lifted and his puffy lips dropped open.

"Angie!" An urgent tone. Now the doorknob turning, but

Lat, always prepared, had thought to lock it. "Why is the door locked, Angie? Open up," said Jeremy.

I have a date with him! I scribbled on my bedside pad and held it up to Lat's myopic eyes. "Never mind your glasses," I hissed. "Read."

"What?" said Jeremy, still rattling the doorknob. "I can't hear you."

"I'm asleep, Jeremy," I yelled. "Go downstairs. Wait for me on the porch steps."

"Why?"

"Go. Give me a minute to get dressed."

"Why can't I come in?" he said. "I've seen you naked, haven't I?"

"Go!" I said, and miraculously, he did.

*N*o matter where I was in life—jailbait, fiancée, an in-law, an auntie with two brats hanging on my knees—Lat was never far away. When I first met him, in the days when he had no dog (and no cats either), we'd dated half a dozen times, and then he broke it off.

"I like to enjoy you," he said. "Is that a crime?"

"So if you like me," I had said, "why are you leaving?"

"That's none of your business," he said. "My business is my business and your business is your business."

"Well, goodbye then," I said, "young lover, etc."

"Angela," he answered, "just promise me one thing. In the years to come . . ." circling my waist with his Popeye arms, pulling me close, letting me feel his potential.

"Yes?" I said, barely breathing. My eyes had steamed, or maybe those were tears.

"I'll be back."

"Whenever you want to?" I guessed.

"Whenever I want to."

*B*ut after my second marriage, to Dr. Woodberg (my first was to Jeremy's father), a wedding white-on-white, Lat disappeared—or to me, he did. Years passed. Once, on my birthday, September nineteenth, I got a call. I wasn't there, so the doctor got it.

"Friend of yours," he said. "I didn't recognize the voice."

"Did you get the number?" I asked.

"He said, 'Remember me to your wife. Tell her from me that it's no crime.' What does that mean, Angela?"

"It means," I said, then stopped. "I don't know what it means."

But I did. Married as I was one year, and still making Dr. Woodberg happy, Lat was back to make me happy. It was my birthday.

But not that day, not the day after, but this Thursday, a few hours after I broke the Maestro, there he was, racing up my legs, and Woodberg's, too. Had he been looking for me?

*W*oodberg sat at our café table but was soon up to make a few calls, to visit the bathroom, to tap the various message machines that connected him to the world's ears, heart, lungs, and scrotum. While he was gone, Lat, a little older but just as squat, just as mean, overheated, moved his chair next to mine. Color was rolling into his creamy cheeks; that awful light was on behind his eyes, and he was emanating.

"I forgot your name," he said, "but I remember everything else."

"I'm married now," I said, pointing in the direction of the phone booth. "I see you have a dog."

He brushed all this aside. "Tell me your name."

"It begins with A."

That's all he needed. The short arms were around me, squeezing, and a kiss offered and taken, while Lat stared into my eyes.

"It's no sin," he said, when he took a breath, a sip of water, and pushed his chair back in place. "So how are you?"

"Fine."

"Who's this guy you're married to? Do I know him?"

Then I felt Arthur's hands on my shoulders, a miracle, because in public, Arthur kept himself to himself. "Here he is," I said. "Ask him."

I got up to go to the ladies', and when I got back, Lat was gone. Certain men don't care for other men's company, even just as filler. Woodberg liked everyone who liked him, but Lat was picky.

"Who is this guy? Some old boyfriend? He's a jerk."

"You think so?"

"You're lucky you met me. I saved your life."

"Yes," I said, touching the still-warm seat of Lat's chair. This was the first staging. By the finish, I'd be a much older woman.

What did Lat Leece have to offer that was no crime to crave on my part either? His tongue, his marble body, the rough, spongy hair of his head, and the milkmaid's cheeks with a harvest of stubble. Where did you come from and where are you going? When will you return?

So, we continued, the doctor and I, to Philip Feder's Fine Penstocks and Repair on 20th. Mr. Feder was in, and nearly cried out when Arthur unsheathed the severed Maestro. He opened his hands to receive it and lay it on a velvet square with a magnifying lens in place just above.

"Is this an emergency call?" he said through his thick mustache, head down, using a fine sable brush to stroke the jagged break on the Maestro's back.

Arthur looked at me and I looked back. "She did it," he said, "because the moon was full. What did you do—bite it?"

Tears welled in my eyes. "Yes," I said.

Both men stared.

"Now," I said, "one side of my mouth is sore and the teeth are chipped a little."

Arthur took me to a chair by the picture window full of pens and made me sit. "Sit here, Angie. I'll handle Feder and the Maestro both. Don't cry."

This is what I liked about Woodberg, a forgiveness that was divine, although erratic. Emergency surgery was performed that afternoon, failed, and a new body was found for the injured Maestro, but not a perfect match in sheen or depth of black, so Arthur felt depressed but didn't want to admit it.

Only once on the way home did he look at me with an open question on his face, mouthing, "Why?" and "How could you?"

I had no intention of explaining. An act of rage is best left a mystery.

Dr. Woodberg took the Maestro to the Geography Society, where he had an office. It was one more thing he'd removed from our common domain, but at least it was safe. I settled my agitations on a rocker and was soon asleep.

I never lock the door—did I mention that? Through it came whom I was waiting for, but even before my eyes were open, the screaming dog, silent now, had its paws in my lap and was trying to climb onto the chair.

"Zita!" its master yelled, and Zita was on all fours, low and cowering.

Next Lat was on my lap, not just on, but swimming over the surface of my entire skin. Soon the face had risen to my face, eye to eye, nose to nose.

"Your name is Angela. I remembered it right after," he said.

I wrapped my arms around him, and we slipped off the chair. The dog, Zita, had couched herself, quiet, and Lat and I performed the mysteries of communion, an asymptote, never complete but always approaching.

When we had coated the floor, the sticks of furniture, the lower walls, and even one window with our secretions and airs, the end was in sight. With Lat the end was never the end but only an interval. He collected his clothing and his sleepy dog and soon was gone.

"Don't say it!" I said, when I saw him spring back from the door, mouth open. Then the door closed and I heard Zita's raw claws on the hard wood.

I lay back on the damp sheet. But it wasn't a sheet, it was the mattress. In our coilings we had stripped the bed of its covers. How cold the satin felt, how rough the quilting. Lat was gone again. It was no crime, but days on days would burn to pulp, organ systems age and dry, and the weather turn a page before another such charm would be laid at my feet. The better, the more perfect the charm, the longer the blank in between—a desert, a vacuum.

Healy walked in to sniff the chair that Lat's huge pet had occupied. Then he jumped up on the blue mattress, nosing over the damp surface.

"Mind your own business," I felt like saying, but was too deflated for words. Healy stretched out against my bare back and pressed into me. It was his way of saying: it's no crime.

$\mathcal{D}$r. Woodberg was just forty. His birthday was last Friday. His idea of happiness was perpetual motion. Sitting or lying to feel the cat hair floating to the sticky surface of your face, watching the dark trees bud in spring, breeding a pure pore of feeling, there for one second then gone—these were to Woodberg a string of premature deaths. Hence (I say hence because I'm lying here in damp desuetude, and it makes me feel the pinch and tuck of logic), his idea of love is eggbeaters spinning. There is a stink of mortality, for him, in the voluptuous, the prickly crawl of sensation, the lacunae of nothing, the enigma of time. This uncertain wave, the aping of unity, for Woodberg, opened the very darkest graves, the deep ones, where maggots stream and the soil grows new and unexpected colors.

There was only one crime and let it be on my head. You've seen my head, a silky stalk, and this is my body, like a long dribble of milk. That gray spot is the flattened cat. In my heart, an emptiness, I was cooking something, preparing something bad for Woodberg, something to take his appetite away forever. Or should I be cooking, I wondered, for two? I drew a sheet up from the floor to cover my gooseflesh. In that tent, I consulted with darkness.

Only once in a blue moon do satisfaction and desire meet on a clear field and combust. Revenge is different, sloppier, easy to miss the mark and still stun or even kill, just with the idea of it. I poured my thoughts into the recipe.

But with all the ingredients listed (a cat skin, twenty feet of bowel, kosher salt and nine BBs, a few pencil leads, pickles, old make-up, golf ball, string, and bad mushrooms) and the blue bowl set on the counter, blenders, choppers, blasters, and pulverizers at the ready, I shrank.

The six o'clock siren went off. It was night. I untied the cat from the cutting board. I washed off the surgical markings from my own belly, smooth but now riddled with signs. I emptied the vials, pitchers, colanders, and vats. I found part of a pig in the fridge and started it roasting. I put my head under the faucet and let the cold and hot water hose away the sweat of iniquity.

I served Dr. Woodberg a delectable repast of pig, curries, cold sauces, and fresh figs. He was heartened.

"Why's the bed stripped?" he asked, coming back from the bathroom.

"Have you had enough to eat?" I said.

"I'm going to eat more. You didn't answer my question."

"Say it again."

"Why's the bed stripped?"

"It needed to be stripped."

"It smells funny in there."

"I've been sick."

Woodberg looked up; he checked the pallor of my skin, the oiliness of my eyes. "You don't look sick."

Then I decided to tell him the truth. "I broke the Maestro's back on purpose," I said.

I watched as wrath creased his face. "I *knew* it, I *sensed* it, but I never thought it could be true."

"It's true."

"Angela."

"Yes?"

"Why did you hit me in my most vulnerable spot? Why do you so loathe me?"

I wrapped my arms around him. "If I did, I don't any longer."

"I hate you, too."

"I know," I said.

"How? How do you know?"

"Why do you think I busted up the Maestro?"

"That's why?"

"I think so. That's what I recall."

"Can we get over this, Angela? Or is it already over?"

"The props of marriage are many, Arthur. They're many and changing."

"I see."

"But the Maestro, you see, once broken, is now fixed."

"It doesn't look good. Or rather it doesn't look right."

"Does it work?"

"That was never a question."

"Let's make the bed, Arthur. First let's vacuum it and put on a fresh fluffy pad. Clean sheets, clean blankets."

"No funny smells?"

"Nothing but laundry soap, textiles, and dust."

"I don't even *want* to know, Angela," he said after a while. "I know, but I don't want to know."

The phone rang. "Answer the phone, dear," I said. "It's for you."

He answered, not just that once, but half a dozen times that night. There were two hang ups. That's how I knew that Lattimore wouldn't be coming back—not now, not for a while.

"It's no crime," I told myself, leaning over, stuck in the flypaper of longing.

But you know something: it was.

Moon, June

I.

I bought a purple dress, second hand, a jersey with ridges. A second-hand dress, even the kind of flimsy thing I buy, has a little life left in it from its other closets, restaurants, walkways, touches it may or may not have received, powder dropped on it, earring caught in its webs, the dry cleaner. It makes for thoughtful wearing, if you need that kind of stimulation, which I don't. My clothes, by rights, should come straight from China, touched only by the assembly-line seamstress, folded and packed in plastic. But I like adventure, so when my eyes feel like they're fading in my head, I'm off to the second-hand to see what the skinny rich woman, my body double, has tossed to the winds.

Where she buys her clothes new, I don't know, because nothing around here has the jerkins, kimonos, sheaths, and Italian jackets that she favors, and whatever's good enough for her, I say, is almost too good for me. But she wears them for a while, takes the nap off, softens the fabric, and boredom builds. A rage builds. She packs the car with cute things and throws them into the arms of the charity that runs this consignment shop. She can't get away fast enough, takes the speed train to New York, and is out on the streets. Her needs are great, fierce, judging from what I've been picking up over the years. Statements, criticisms, last word and testament, jokes, banging her own drum. That's what the clothes tell me, but once I've worn them, I flatten that effect right out. The clothes die, and fast. On me they're just curtains, although—worn to a nub—sometimes you can see my body right through them. She'd never stand for this. Most people buy their clothes to keep the outside out. I buy the worn-out things that put almost nothing between me and the world. I like it that way. My body itself is a set of clothes: my bones are corset material, my skin a good silk, the organs inside, that's the true jelly. That part you don't want slopping around, or people to grab it and squeeze.

But Jane, I'll call her Jane, is a real shopper, and nothing of herself faces outward for low-lifes to inspect and to handle. But she wants them to look, so our outfits are claims on their attention—a pretty tuck, a long, elegant seam, or just this soft purple jersey that looks like an oblong, but once the body slides in, a nice geography appears, just a suggestion. Her legs must be perfect, longer than mine and no funny, long hairs on them. She's had maybe two, three husbands, the last of them good-natured, rich, and quiet. He believes in clothes and likes his wife's legs tanned and hard, exposed a bit more than suits her age. And freckles are cute, too; her legs are covered with freckles. She never rages at him; she takes it out on the clothes. Even by the time I get them, they're a little askew by dint of the forceful thwack they've gotten, landing on the fabric counter. Here and here and here! Once these clothes are gone (and on my back), she's got some breath to spare and boards that train. Fresh clothes get their own special bag and are sometimes wrapped in paper. All the stiffness is still in them, and that stiffness matches hers, starch on starch. She goes home on the train, and the husband is waiting in his black car to take her and the clothes home. He takes them out of the bags and out of the paper they're wrapped in; he does the hand-washing if the starch is too scratchy; he does the hanging and folding, while she lies on their bed with a wet cloth over her eyes.

"I love you, Boy-o," she says, while he works.

This economy works in my favor. Like a princess, I throw clothes over my head and feel nothing but fineness, thinness, liquidity. And up to now our exchange has been fruitful. Up to now and this purple dress with its fine indentations.

"Get a new dress?" said Bruce, my own boyfriend, seeing the cotton rag hanging on my closet door, airing.

"Yas," I said, though my policy with questions is don't answer them.

I could see Bruce reflecting. Was there something wrong? Was the dress speaking to him in a tone, telling a secret I didn't yet know? I'd worn it once to a luncheon party but hadn't broken it in, much less sniffed out its history. He was studying the dress.

"Purple," I said.

"Yes," he said, but I could tell he was still thinking. Mysteries were opening and not closing. "Put it on," he said.

I was lying then naked on the bed; my skin's a little purplish and, as I said, already is a kind of dress. "You don't like it?" I said.

"Just put it on."

Suddenly there were three of us. There was a taste in the room that was not mine, and not yet his either. To see what was what, I put it on, a slithery thing, column of gentle purple, ease everywhere, no fit, no tuck.

"They had a name for that, I remember," he said. "Sack."

"Oh no," I said, "not sack."

"Yes, sack."

"No one wants to hear that, Boy-o," I said.

"My name's not Boy-o," he said. "Why call me Boy-o?"

"*He* wouldn't say something like that," I said, already the tears peeling out of my eyes and wetting the purple bib.

"Who's this Boy-o?" he said. "Do I know him?"

"He's rich," I said, "and he loves clothes."

"This is his?" he asked.

I sighed. Sack dress, or just sack. I put the purple sheath back in the closet and returned to the bed with my everyday skin dress on. Not only had my life been attacked, but Boy-o's and Jane's too. And they didn't even know it. I had brought this on their heads, that which they had sought to avoid by keeping all dresses fresh and up to date, stiff and resistant.

"Let's go to a party," Bruce said, "and try it out. Don't feel bad. Life is short. You expect everything to turn out nice, but sometimes it doesn't. For you," he added, in a dry tone.

"I heard that," I said.

So we went to a party. First we waited until one rolled around. By then I had bought a dozen more dresses, but he remembered the purple one.

"Remember that sack that hung on your door? I've seen old sheets that had more life."

"No," I said, but he was already in the closet, fishing it out where it hung, behind everything else, yet emanating plain-Jane spirit.

"Yeah," he said, laughing. "Boy-o's dress, remember?"

"Yes," I said, slipping the purple tube over my big head. The dress was warm, and I sucked that warmth into me. I'd need it.

The party was fifteen blocks away, in a nice district, not far. I put on thin, tottering shoes and combed my hair over my ears. With sunglasses, I was in full disguise.

"Take those off," he said. "And pull that hair back."

This Bruce was a sharp fellow, nice duds, refined shoes, nothing out of place or out of kilter. His head was Roman bust, the early ones, before the vices set in.

"Okay," I said, looking at him, rosy in pure black. He was tanned, muscular; his jacket seams hugged the lines of his body. His back was straight; his handsome face gave away nothing. Used? Worn? Maybe, but still the pick of the litter.

"If you're so bright and snazzy," I said, "how can we measure the impact of this sack?"

"Don't shy at shadows," he said.

So off we went. The street was empty, but near the house were a few stragglers, edging toward this party. We crowded on the porch, and when the door opened, the party bubbled out.

"Oh, June!" I heard addressed to me.

"This is Bruce," I said.

"A new one?" I heard.

"Not brand new," I said.

"Well, pleased to meet you, Bruce. You did say your name was Bruce?"

Poor Bruce climbed into his shyness. He didn't like direct address, especially from a stranger. But women like shy men, so Ursula, our hostess, unwrapped Bruce of his cashmere coat, touching its nap, and his, too.

"See to June, Bailey," she said to her husband, and Bailey stripped my back of its moleskin, sniffing it.

"Animal skin," he said, "with a hint of Opium."

Bailey and I walked into the room, arm in arm. He knew all ladies' perfumes. He liked ladies—their true scents and false.

It was only then that he noticed the sack. "Huh," he said. "Got a new dress?"

I looked at him square. "I don't know you well enough, Bailey, nor you my closet, for you to make a remark like that and not risk an implication."

"Oh, June," he said. "I don't care what you wear, so long as you're always a sweet tart."

"Fine, but . . . ," I said, and felt Ursula's eyes on my back for occupying her husband for more than the exigent minute. "What do you think?" I opened my arms so the dress could hang clear.

"Lovely," he said. "It's like a small house and roomy too."

Bruce was there. He heard. "See!" he said.

"I didn't catch your name," Bailey said to Bruce, "but I've known your girl here for ages." He winked at Bruce, and Bruce didn't go for it. So little did he go, that he wouldn't, with Bailey, pursue any idea of the dress.

"Is it any better in the artificial light?" I said, opening my arms again.

"No," said Bruce, pulling me away. "If anything, sunlight gave it a little something that's lost in this light, especially compared with what's around you."

I looked around: pouf skirts, slinky numbers, off-the-shoulder and tube skirts. Stun-gun color or dead black. "This, I guess, is just like a murk passing over the sky," I said.

"More or less," Bruce said, catching the legs of a young thing in a dress big as a kerchief with about two cents' worth of fabric. The skimp skittered off, a drink in each hand, and Bruce and I leaned against a wall to watch, as we always do, because Bruce, a thinker, doesn't waste breath.

It was then that I spotted, across the room, looking into the windows of a dollhouse, a spectacle of more than slight interest. On her back, a cream-colored frock, a flapper's dress, rigged shoulder to hem with wavy ribbons. Voile on silk, like something Daisy Buchanan would wear to West Egg on a day when Tom was sidetracked. I heard the gasp of pleasure that I knew so well but had never heard before in public.

"Unfair!" I said.

"Sorry," Bruce said.

"Never mind," I said. "You know who I think that is?"

"Who?"

"I just know," I said, and sure enough, she whirled around the way people will when you're staring through their backs, and glance met glance in a flat minute. It was her sack I had on, and it was my soon-to-be ivory frock on her back, if I chose— and I transmitted this idea in a witty flash—to buy it!

Of course men will be men, and Boy-o, at the hors d'oeuvres table and sensitive to his lovely spouse's moments of vision, with a caviar toast halfway into his mouth, thought to look, and stiffened. The look on his face showed that the heart attack soon-to-occur was advanced by a shock that, for the second, cost this elegant man the use of his marbles. He laughed, choked, and coughed up egg yoke and bit of onion, and the toast dropped to the floor. Spread with a sheen of black eggs, the toast left behind a path of tarry smears. So much so that I laughed; then Bruce, with 180-degree sight, jogged his martini so the speared onion somersaulted out of the glass and onto my shoulder. Cold, it was. I swept the pick off and it stuck Bruce straight in the throat, pinged off, of course, but blood bulbed out, drop by drop. The hostess lost her cool. She'd been carrying, on a bowl of shaved ice, fresh egg yolks and dark red caviar. Laying the tray on the floor, she ran to Bruce, but for once, he didn't want a lady's attention and swiped her off. Some fool had, by then, kicked the tray: ice skidding and a heap of yellow yoke dust, shattered glass and amber beads. My blood pressure fell; I could feel blood pooling in my feet. In a second I'd be down, so I grabbed Bruce's black-cloth arm and squeezed. Bruce screamed. (My nails had engaged and a ring with sharp teeth). Bedlam, but for the girl in ivory, who said, "Gemini," tapping her heels across the floor. "You're a Gemini!"

"My name is June," I said.

"I'm a Gemini, too," she said "and I could feel something in the air. I looked at your face" (her eyes locked above my neckline), "and I knew."

"What a mess," I said.

Bailey entered with wet towels and mop. "Your boyfriend's bleeding at the throat," he said to me. But Ursula, I saw, was sticking an ice cube on his skin—wrapping it in a fine tea towel—and an extra, double martini for his hand. I saw all this, but also felt the scan of "Jane's" expert eyes.

"Don't ask me if I have a new dress," I felt like saying, and maybe my eyes already said it. She drew me off to two chairs, spindly and gilded, and we sat.

"Tell me about your birthday," she said. "It is June, isn't it?"

"I'm not your age," I said, "but we do have things in common."

"Oh, you're young enough," she said, fondling the sleeve of my dress, "to be my daughter. Maybe my daughter's daughter."

"I only look young," I said, "and my birthday is June. Pure chance," I added, "because June is also—as I said—my name."

"June?" she said with wide eyes and tears in them. "That was my mother's name."

"Tell me something about her," I said.

"Okay," she said, patting my arm but, in doing so, running a finger over the fabric of the sack. "My mother was refined," she started, not shutting her eyes but turning inward the way people telling old stories will. "Every night, before putting me to bed, she'd lay out on my little chair all the dainties I would wear the next day. First she'd say, 'What dress or playsuit, my daughter?' And I would say, 'Mother, what about the French blue shirtwaist?' She'd squeeze my hands in pleasure and run to the closet to fetch it, then to the dressers to find the proper ankle socks, the camisole, and underpants to match the French blue. A ribbon or buckle for my hair."

I nodded.

"We're not finished. Before I knelt down to say my prayers, she lay out the doll's clothes."

"The doll's clothes!" I said, my heart racing.

"I had a roomful of dolls, but one was dressed just like me, in her own little French blue clothes."

"And matching underwear?" I said, uneasy.

"A match," she said.

"And all laid out the night before? By your mother?"

She folded her arms, because she knew my end of it, where I bought my clothes, where I'd gotten the purple sack, and where I'd buy, if given half a chance, the ivory flapper's frock.

"So that's how it worked?" I said.

She moved her head close to my ear. "They told me," she whispered, "at the second-hand shop, but I didn't know it was *all* you."

"It was all me," I said.

At that she took my hand and squeezed it, and rose from her chair. Boy-o was there somewhere.

"Before you go," I said, "does he lay out the things now? Boy-o, here."

"Boy-o where?" she said. "Have you met my husband?" And up came, from the middle of the party, the tea towel still knotted around his neck which had drawn one perfect red spot, Bruce. "You don't mean Bruce?" she said.

"Oh no!" I said. "No, no. That is mine. Your Bruce," I said—standing and surveying the room until, yes, there was Boy-o—"is there."

"Francis," she said, "come and meet June." And over came the Boy-o called Francis. "This is my *ex*-husband, June. He still lives with me, but he's available."

"He's available!" I said, or maybe screamed.

"Bruce will be, too, won't you, Bruce?" she said. "He's got a wound but, otherwise, good as new."

"Bruce," I moaned.

He looked at me. "Life, my dear June, always has a little roughage. Can you live with that, June? Can you accept it?"

I looked down on the ridges of my purple sack. Not a stain on it, not a crease. I realized already how my life was woven into it. My hands ran, then rubbed, along its nap. Under the nap were the bones. This was a private act of desperation, and soon Jane was at my side, clutching at my hand.

"No!" she said.

I drew myself up, still touching the dress. She tried to slap my hand off it. "No!" A rough piece of action might have ensued: if it weren't for the quick-thinking buffering by Bailey, my dress, the purple sack, would have been a fringe of ribbons, ripped along those ridges I so prized.

"Don't touch!" Jane said. "Never again," she added, and off she went with Bruce, and Francis Boy-o trailing behind.

I looked my host, Bailey, square in the eye. I liked things used, but I was no doll.

II.

When I was eight, my father gave me a hundred-dollar bill and said, "Run up to Cato's and buy a loaf of bread." But the laughter behind my back made me halt. "Look what you got in your hand!" my father jeered. The thought was that—not paying any attention—I could be fooled. And it was April Fool's.

If you're tricked enough times, and by the right people, it gets easier to take. But Bruce was not going to get away with it. I started collecting string, I pilled my cat's extra fur into a woven ball. I went out and bought a case of ice cream.

I waited for the phone call, and it came.

"June?"

I said yes, June.

"This is Bruce," he said. "I want to come home, right now."

"Home where?" I asked.

"Well," he said, "my own house, but also yours."

"What about hers?" I said. There was silence. "Cat got your tongue!" I said, and hung up. I mixed a little cat hair and chopped up string in a pool of melted peppermint stick ice cream. I poured the mixture into an ice cube tray and froze it.

A week passed. Down at the second-hand store, there was a new item: ivory-colored dress, silk satin and voile. There was an egg stain on it, but I bought it anyway and paid top dollar. In another paper bag, I was carrying a second dress: green striped with black. It was a gift to the shop, I told the sales ladies, all friends; it was new and it didn't need dry cleaning or pressing.

A week later, with the freezer full of fresh, smoky-looking ice cubes, some still in their trays, others dumped into a blue bowl, I returned to the store. The green and black stripes had sold. In its place, nothing that I hadn't already seen before. I went to the spot where the striped dress had hung, crushed among the others, on its bent hanger. I felt for the place—empty—to confirm what my eyes didn't see. Then I went home to plan my party.

"Come to an ice cream social," the invitations said, picturing a cat with a ball of yarn and pretty summer tables set with a bowl of ice cream and candy apples. "Come at three and stay till five," the words said. I invited Francis, Jane and Bruce, Ursula and Bailey, my mother, three sisters, and their three children. Dress, the invitation said: "pretty afternoon clothes." I hired a soda jerk from Eddie's and instructed him to make individual sodas to order. I opened my freezer and showed him the thousand pre-frozen ice cream cubes. Use your own stuff from Eddie's, I said, but throw in some of these to cool things down.

For the party I had my house painted, every wall cream-colored; the smell of paint still in the air. Pearl-colored balloons, white streamers; I covered the paintings in white batiste. My sisters, my mother, and my nieces arrived, wearing their custom-made dresses.

"Don't drink any sodas," I said. "Try the sundaes or a plain bowl of ice cream." The kids looked glum—the ice cream was all vanilla and no sauce. "Yes, sauce," I said, pointing to silver bowls of fondant, white chocolate, meringue, and coconut.

We waited. The guests came on time, first the triplet, then Ursula and Bailey.

Our family stood, once the ice-cream man had let in all these guests, just inside the living room. We presented a wall of green and black stripes, a hive of awful bees or strange cats. The party at the door split apart, leaving stranded the one dressed to match, in simple black-green. Our eyes converged on that one pair of eyes until those water-filling eyes closed and head hung low. Into the bedroom marched the striped look-alike and therein shed the stripes, emerging garment in hand, to lay it at our feet. She was dressed in a plain slip.

"That's still a nice dress," I said.

Then we all took off our dresses and underneath were white ones just like hers.

It was then that Bruce excused himself for the ice cream table, where the jerk fixed him a soda. Francis Boy-o was right behind him, and Ursula and, finally, Jane, behind them. Bailey stepped forward and stood before my dolled-up family. We'd all covered our slips with green, black stripes. He looked, starting from the right, at each of our faces, then he shook our hands. We could hear the gagging and choking in the ice-cream room, as little by little, the guests ate and left. Before leaving, Bailey shook all our hands again.

In life, I told myself, later that day, when my family had left, and the ice-cream man had loaded his truck with the tubs and spoons and tulip glasses, removing the special ice cubes in a garbage bag, there are three possibilities (original, imitation, and crime), but when all three are exhausted, it doesn't mean you go back again to the first.

III.

The purple sack hung in the closet, the weight of its jersey stretching its ridges, the hem ruffling a little, as time went by and it was never worn, never sought. Bailey dropped by every other day, but nothing doing, I said, go home. He went home, but he also came back. My clothes all came from China, and I led a solitary life because every number's, I told myself, been played and played out. Harsh fabrics and knife-sharp labels sanded my skin. I was a living rash. The synthetics were especially rough, but nothing went easy. Shadows formed under my eyes. I faded to dead white, and all was cream around me. This was a revenge, action was taken and bounced right back. Darkness was mine.

I heard through the grapevine that Jane had spent her February and March in a clinic. Bruce and Boy-o were keeping house, but not the same house. When Jane was brought home, she weighed a hundred pounds, not quite. Nothing fit, including the striped dress—the one she'd worn, I'm told, day and night.

I packed an Easter basket (it was almost Easter) and donned the now-pale purple jersey, which had grown a few inches from its own weight. I made a crown out of real flowers and placed it, whole and wet, in a Tiffany box. To the house of illness I went. Jane was padding around on stocking feet, the stripes still glued to her back.

"Do you ever wash it," I said, "send it to the cleaners?"

She sighed and showed me how, under the dress, her skin had taken on a striped character, just a hint, but you could see it.

"Jailbird," I said, grinning. But it was no laughing matter. Boy-o and Bruce were sitting on the couch. They'd lost flesh too. No one seemed glad to see me. "I brought an Easter basket," I said, and showed them, buried in the colorful plastic grass, a foil-covered chocolate egg, one hard-shell blue and one pink egg, and a few baby chicks all gritty with yellow sugar, the jelly beans fallen to the bottom, and a chocolate bunny. They looked. "Happy Easter," I said.

"Is that your Easter sack?" Bruce said, brightening a little.

"Not even," I said. I pulled the dress up over my head and lay it on the floor, so the ridges ran north-south. I pulled the cobwebby striped dress off Jane's body, where it was half stuck to her back. I sat her on the purple sack, now a beach blanket. On her head I placed the flower crown, fresh flowers, freshly woven.

"Name that tune," I said to the gentlemen.

"Venus rising," the husband.

"The triple crown of the three graces."

"Mary, Mother o' God," said Boy-o.

"Okay," I said.

By little and little, wounds were healed, breaths taken, light food and bites of candy ingested. When the Easter basket was emptied, the May wine drunk, and a muffin cake baked fresh, Jane (or Miss Jane, as I called her) was back on her feet. It was almost summer.

I started making my own clothes, but eventually (sadness being what it is), I went back to buying seconds. There was a new husband for Jane, and the old Bruce had become the new Boy-o. The old Boy-o, all handled and picked over, was beyond seconds. He tried to enlist in the army, but too old, just a hamperful of dirty clothes. He rented a bachelor pad and sulked alone. He would be renewed, just like the rest of us, but only in the fullness of time.

The dress, the purple sack, was cut in two and used in two households as a clever, suck-all duster. When Jane and I did our own dusting, we used our dress on the dust. Life goes on. Purple and black-and-green are played out, lost for now. Our mothers and female collaterals are out there somewhere. Fresh dresses are their daily bread, their mutual friend.

—FOR ALEXANDER S. C. ROWER

Better Than Real

First I coughed in his face, then lent him my woman's hankie. He took it, but just held it in his hand. My cough had not spread any wetness. He handed back the hankie, and I refolded it.

Nice, I said, isn't it?

Sure, whatever you say, he said.

I hope I'm not being too bossy, I said.

Whatever you say, he said.

I could just as well go home, I said, my voice lemony with anxiety.

Where would you go? he said.

You got me that time, was all I had to say, but off I went and sat in the parlor with the cat on my lap. Put the light on over your head, he said, if you plan on reading. But I didn't want to read. I didn't want to sit alone and not read, either, and the hell with the cat, so I knocked it off my lap. Get in here, I said, but there was no answer.

In his own time he came in, watering can in hand, and watered all the plants. Neatly, too, no puddles to rot the furniture, no overflow. When I water those bastards, they squeeze the water right through them and blow it out the hole, fill their dishes, and overflow the banks. They're dry, but everything else is wet. It's because of the way you do it, he has said to me. There's nothing loving about it. They can tell.

Of course they can tell. I watch while the greens suck in the silver stream from the perfect vessel. I already feel better, I said. I knew you would, he said. He put the can away and sat on the couch with a stack of books and a clean writing tablet. This is heaven, I said, just watching you peel into those pages. Do you remember what you read?

But that's exactly the kind of comment that doesn't deserve an answer, not in my house. I kept watching. Sometimes he looked out the window to think. Soon the cat was back on my lap, and we both watched. It was a full hour of work, and the cat and I felt the tension and release, and all the little textual surprises, or at least those we could read on his face.

I'm not going to say "his" anymore. There's too much separation in it, and not enough. What's your real name? I shouted out, although many times he had told me already.

What do you mean real?

I mean what name would seem real to me?

Depends, he said. I could offer a sample, but I don't want to put a lot of time into it. Just exactly why not? I said. Am I not worth it? You're off the track, he said; get back on the track. Edward.

Hi, Eddy, I said, a big, goofy smile on my face.

Don't call me Eddy, he said. Edward.

Edwood?

Edword, he said.

Okay, I said, fine for now, Edwood. What do you call me for short?

Eee, for Elaine.

And the cat's name is what?

Esther.

He's a man.

Estero.

Are you finished working yet? I asked. Almost, he said. Go cook the dinner.

Okay, I said, and wiped Estero off my lap. Into the kitchen I went, although my ears strained to hear what was going on in the living room. I heard nothing. I can put up with this for a while, I told myself. After a while, I'll check up on him. He won't be there, but knowing that, does it make it easier? Nosireebob. The cat heard his other name, Bob, and walked in.

I cooked in a wild fury. Hot peas, elephant garlic, buffalo wings, tangerine slices covered over with fine coconut flakes. A pricey wine from the 1980s to wash it down with. It's ready, I said. It's ready, I said again, when no answer came. Do you hear me? I shouted, cocking back my head and aiming my voice at the ceiling. Instead of answering, he walked in, sat down, and unfolded his huge linen napkin. Is Mrs. Reardon, he said to me, ready to dine? She is, I said, sitting in my place. Will we have Grace? I said. You say it, he said. You say it, I said. Bless us, O Lord, he said. And these thy gifts, I said. Which we are about to receive. From thy bounty, I said. Through Christ Our Lord, and we both chimed in, cat too, Amen. Good, I said, good. It's just like real. It's better than real, he said.

Eat, eat. The fun of it's in the beginning when the first savor flicks the nose and dives down the throat. After a while it's just more of the same, unless passion has entered in, in which case, who could stop eating, even just to catch one's breath or un-knot one's pulsing organs? When does passion enter in? I asked him. A smile warmed his bony face, and across the table shot his forkless arm to cover my hand with his. A nice gesture, but meaningless, and he read my face like a book. You didn't mean that, right? he said. Do you call that passion? I said. It's passion to the same extent that eating is pleasure, he said, after the first or second bite.

It took my appetite away, reeking as it did of mortality. He read my face like a second book. Eat, he said, you're a fine cook. And you, I said, are an amiable husband. But not yours, he said. But not mine.

Eating soon stopped. Each day came to an end in the same way. Joy, food, bravery, games, talk, absolute defeat. At least we breathe the same air, I said. But we both knew what we thought; what we thought was this: we were living on borrowed time, and yet that time coffered each day a new pearl. The pearl of love, you might call it, or the pearl that has a coffer for its limits and even when strung together, a half hundred of them, already losing something, becoming the same, gathering tedium in that duplication of moons.

The food flattened on our plates, our hands entwined, our jokes and japes were over for that day and nothing left but goodbye. So goodbye, I said. Welcome to the interval of darkness, he said. It's not that dark, I said, it's still life. Oh, life, he sighed, yes, for you, who are such a romantic. And you a precisionist? I said.

But now was time for silence, which can fill up with mystery, or it can fill up with nothing, or can just be sore like a big fresh bruise.

II.

Bambi entered the room blowing air through her nose. Edward heard it and thanked the gods that there was still enough air in her to honk it. What a sad face she had, all smothered in fat and fruit-acid lotions. He saw it out of the corner of his eye and did not remark it. She could make it disappear so fast, and everything else with it, and then stretch out a toothpaste smile that was a million times sadder. Did you say something? she said, stopping by his chair but scared to look directly into his face. She acted like a blind woman, always pointing her face otherwise than in the direction of his.

No, he said, I'm just sitting here enjoying the cool of the evening. It is evening, isn't it? she said. I hadn't even noticed. That's because we live in an apartment, he said, a high rise. Oh, she said, interesting, but we have windows. Yes, but you like to drop those thin, sideways shades over them just as the sun goes down, so how would you know? You're very wise, she said, and started to walk out of the room. I'm going to wash my face, she said, at the doorway. You just washed your face, he said. True enough, she said, but it's already oily. I can feel it and it makes me want to take a scouring pad to it. Why must I be, she said, so oily, and you so dry? He could read this like a face and lapsed into a silence as thick as asbestos. Good-bye for now, she said. I'll be in the bathroom if you need me.

He reached for the phone and called me. "Elaine," he said, "superdoll."

"Hi, Ed, is that you?"

"Oh lover, darling, sparrow, toothpick."

I listened with my full heart. "Say more," I said.

"Can't," he said.

"Where's Bambi?" I asked, then I answered my own question. "I know where she is. How can she have any skin left?"

"Goodbye for now," he said. "See you next Sunday."

Sure enough, Bambi reentered with a face red as a hotball. She found her small chair and knit a few rows.

"Sit on the couch," he said and she gathered her yarns and followed his advice. "Isn't that better?"

But that made her cry, so she rushed out of the room, leaving behind the knitted square which the cat made for and used as his bread board.

"Scat." he said to the cat, but the cat bared his teeth, took the red square by an end, and carried it away, dragging the needles and red balls behind him. "Bambi!" he yelled to his wife, who had bolted the bedroom door. "Gary has your knitting."

Soon it was bedtime, and after many applications of acidic liquids, Bambi felt her skin dry enough to sleep. Dry enough? he thought, it's scaling like an old snakeskin. Together they lay with no portion of her body skin touching any point of his private self. That was the given, but Edward felt the need for something, so he rolled over and grabbed his big roll of a wife around her waist, kissing her but avoiding the papyrus cheeks and forehead.

"Are you really kissing me?" she said, talking directly into his mouth.

"No," he said.

They kissed anyway, and he plugged himself in, and they both remembered the old days when a sheet of an entirely different feeling covered them and this.

"Is it as sad to you as to me?" she asked her husband.

"There's no good answer to that question. Goodnight, Bambi, queen of hearts."

"I love you, Edward."

Next day she was up early, reknit with fresh balls the awful snarl the cat deposited on his food tray. It was his now. Bambi started fresh, and before the sun was half up, all the new stitches were in. It was a coverlet for Edward, either for the foot of the bed or to wrap around his neck on a cool evening. When the square was remade, she lit the stove and cooked a frittata and a little fruit pie, baked with the cherries from their own tree. Edward and Bambi had a summer house and garden, but Bambi hadn't seen it in a year, two years, because Edward liked her to stay in the apartment with the air conditioner on and take care of the cat. He spent every day at the summer house, doing chores and tidying up. Edward had his own money and work was optional; every once in a while he took a job, did it, invested the pay, and the nest egg grew and grew. Sometimes he showed Bambi the bank balance. Often he picked fruit at the summerhouse and brought it home to Bambi. Elaine did not want any summerhouse fruit, although she often ate it, picked from the trees, when she was on the premises.

"It's a delicious pie," he said. "Did you make yourself one?"

"No," she said. "I'll eat later."

"I'm off," he said. "See you tonight."

"Can I call you there?"

"As often as you want to," he said. "I'll be right by the phone, unless I'm out in the garden."

Instead of going straight to the summerhouse, Edward knocked at my door, entered, and decided to spend the day with me. He read the papers, stocked the birdhouses with feed, and trimmed all my bushes. I watched him from the window. "Who's going to get you, Eddie?" I said. "Bambi or me?"

He laughed. "It's entirely up to the two of you." He had approached my window and lay down the pruning shears, poking his head in the window to bite my fingers. But, as I said, we started high, feisty; we ate, danced, sang, raced around the property, and then the mood sunk to absolute defeat, and Edward sailed home to Bambi. Sorrow answered to sorrow. No one was getting any younger.

III.

One time we tried something different. For one week of the summer, we all moved to the summerhouse, together with Ed and Bambi's sole son, Frederick, a board-school boy they saw once in a blue moon. It was a long week, seven days of the most mannered conversation and the most delicious food: we all cooked; even Frederick had a shot at the stove. Evenings we set the table deep into the garden under the fruit trees. Only candlelight and the dark world, twittering, cracking, and buzzing around us. We tried every recipe on earth and kept the conversation even. If I said: Isn't it funny that people used to think God is dead and thought it would stay that way, just where they left it? Frederick would pipe up with how many boys studied theology and believed what they read. Edward said computers had replaced God, but people were afraid to admit it. That's just like you, Edward, Bambi said; it's why you're irresistible.

I wouldn't agree, I could have said, but this was a subject best to avoid, especially with the boy around. One night of that week, Edward, who slept with me in the studio room built into the fork of a tree, said: What do you think he thinks? What did he used to think? I asked, when you and his mother lived in two separate houses, visiting occasionally. Yes, yes, Edward said, but here you are, a strange new woman, and living right in the house with us. A friend of the family, I said. He's not a fool, Eee. Do you want me to go home? I asked. No, he said, I just wanted to tell you what I thought, what keeps me awake at night with Bambi by my side.

The next night, Bambi came to my tree room. Pleased to meet you, she said. I knew there was someone. She sat on the bed, her back curled and her head hanging. I rubbed her back. She said: Do you think you're helping me? I stopped and started packing. Do you think there's anything you can do to help? I sat on the bed. I could kill myself, I said. We both laughed, but I repeated the offer nonetheless. Then I'd have your life on my head, instead of your body on my husband's; no thanks. I'd rather go back to my knitting, live life the best we can. We're in this together, Elaine, and don't forget it. I never do, I said. You're stuck with me and I with you. And we're both stuck with him, and Frederick's stuck with us, at least for now. Things could change, I said. I won't hold my breath, she said, then added: I don't want them to change. They might get worse.

IV.

And then they did get worse. One night, just as the moment of absolute defeat came on, and all the lights were on and the shades pulled, candles lit and music playing, Edward said, I'm not going home. What? I'm staying. With me? I said. I'm staying here. Are you sure? I said. Are you nervous? he said. Are you? I asked first, he said.

I ignored it and said: Okay, then, call Bambi. No need, he said, she'll figure it out. Don't make her figure it out, I said. Call her and fully inform her of the number of days you expect to be away from home. Forever, he said. You're living here with me? I said. Don't keep asking me the same question. If we're here together, the last thing you want is repetition or boredom creating indifference, which, as you know, Elaine, can come fast and never leave. Human condition, I said. That's more like it, he said. Are you calling Bambi, or am I? I said. I'll call in my own good time, he said; meanwhile, what are we going to do with ourselves now that the competition and intermittence are gone forever?

That took my breath away, and while I was collecting fresh, I was already imagining how to get Bambi to move in, too, or, more sneakily, how to get our lives to have a built-in Bambi without Bambi, but I was already feeling bad for her. She was part of it, so I called her myself.

I can't talk right now, she told me, straight off the bat, before I'd even had time to open my lips. Why? I said. I've got doctors here, she said, and after they finish wrapping my face in cool cloths and rich ointments and giving me shots for infection, I'm going to a spa. I plan to swim twelve miles a day. I'm allergic to the cat, and he's outta here. My lawyer is working on a divorce.

Is it over, Bambi, I said, what was between you and Edward and me, too? Because that's what I was just going to say to you. Ha-ha, she said. Think I didn't already know that? I've been waiting for this day since June 25th, 1988. Remember how hot that summer was? And Bush won in the fall? That was the day Edward met you. He came home cheerful for a change. A thick smile on his face, something I'd never seen before, not the depth of it. Just what's happened to you? I asked him. He told me he was in love, his life was saved, but nothing would change at home. He wasn't moving an inch. This was real life, his life with me, and you were love life. I was furniture, cars, bills, joint checking account, and mortgage. You were LSD, Spanish fly, stolen moments. But little by little, superdoll, I started putting what I was onto you.

I let out a big stream of air. Bambi heard it and said: Enjoy yourself. You've got everything now. What about Frederick? I said. He's coming too. The cat's coming. They're probably on their way. Goodbye, Elaine. You're a nice person, but you don't look both ways before you cross a street.

I hung up the phone.

Bambi's a different person, I said to Edward. She was always different, he said. You just didn't know her. What about those stories, I said, you know, the knitting, the skin, the early morning breakfasts? Some of it's true, he said. People do things, Elaine, just for their own pleasure. This is something you don't understand yet. Twinned destinies and all that—those are all ideas from the poets and your own head. The rest of us are out here, turning on our own gyres. Get it now?

How much do you love me? I said, and I could already hear my voice thinning and rising.

Take a good deep breath of air, he said. Then blow it all out. The dark night is going to close over us, Elaine, superdoll, and what will it matter whether I'm balled with you or by myself, or with my darling Bambi? Don't try to trap love, doll, love is motion.

Partly Him

I.

It wasn't the end of the line, but it was close. That's what made the straight shot up the coast so pleasant. There were hours of passage, lined up with strangers, reading or gazing at rocky beach, grassy marsh, shambling towns with windows facing inlet, pond, harbor, sea. By the time Alice arrived at her station, all the knots had been worked out, and her face was clear, the eyes as if filled with sea water, gray or blue—different, she thought, from glass or blood—and no memories hanging in them like a line of wash left overnight in the rain. This no one wanted to see. You could come empty-handed—that was fine—but don't bring the indigestible lumps from life at the other end of the line. Come empty—that was all they required—and Alice emptied, little by little, all the way up the coast. The work was pleasant.

Alice's mother—there she was—stood on the platform. Alice wondered if the train would stop. Theirs was an irritating little state with its two depots and, in between, nothing but woods. Lost time could be made up here, and was, full-throttle, once the country station was cleared.

Standing on the platform, they felt the rush of air as the 174 screamed past. The hollow train would clock in at Boston South Station right on the minute.

II.

Daddy—as Alice and her mother referred to him—had come along for the ride.

"How are you?" Alice asked her mother. "You look well."

"He's not good. He looks terrible," her mother said, charging up the platform with Alice's soft suitcase. "You'll see."

"I asked you," said Alice, right behind her mother, "how you are. I know how he is."

"See for yourself. I'm fine."

Alice was still talking to her mother's back. Ahead she could see the blue car and egg-like skull—was that him?—through the side window. He was in the backseat.

"Hi, Dad," Alice said, opening the car door, bending to kiss the rough cheek. But he didn't want the kiss. Instead, flung in her face was a bony hand. Alice caught the hand in both of hers and then felt the squeeze that was his (painful) way of showing how much he wanted to say, or felt, but couldn't yet. He didn't let the hand go. He was shaking it in his, squeezing tighter.

Her mother drove. Alice sat in front, listening to the barrage of questions, unanswerable questions, part of the necessary music of finding themselves, all three, back in the family nest. Alice held onto the door handle. The night sky on these lonely roads was deep and black; the stars in their profusion stood out, each in its own layer of space. Under the same sky, never as clear, pinkish and low, was Timothy—where would he be? He could be anywhere in his web of offices, courtrooms, classrooms, restaurants, and phone lines, but he wouldn't be seeing this sky or stars. He was no skywatcher. Alice's father was asking about Timothy, asking and telling. What Alice, he felt, seemed not to understand was that Timothy Massie might be Alice's husband (*second,* he always added with a grimace), but since *he* was Alice's father, in picking Alice, Timothy had picked Terence, and their names (this wasn't important, but anyway) began with T.

Terence was Terence A. McCarthy, and Timothy was (he tried to remember—it was hard to remember because that asinine Alice hadn't taken his good name) Timothy ——. And now the subject was changed, and he'd lie awake that night in a rage because *then* he would remember, again and again. That goddamned Alice—she always did it to him.

Timothy was—Alice ventured again, having answered pressing questions and asked others, provoking an argument between mother and father, which, now flaring, would supply the material and interest for the rest of the ride—where? Alice's imagination could never—and now wouldn't try—to do justice to the variety, the play of Timothy's days. Timothy, husband of four years, was defense attorney to the poor, part-time professor, columnist, advisor to governors and mayors, amateur musician, cook, and occasional public lecturer on criminal trials of note, historical and contemporary. Where was Timothy? No one—including his secretary—could answer that question with confidence.

"Alice!" she heard. "Are you deaf?" A bony knuckle was knocking her shoulder. "Did you hear what your mother said?"

"No, I didn't," said Alice, turning away from the night sky.

"Are you hungry? Would you like to have supper out? We planned to stop on the way home if you want to, if you're hungry. We won't, if you're not, but we haven't eaten either," her mother said, "and I'm starved."

The knuckled weight fell on her shoulder. "Baby Alice," the father said, "my baby Alice, blue gown. Don't tell me you're not hungry. I've been waiting all day. . . And here you are finally, coming on that stupid train, and the damn thing is late. As usual. Sitting out here in the freezing cold, for how long? What was it, an hour? Half an hour? I'm half dead."

Alice smiled. The train was fifteen minutes late, but her father had likely built his whole day around the trip to the station. He was dressed and ready, shoes tied, throat dry, and stomach twisted in apprehension of the number of things that

could, and would, go wrong, and so, drinking, to ease the torment, most of the six-pack, some vodka he'd stashed in his
dresser, a pint bottle, and then having to find the paper bags or
dish rags or face cloths or t-shirts, or whatever he could lay
hand on, to wrap it and bury it deep in the garbage (not the
recycle box—oh, no!—where she was sure to find it), and
making a quick stop, when he went to fill the tank, at Mai Tai.
He knew all the bartenders, chinks or whatever they were—
all friendly and wouldn't squeal. He knew that much. Even
when they picked him up (he'd fallen and cracked his head) on
the asphalt, and he was out cold for, what, 20–30 minutes,
they wanted to call 911, but they let him sit and catch his
breath instead. He was fine, he kept saying, although blood
from the gash was dripping in his eye, and he wouldn't take a
clean napkin (nah, he had a handkerchief, but where was it?)
but hoisted up (they were all watching) after a bit and hauled
into the men's to see (holy Christ Almighty!) the gash and treat
it with wads of toilet paper, then dunked his whole head in the
basin, run the water over the gash, more toilet paper. There!
He showed them, Charlie Chan or whoever his name was, running over with a Band-Aid. What—was he crazy? How was he
going to explain the Band-Aid? Didn't have to explain a thing.
Went home and got into bed, light off, no questions asked.

They laughed at it now. At Mai Tai, he was a regular.

Did Alice answer? No one knew for sure, but here they
were, barreling into the Harvey House parking lot—steak,
Italian food, shellfish, blue plate, and good drinks. They were
famous for big drinks, a drink and a half, and it was happy hour
to boot, so three drinks, really, for the price of one.

*I*t was walking in, with his arm hooked through hers, that
Alice could see and feel how he had failed. His forearm was
like a twig, and trembling. His step was irregular, uncertain.
He had barely the strength to pull open—straining and swearing with the effort—the Harvey House door. Once inside, he

shuffled ahead, greeting waitresses, barman, in that loud, gruff voice, suddenly animated, in the glaring lights and din of happy hour, the suffocating air dense with the smells of deep-fried fish, thick red sauces, grilled steaks, the sweetish odor of spirits, and the acrid odor of smoke and old beer. He came alive, but what was there to fuel this sudden life, Alice wondered, seeing the loose jacket and empty trouser legs and the cruel bend in the neck and upper back? They had walked a few feet of parking lot, up two steps and into the hallway, and he was gasping, bracing against a wall to cough, then sunk onto a bench, waving at them to go ahead, take the table, give him a minute—he'd catch up, don't call attention. He had no breath, Alice noticed, to yell at them. Just enough to wave that stick-like arm in its bulky wrappings.

"See what I mean?" her mother was saying, as she lowered herself into a booth and slid over. "He's worse."

"What does the doctor say?"

"I don't know. I go with him, but he goes in alone. I ask the doctor—he's young—but he doesn't say anything I don't already know."

Alice and her mother had finished their first drink when Terence McCarthy, still puffing, showed up at their table and waved his wife a direction—move in! He didn't like to sit too close. If it had been Alice next to him, that was different: she was young (well, not young, but not old). He didn't like old and fat next to him; he'd made that clear without words.

Deep into her drink (a martini), Alice was wondering again, while her parents discussed the menu they knew by heart, where Timothy was.

"Where's Tim tonight?" her mother chimed in.

"Hey," her father added, "I like him. I *like* him. How's he doing, Al, how's the practice? Has he been making the front page?" And he was off on his favorite subject since Timothy, a Jew, had been brought into his life. At first, he was alarmed. A Jew lawyer? But times had changed. You could always have your Jew lawyer, and more power to you if you did, but now you could marry them, at least someone like Alice could. She did whatever she wanted to anyway. No one could stop Alice; she always went too far. But, in this case, he was thinking, it worked out.

"It worked out fine," he was saying aloud. "I like him. A nice fella. Talkative, a good mind—oh, you bet your life—smart! I'm dumb, but he's smart. He never talked down to me, though." And he looked at Alice—big, goofy Alice, his favorite—and winked. "He doesn't, does he? You'd know. Does he?"

"No," said Alice. "No, he doesn't."

"Of course he doesn't," the mother chimed in. "Why would he?"

"What do you mean, why would he? We're nothings. He's . . . What is he again, Alice? Chief superior district court of appeal attorney general? What office did he hold? Doesn't anymore, though, right? Lost that election. Not a politician, Alice. I could have told you that. Bright, though. Doesn't matter. He's doing all right, and so are you. You're making pretty good money now, aren't you? You must be. You've been doing that job, what, ten, fifteen years now? They must be paying well. Just keep going like you are, Alice. You're doing fine. Nobody—I don't want to hurt your feelings; it's only your father talking—but who would have expected it? There were years, Alice . . . " Here he stopped. The waitress was laying three coasters on their table and now his three beers. Hand shaking, he hoisted one and drank half of it.

Some went down the wrong way, and now he was coughing, choking, and Alice's mother was hammering him on the back. The waitress returned. "Are you all right, sir?" He couldn't talk. He was coughing into the napkin. Alice's mother was trying to push him out of the booth and into the lobby, men's room, anywhere, because he was making such a racket. But the coughs subsided. He dabbed at his streaming eyes; he was mad, but too breathless to let any out. Alice's mother returned to the menu; Alice's father hung his head and waited, glass in hand, for his throat to clear. It was only seven o'clock, but Harvey's was packed.

"How's your father?" Timothy asked—not first thing, but after an account of where he *had* been (mayor's council on veterans' affairs, cocktail benefit at the museum, trip to the gym for swim and sauna, dinner—alone?—at his neighborhood sushi joint, and now two rented movies; he'd probably go to bed early, so he could put in half a day tomorrow before flying to Boston) and who had called, both for Alice and for him, that day's mail and faxes.

"He's bad," Alice said, in a whisper because the walls here were thin and no one slept.

"Is he worse? How could he be worse!" Timothy laughed.

"Maybe he isn't, but he seems worse."

"Have you or your mother called the doctor? No, I'm sure you haven't," Timothy assured himself. "You don't believe in doctors. Well, say hello to him for me. He's not coming, is he? Does your mother still want to come hear me? That's nice of her."

"She's looking forward to it."

"Are you?"

Not long ago—two weeks, two and a half—after a cool and oddly strained dinner with friends, Alice woke up in a knot of bedclothes with rings of sweat around her waist and neck. Too much wine and too much listening to windy, frustrated wives, while their joking or ranting activist husbands were comparing notes on doomsday scenarios—the end of capitalism, the end of *advanced* capitalism, the end of life as we know it. She sat up, uncoiling the sheets. Where was Timothy? He was there a minute ago, because a cry in his sleep was what had wakened Alice. But he was gone. She felt the hollow, still warm, where he had lain in a ball, facing away. Then she rose and padded through the living room, sitting room, dining room and hall, into the narrow passage that led to the kitchen. "Timothy?" she called, but there was no answer.

He was there. He was leaning over the counter in pajamas and bare feet. In the dimness (a nightlight burned over the sink), his flannel back curved in an arc, his head just above the counter top, where it rested on his fist. What was he doing?

Alice halted. He must have heard something, but he didn't react. After a few minutes, she heard the sob. She pulled out a chair, tried to guide him into it, but he stiffened in place. Alice sat on the chair, then moved to another one—not so close, with a clearer view. But he wasn't crying, or if he was, it was now silent.

"Are you in pain?" she asked him, her voice deep, soothing.

"What?" He was talking through his fingers. He *was* crying.

"Are you sick? Shall I call the doctor?"

" Leave me alone."

"Why should I leave you alone. You're in trouble, aren't you?" Alice was surprised to hear how the rich quality of her voice, ready for these occasions, had thinned.

Hearing it, he turned. "You know, don't you?" he said, his own tone thin. No tears now.

When she didn't answer, but hooked her leg around the chair leg and tightened it, he said: "I thought you did. How could you not know."

"Know what?" she said, after a while, although it wasn't necessary. He was ready now to talk. He sat in the chair Alice had pulled out for him. She was ready to ask if they needed more light, but was checked by the look he gave her, and then by the news that he was "in love" with someone else and had been for some time. His face looked aged, some mysterious suffering had parched the skin and knotted the muscles. She couldn't look into his eyes, although he was looking into hers.

She tried to get up from the chair, but sat down again. What was it? It couldn't be clearly grasped; the shape was there.

How were all those days, weeks, to be filled in? She wanted help from Timothy, but Timothy could give no help. He was almost gone. This part of it was clear.

And now he must answer questions. First, he refused, and then he answered every one, sometimes cried out the answers.

How much time elapsed? Three hours, four. They moved eventually from the dim kitchen to the bedroom. Alice did not cry. She didn't say much, but in the nightmarish trip, walking—sometimes staggering—from kitchen to bedroom, with its silk-shaded lamps burning brightly, she had blacked out, a first. It was enough to stop, to stand, to hold onto something—Timothy, the wall—and she was steady again, enough to walk the few steps to the bed, where they lay together, at first in silence; then the talk began again, and finally Timothy gave way to raging tears, sobs of despair that could not be quieted until they found themselves embracing as if for the last time.

It was still obscure, but dawn had seeped through the cotton curtains, spoiling the lamplight and smutching the scrambled bedclothes.

The affair would end? Maybe yes, maybe no. The marriage would go on? Maybe. What would happen? How would they live? Timothy didn't know. He couldn't say. He didn't know his own mind. His life was falling apart.

Do you want me to go? he asked Alice.

Go where? she felt like saying. She knew where. But if he went there, to the "someone else" he loved, he wouldn't come back. And she wouldn't want him to. They both seemed to know this. So nothing was done. Timothy didn't want to decide right then and there; he didn't know what to do. He would leave, though, if that was what Alice wanted. Did she want it?

III.

When Alice got up, it was only 7:00, a beautiful, cold winter day, but the burbling of the coffee maker must have alerted Mr.

McCarthy, who napped all day and lay awake all night. Through the wall his bedroom shared with the kitchen, he shouted: "Who's out there making all that racket?"

Alice said that it was Alice.

"Is it you, Lillian? Speak up," he shouted.

"It's Alice!" Alice shouted to the wall.

"Oh, Alice, it's you. You don't have to yell. I might be old, but I'm not deaf. Wait a minute, I'm getting up. Don't sneak back to bed."

Alice sat down, cup in hand, but Mr. McCarthy went first to the bathroom, then returned to his bedroom.

"Aren't you getting up?" she asked, when ten minutes had elapsed.

She heard coughing, then nothing. She walked to his darkened room. He was standing, bent over his bureau with his arms spread, each hand well apart. This was something new. "I'll wait for you," she said. "Take your time."

He didn't answer; he had no breath to answer, her mother said. She was in the kitchen now. She didn't need to look; she knew what Alice had seen. "It takes him a while in the morning. Sometimes he doesn't get up till noon. And it's still hard."

But he must have made the extra effort, Alice thought, seeing him emerge from the bedroom and pick his way into the kitchen, where he halted at the breakfast bar to brace himself again, arched over his stiffened arms, panting.

"His lungs are wet," her mother explained. "He's better after he's been sitting up awhile."

But he wasn't better. He lowered himself into an easy chair and bent low over the hassock, head in hands. Alice watched. His rib cage—you could see every bone through the t-shirt—swelled, but nothing rose to fill the straining lungs. They swelled again; they ballooned. She could hear the hollow tubes with something whistling against them; she could hear the intake of breath through the open mouth, but even there, it was blocked by mucous. The mother had handed him a roll of paper towels, and he had honked into several sheets. She fixed him his coffee. Sometimes the hot liquid would break the barrier, she said, or he could cough himself clear. "Take your shower. He won't be available for a while. You have time."

When Alice returned with wet hair and a bathrobe wrapped tightly around her, he was ready, more than ready.

"Alice, you look good!" he was shouting. "Look at me. Don't hang your head. Put your arms down. Let me see you. You never let me look at you. Stand up straight. Good! You're a good-looking woman, Alice. Nothing wrong with you. You're built nice. So why does she wear," he turned to Alice's mother, "those weeds? You look like *my* mother. Why can't you wear a color, a nice suit, a pants suit? You've got the figure, Alice. I don't know why you kids do it. Does Timothy like it? What does he say?"

Mr. McCarthy was on a roll, and he'd stay on it until he took wife and daughter to the Providence station—a big trip for him, but he insisted on making it. Her mother drove in, and Terence slumped in the back seat. Alice could see him in the rear-view mirror, shrunken, dazed by the light, exhausted from the stream of talk. Depressed, too, offended because Alice wouldn't engage with him. Yes, no—she responded to his questions, when she responded at all. Mostly she sat there drinking her coffee, sunken into herself. She wouldn't look at him.

"Look at me when I'm talking to you!" he had to say at one point, and she laughed to make light of it—and the strange, energized rant that preceded it. "Don't you want to talk to your father?" he said. "No," he answered himself. "You never want to talk to me. I've got nothing to say. Who would want to listen? I'm not smart. You're smart, Alice," and he was off again. "*She* doesn't talk to me," he said, pointing with his thumb to Alice's mother, busy frying bacon for their breakfast. "She's had enough of me, forty-three years. She's heard it all." He laughed. It was okay; now he was taking it well. Everyone relaxed. He had turned it around himself; it could have gone either way, but he had rescued it. They all had a good laugh at his expense, but now, as Alice glanced at him in the mirror, she could see the effort had worn him out and left him with nothing.

IV.

It was cold in Boston, a gusty, gritty cold that took the pleasure out of walking even the short blocks from the Parker House, where they'd settled in their rooms, to Filene's. Mrs. McCarthy, out of the house, free, wasn't content to see the usual: Beacon Hill, Faneuil Hall, the Public Gardens, and Common. It was three in the afternoon, the sun still shining, and she wanted to make at least one trip to Filene's basement. She had made it—it was the highlight of the day—and now Timothy wanted to go. There was time. They would meet for a snack at five, and the Old South Church was just a few blocks from the hotel.

Timothy made two trips, the second one three-quarters of an hour after the first, when he insisted Alice come along. There were so many things—shirts, jackets, ties, overcoats— he wanted to show her. Everything was so cheap.

Alice didn't want to go to Filene's basement. She didn't want to see the tables heaped with boots and sweaters, the rows of shopworn cocktail dresses and dusty evening gowns, automatic markdowns under the low ceiling. There was a sub-basement where things were cheaper still. But Timothy insisted: Italian-made shirts and suits at half the price of Barney's or Saks. She had to see. No, the shirts were not seconds; they were wrapped, folded, pinned, fine fabrics and beautiful tailoring. So she went. Dusk was falling in the caverns of old, gray Boston, although the nearness of 5:00 quickened the pace of the wind-whipped walkers. Timothy, holding Alice's bare hand in his gloved one, was surprised to see the difference half an hour made in the density of shoppers—mostly women—mobbing the tables, arms reaching through the thicket of coats to finger silk scarves or to open purses, to shake out a folded shirt, or to find the matching slipper. Timothy stopped just at the escalator. "Keep moving," Alice whispered, and sure enough, a crowd had massed behind him, impatient and eager. They rode the escalator hand-in-hand. Timothy found the jackets, shirts, and ties he had set aside.

Alice was lined up at the cashier with a belt, shoes, and undershorts, while Timothy still stood over a table of imported dress shirts: he had two whites and a blue under one arm and was deciding about a tattersall and pale yellow. Then he found another room, and he hadn't yet seen the sub-basement, but Alice left him to return to the hotel. "Keep an eye on the time," she told him. "I know," he said, but his back was already turned. Then, pacing toward the subway exit, Alice felt a tug at her arm. It was Timothy. "Alice," he said, stopping her, pulling her out of the wave of shoppers making for the exit.

There was a coffee counter, but no one to make coffee. They sat at the counter. "Why don't you look at clothes for yourself?"

"I don't feel like it."

"What would you rather do?" he asked. "I don't mind leaving. I can leave now."

"I don't want to do anything. I'm going back to the hotel."

"Is that all right? Are you okay?"

"I'm fine," she said, and he was gone again. But she wasn't going back to the Parker House; she was going toward the subway exit. When she arrived at the doors, she stopped: fresh, cold air from the street came this far; here it met the rush of heated air from the store, but just half a foot to the left, closer to the stairwell, was the air from the underground, spicy with diesel oil, damp wool, and a mustiness from the tunneled-out earth that never quite dried. She listened to the screech of brakes, and soon the stairwell filled with office workers, forcing their way up to Summer Street, to go left to South Station or right to Park Street. This seemed to be the heart of Boston, her feet were on the heart. But it was her heart too. The rag in her chest was nothing. The pounding from underfoot, brake valves screeching, doors parting for the outflow of padded bodies and the inflow of cold wool and dusty boots—this force she could feel through the soles of her own thin boots. Her whole body, so still and alert, rumbled on this hub of criss-crossing passage.

It was dark outside. There were no revolving doors at this level, so Alice left the heart and went up a flight of steps into the maze—pink, yellow, glowing in coned light—of cosmetics and perfume. The aisles were spacious, the footing smooth, and at each booth, with hands on the warm, lit glass, stood a queen or princess, red suit, pink suit, black and white, lavender, yellow, and cool peach. Their heads were burnished helmets of a rich, ripe color, and their faces creamy ovals, jeweled or enameled—breathing, if they breathed, this heavy burden of flowers. The air was weighted with flowers, or burned by spice and incense. Oils, creams, and lotions open on the counters enriched the air. Alice glided through this radiance and past painted boxes, legends, mirrors, and the cells of lighted glass. Her eyes were filled with tears. Only in the cold dark of the street did her face dry, and lips already chapped.

She hurried, but the sidewalks were crowded, the streets choked with cars, and passage in every direction impeded.

V.

Mrs. McCarthy's single in the Parker House was a closet-like space with the bed squeezed between door and wall. She had rested before Timothy's performance, then had called Terry. He was there, sounded fine, always sounded fine when he had the house to himself; but one day or one hour or five minutes too long in isolation, and his pleasure would turn to something else. Feeling abandoned, helpless, and hated, he had his own weapons for redress: he'd stop eating; he'd drink three times as much as his shrunken stomach could safely hold; if he felt up to it, he'd go to the Mai Tai. Mrs. McCarthy could estimate how the time alone was shaping up for him and what margin was left for her. He paced himself. If she went for an hour, he allowed two hours; if she planned a morning's excursion, he'd give her till three, three-thirty, but after that, even fifteen minutes more would unbalance him, poison his mood, and he'd set to work on the payback. But it was too early in the two-day jaunt (long, yes, but he'd encouraged her; he could handle it; he could space out the few events and treats of his tedious days) to worry. He was holding himself up well; some resources were used up (he'd called at the Mai Tai on his return from the station; he'd talked to the other daughter, Paula, twice already; a friend from work had called out of the blue; and he had watched his favorite video, *Patton,* gift of Tim and Alice (but he knew *Tim* had picked it out for him). Yes, and eaten lunch, but no dinner. He was tired; he was going to bed. No, not right away; he was going to sit and watch the news, hear tomorrow's weather, for tomorrow he'd drive to the country station at 4:42, train 64, the Yankee Clipper (he had it all written down) to pick them up. He had that day planned, too. He'd leave the house no later than 2:30, but he'd be ready to go at noon, with all the little bottles wrapped up, and the cans, to make a special trip to the dumpster. He wasn't fool enough to drop them in the recycling. His whole day was planned. He could see it unfold hour by hour, step by step.

Mrs. McCarthy had hung up, she told her daughter, knowing he was cheerful and sober. Was Timothy all dressed and ready? What had he bought at the basement?

VI.

On the dais—there was no altar—raised above the nave with a double curving staircase, was Timothy in a dark suit and gilded tie. He talked, he debated another man, he summarized, he opened the discussion to the floor. Those with questions filed down the center aisle to stand under the dais, where Timothy now stood to receive them. Alice and her mother were sitting to the left, sharing a pew with high wooden walls and a latched gate. It was a family pew, paid for 150 years ago by the Motleys, still used to this day, with black prayer books propped in their wooden cases. Alice had opened hers to see records of the Motley marriages, births and baptisms entered in a faded ink on the flyleaf. While Timothy's panel talked, Alice and her mother studied these records. The Motleys had three branches: two had moved to Beverly Farms, but one branch still lived on Chestnut Street—Warren, Phillipa, and grown-up children Clementine, Frances, and John James.

"Look," Alice's mother whispered. Alice gazed at the platform. "No, there," said her mother, "and there, and all over," pointing to the four corners of the air space.

"I saw them," Alice whispered back.

"Who are they?"

"Founding fathers," Alice said. "Don't you see?"

At the four compass points were four Boston signers.

"Look back," the mother said. "There's more. Look up."

There must have been ten, twelve effigies. They weren't just colonists, although the latter congregated on the ground level, closest to the pulpit.

There were still three people standing in line to ask their questions. When they had asked them, they walked across the front of the church, under the dais, and down the side aisle. Here was the oddity. The signers and rebels, the orators, lawgivers, merchants, warriors, and writers were faced in all directions. You couldn't help but meet some eye, but the questioners approaching the mike or filing back to their places seemed to walk right past and through them.

It was in their nature to be seen through, Alice thought: they were made of clear Lucite; they were flat, the lips and eyes and hair, the stock and neckcloth, the waistcoats and tailcoats, the gloves, breeches, and boots were mere suggestions.

They were there and not there. You could see them and see through them. Some reflected the light, some were in shadow—blue like the air, but darker.

The forum was over. People were clapping. Some were standing. When they stood, the plastic effigies vanished, but, as the crowd dispersed—some waiting to shake hands, to ask more questions—the long-dead patriots were in place. Some were in the benches; some were in the aisles. Alice caught her mother's eye and touched her hand. Then they gathered up coats and scarves. Timothy was working his way to their pew; he was bringing someone with him. Mrs. McCarthy whispered, "I've got goose bumps."

"I know," said Alice, and here was Timothy with the panel moderator.

The Boston night was black and frigid. Timothy, Alice, and Alice's mother took a cab from the Parker House to Arlington Street. An Italian restaurant with Tuscan-based food, trendy and youthful, was crowded: there was a long wait, and the bar was also packed. Every surface was metal, hard wood or enamel; the ceilings were low so the voices were piercing. The three were tired; they didn't have the energy to roar over the crowd, to fight it off, or to enjoy its stimulation. At least Alice felt she didn't, and one look at her mother's face—the glassy eyes and stiff smile—was enough to shout at Timothy, who was making his way to the free table. When he finally reached it and turned around, Alice could see that even Timothy, all keyed up by the talk and its aftermath, was shielding himself, still stuffed in his coat with his wool hat pulled over his ears, from the shattering din. He was quick to agree, and in minutes they were seated in a well-padded, pink-lit breakfast room with pastel murals of the Public Gardens. Just the sight of the cobalt blue goblets filled with ice water, the muted sound of a recorded string quartet, the carpeted step of the white-coated waiters, and the murmur of conversation made all three of their party meet each pair of eyes with gratitude. Their day, every moment of it, had been such a triumph.

VII.

By morning it was over. It was time to go home. There had been a free hour for a dash to Filene's, but instead Timothy took a conference call, and where was he? Alice's mother kept asking, but when they tracked him to the gloomy corridor reserved for businessmen in residence (Mrs. McCarthy opened a door; the room was empty, just a bare table and chairs, and every other room—B, C, D, E—just like it), no Timothy.

Mrs. McCarthy didn't want to wait. Wherever he was, didn't he have a noon flight? Didn't it make sense to just let him finish up his business and go? He hadn't counted on seeing them—he'd said goodbye at breakfast—and with the extra time, Alice's mother explained, not having to chase after Timothy, they could go to Quincy Market, just a few blocks away, and buy souvenirs. They had bought nothing for Paula's children, and they might pick up something for Terry, even though he had everything he needed—his dressers and closet were jammed with Christmas and birthday presents, and what did he wear every day to sit (twelve hours) in that lounge chair? An old sweatshirt, work pants.

So, without seeing Timothy again that day—or the next, as it turned out—Alice and her mother trekked to Government Center and down the stone steps to the market, quiet in the late morning. While Alice stopped for coffee, her mother bustled from stall to stall, returning with an armful of shopping bags. Toys for the kids, bath powder for Paula, and—look!— a clean new sweatshirt for Daddy. It said BOSTON. It wasn't much, but she couldn't find anything else, and at least he'd wear it. It was white like the one he put on every day.

A half hour later, the two were ready to board the train at South Station. The sky had clouded over, and it was cold again after a dazzling bright morning. Mrs. McCarthy made one last phone call home. There had been no answer an hour earlier. It's not possible, she said to her daughter, that he's started out that early? Alice laughed. She knew what was possible, and could picture him at Mai Tai, or at Richard's, which was on the way. She didn't have to say it. They could both picture it. And here was the train, inching down the platform.

They thought they could picture him (at Richard's or Mai Tai), but these pictures were useless and could not be summoned when mother and daughter arrived at the country station and waited while other passengers were received in person or by a waiting car with the motor running.

Where the platform ran north toward the city, the four train tracks seemed to merge into one. Cold and distracted, Alice paced up the platform to a point where the tracks separated out again. Bare branches crowned platform and tracks. The sky above was pure white steam, when she heard the car.

Mrs. McCarthy was on the platform walking south. She also heard the motor, wheels grinding the gravel. They turned and looked, but the car wasn't the McCarthy's blue sedan, and it didn't nose into a parking space. The car, green—familiar, but whose was it?—stopped in the center of the lot, and someone jumped out. Who?

When the party approached, Alice and her mother saw that it was Mike, Paula's husband, who'd left the car in the middle of the parking lot with motor running. "Dad's gone," he said.

"Gone where?" Alice heard her mother say, and by then, Mike, without answering, had herded them into his car. Mrs. McCarthy pushed Alice into the front seat.

*A*nd he *was* gone. He was there—Alice and her mother insisted on seeing him—crumpled on the floor next to his chair, a few angled bones and silver-bristled skull. His shoes were on, his watch was on, but the lamp was knocked over, smashed, its shade ripped, the bulb blown out.

He was gone, but gone *where* was still a good question, because Alice, in the first choking burst of grief, sensed he hadn't
completely left the tiny house. It took months, and several re-
furbishings of the living room—new lamp, drapes, new rocker
for the discarded lounge chair with the dark stain on the head
cushion (not blood, just the daily, hourly pressure of a human
head)—to eliminate his traces, and he still wasn't completely
gone.

First, they'd carried him out. Alice happened to be outside
on the lawn when the hearse pulled into the driveway. Five
minutes later, through the back door and down the back steps,
they carried a canvas bag—it looked like canvas—with contents so light that they didn't really need the fold-up gurney,
but, for appearances' sake, so they wouldn't appear to be haul-
ing trash, they lay the zippered bag on the gurney, and Alice
watched while her father made his last trip down the driveway,
past the shed, and then hoisted into the limo's hatch. She stood
on the lawn until the black car disappeared.

Inside was disorder, extra family members, two state police
searching the house for poison and pills. They *did* turn up
empty liter bottles of vodka, tucked here and there—one right
under the lounge chair—but Mrs. McCarthy had explained
that Mr. McCarthy couldn't, in his present state, have drunk
himself to death. It was not likely—Alice heard her mother
say—but the big bottles were upsetting to see. The question
held them, but they resolved it. He might have, yes, but not any
more intentionally than he did anything else. Everything he did
was life-threatening, but no one thing could be singled out.

The priest was at the door and, behind him, the undertaker,
whom Paula had called right after phoning the rectory. Coffee
was made. Alice couldn't speak, but Paula and her mother answered questions for the death notice. They had until tomorrow, the undertaker said, to flesh out a history for the formal
obit. The undertaker, a young woman, daughter of a longtime
family friend, would help.

When the visitors left, more calls were made. Children were collected from where they had been left—with a neighbor—when Paula, there to take her father to the train station, saw the paper still rolled up in its plastic bag. She had called many times, no answer, but seeing the morning paper lying on the blacktop at 3 P.M. was certainty. She walked her children to the neighbor's, to spare them whatever was waiting for her.

The house was now quiet, the busted lamp on the carpet, the juice glass lined up on the breakfast bar next to an inhaler still in its box. Alice moved to the lounge chair and was using the lever to fold its foot, so as to gather up the fragments of glass and the coffee cup, but Paula was right behind her.

"Let me do that. Call Tim. Don't you want to call Tim? Call Tim, Al. He'll want to know, and he can help."

How? Alice wondered. How could he help? But she did call, got the answering machine, launched a swamped, choking message, and someone picked up. "Alice!"

Timothy would clear his calendar for Wednesday. There were no court dates, anyway; he'd come for the wake and the funeral the next day. He couldn't stay longer, and he didn't ask when Alice was coming home. He understood, he said, that Alice didn't know.

"How's your mother?"

At first, Alice didn't know how to answer. "She's taking it hard."

"Of course."

"No, really," Alice said.

"I know. It's natural."

"Yeah, but we both know," she said in a quiet voice, "what a pain in the ass he could be."

"Didn't we, though!" Timothy said, but Alice said she had to hang up. "Why?" Timothy said. "Talk to me."

"I can't."

"You're not worried about *me,* are you?"

"I wasn't even thinking about you."

"Well, don't. You don't have to. I'm by myself."

"You're 'by yourself'?" Alice repeated, struck by the childish phrase.

Timothy let the subject drop. "Your father was very sick, Al. Don't forget that. It's easier for him."

"He didn't want to die."

"He didn't?"

"How can you say that!"

"I'm sorry. I didn't mean to slight him."

"Nobody wants to die, Timothy."

"Really? I don't think that's true."

Alice sighed. "I have to go now. We can't find my father's insurance papers. We can't find anything."

"Maybe tonight you shouldn't try."

Alice didn't answer.

"Let me talk to your mother. Shouldn't I say something to your mother?"

"That's a good idea." Alice turned from the phone. "Ma?" she said, but her mother was already there. She liked Timothy. They all did.

The next day Alice picked out her father's casket: maple. It looked like a twin bed set they had once owned. White satin lining and brass nameplate. The casket, the undertaker explained (they were in the basement of the funeral home), would be sealed in a concrete case. That's why it wasn't necessary, she said, to buy a steel casket—although sometimes people did. The metal boxes, twice as expensive, were hideous, Alice thought: silvery, bronze, and dead black. They gleamed like new cars. It took ten minutes to pick out the casket. No need to spend hours in that basement room, smelling of flowers and formaldehyde, although—her mother pointed out on the way home—it was upstairs where they did the embalming. No, Paula said, they were both wrong. It was in that big garage next door. Hadn't they noticed?

Over the next day and a half, the other sister and brother flew in, along with Timothy and the spouses. Each night while they were all there, someone took a turn sleeping in the father's small bedroom. "It breaks the ice," Mrs. McCarthy said. Timothy and Alice's brother gave readings at the funeral mass, where the family walked behind Terence McCarthy, wheeled up the center aisle of his old church. The casket was draped in a white cloth and the priest vested in white.

After the mass, the funeral cortege drove past the McCarthy house on Fenmore Street. This was an Irish custom, and so thoughtful for Patricia Healy O'Connor, the new funeral director, to think of it

You're going now, Terence's oldest daughter was saying under her breath. You're going now, Dad, so say goodbye to the old house.

Timothy, on one of the jump seats, must have heard. He smiled at his wife. "I know what you're doing," he leaned over to whisper in her ear. "I can see."

"What? What am I doing?" she said. She hadn't meant it to sound so harsh.

Alice stayed with her mother for a week; then work called her back. Only once in the two years following did Alice see her father. It happened the summer after he died. Alice had been visiting her mother.

"How are you doing? Are you getting used to it?" Alice asked on the drive from the station.

In a tone she'd never heard before, and after a pause, her mother said, "Somewhat," and nothing more.

But it wasn't at home or at the train station in Saugatuck where Alice saw her father. It was at the other end of the line, at *her* station, where she'd been looking for Timothy, who usually met her at the gate. Alice rode the escalator with her suitcase. She pushed through the glass door and stood. Then she walked the length of the waiting room. Just at the spot where the airy, sun-filled station was cut by a broad causeway, Alice spotted him. He was sitting on a bench, facing away. Those were his limp, roomy trousers, hiked high, the crew socks, the sneakers fastened with Velcro strips. Alice stopped at the information booth. She rested against the counter.

"Alice." She heard a familiar voice, and then a footstep, and now the view was darkened and hot breath was pouring over her face. She shifted away to where she could still see.

Of course, Timothy—for it was Timothy—saw too.

But they couldn't stand there forever, staring. There was motion around them, and soon the old man, although in a world of his own, would notice.

But Alice still stared. It wasn't him, but she wasn't finished with the one it was, who was surely partly him, or the new him, or something related.

"Alice," she heard—that voice, the legal voice, had a certain vacuum-like force. There was nothing between them now but this attention-getting voice. The space between them had been swept free of everything else.

For a moment, she was in between, frozen still, but in another minute or two, she'd break out, begin to move. She was home now. Timothy would lead the way. He was already ahead and almost out the door.

Lavare

A lady stopped me in the Laundromat to say: don't forget. Don't forget what? I said, but regretted it because already a little too rude for me, too much of me coming to the surface for the sake of what? And sure enough, without a flicker, she passed me by and went over to a steel case bolted to the wall, plugged in her quarters and out came a puny carton of Duz, something they don't even make anymore. Quiet now, I said to myself, don't waste a day's energy on this imbecility.

Was she an imbecile? She poured the snowy contents of her carton into a load of whites, flipped a switch to . . . whatever it was: annihilate, petrify, because you could tell right away she washed the hell out of her clothes, especially whites. I could hear the water coursing in, at least two fast pipelines, and then I got her attention: forget what?

"Don't forget yourself, little girl," she said. "Just that."

"Just that?"

"Take it in," she said and plumped away, sat on a pink plastic chair, and pulled her rosary out. "Our father, who art in heaven," I could hear her muttering.

"No," I said, "not our father, who art in heaven. Glory be to the father and to the son and to the holy ghost. That's where you start."

At that she dangled her rosary in front of my eyes to show me, fool, that she wasn't starting at the beginning. She was already on the first mystery and its first bead, the one right over the medallion.

"Okay," I said. "Sorry." Sighing, I sat down next to her. After all, she was my mother, or she could have been: right age, right size. In my pocket I had a little translation I was working on, but no dictionary, not even the tiny one I usually kept in my bone-leather purse. So I did a free translation. On my left knee was the original (I love that word), although only a photocopy from a page of a real book borrowed from the library; and on the right, a sheet of stationary, pink with a rose on top.

"Nice," she said, flicking the right-knee paper with her pinky.

"All I could find in the stores you have around here. Do you still call them stores, or are they all outlets, commissaries, retail depots?"

"What?" she said.

The first line of the poem was easy, and I had already translated it, but I wanted to copy it to have the feel of the beginning under my fingers. I took up a "Pennysaver" to stiffen the paper.

Atlas came into it. And every night I dream of Atlas, the only man who'd have the guts to squire a translator with a little monkey face like me and swell legs and shoulders by Praxiteles. The first line was so lovely that my pen hand dropped, and I was gazing into space, but not gaping: when I'm outside my own frame house, all my controls are on, switches and meters. My body takes care of itself, so I never look like an idiot when I take a little mental vacation. Or speak under my breath like the lard-queen sitting next to me. She fills her skin to bursting—a way to avoid wrinkles and to keep the feet and hands, prone to bony pinnation, fat and round.

The second line of my poem had Hannibal Africanus in it, but two words I needed to check. I'm no good at languages; my talent lies in making the English sound and look exactly like the original and be pleasing in itself. What a lovely job you have, I said to myself. Lonely and desperate though I was, I always had this delicate work to do which satisfied me to the gills. That's something, I thought, this wash hag could never understand, not in a million.

She was now tucking cloth flats into a huge steel-gray dryer. I was outraged at the disproportion, but soon I saw her return—flop, flop, flop—to four other machines. And here's the beauty of it: not only had she separated her whites from cottons, and fines from medium average, she had (I suck my breath to think of it) a washer of red, of yellow-brown, of print-pastels, of violet blues.

But they were all—after all the careful sorting—smucked together in that industrial-size turbulator. Why, I thought, why? The skin around my eyes (violet just like Liz Taylor's) stretched thin with the effort to keep them in my head. That's what an intellectual life does (although no one will tell you this)—makes you the butt of ordinary life. Everything kills you because you want to grind it down so fine, and it won't be ground, or it will, but you'll never get that grit out of your mouth: there's too much of it, and it's everywhere.

Why, why, why, I asked myself, could it matter so much to separate and then matter not at all to mix? Now she was playing the big lunker for everything it was worth, dropping in quarters enough to work for an hour, two hours, until nothing would be left but heat and a beach ball of cloth. Why was she worried about me forgetting myself when my laundry, here beside me in its see-through bag, was perfect? I saw them do it: a rational degree of separation, tepid fluids and thimbleful of mild detergent. Of course they weren't clean here in this bag, if by clean you mean weave dissolved, nap shaved, and just a cobweb chemically purified and baked. My clothes retained a semblance of being-in-the-world, and I liked it that way.

It meant no drastic before and after. That's why I also liked translating poems and not narrative, which took you up, messed with you and left you high and dry, never the same—always a little worse for the action.

"What are you writing there?" she asked me, en route to the steel box to buy a bottle of beat-em-up fabric "softener."

"A synopsis," I said, when she had purchased her purple plastic bottle and passed by to return to her drying drum.

"Oh," she said, as if that answered any of her questions.

The word "lean" was in the next line. Lean was only one possible equivalent, but I like the meat associations.

"I never worked a day in my life," she was now saying, trailing back to her chair (the big drum rotating, shaking, knocking, but not yet white-hot), "for pay."

"Oh," I said. "Yeah," as if it were so hard to understand, or so meaningful. "Housewife?" I said. "Mother?"

"You can say that again," she said, raising her rosary hand to swipe the air, a gesture of a certain age, but still with some capability. "You don't know the half of it," was one thing it said.

"I know what you mean," I said, trying to show by my own gestures that I was shortly going to return to my work, which was not exactly housework. But before I did, "Why did you say that to me?" I asked her. "'Don't forget yourself, girlie or sister.' Why? What was I doing that aggravated you to speak to me, a stranger, that way?"

Tears were forming in her eyes magnified behind her glasses. "And now you speak that way, and in such a tone, to me?" At this, she took the rosary hand, released an index, and pointed at a button high up near the neck of my blouse.

"I think you're turning things around here," I said. "You spoke to me. I hadn't yet spoken."

"I forget the details," she said. "Alzheimer runs in my family."

"Okay," I said. "It doesn't matter anymore, especially if you've forgotten. To show you how quickly I, too, can forget, my name is," I said, sticking out my hand, "Dr. Helen Ann Souplice. Pleased to meet you."

"And mine," she said, gaily and with relief, "is Mrs. Dick Henly."

"Hello, Mrs. Henly," I said. "Dick's your husband's name, of course?"

She ignored this question, as she would ignore every important issue that emerged then and always. "Do they call you 'doctor'?"

"Sometimes," I said.

"Are you a medical doctor? No, I don't think so," she answered her own question, shaking her head for emphasis.

"There are," I said, "women doctors, you know."

"I know," she said. "What—do you think I don't know anything?"

"You're starting up again," I said.

"I have other problems in my family," she said. "It isn't just Alzheimer, so lay off, will you?"

"That's harsh, too," I said, "or don't you even hear your own tone?"

She laughed. "My husband hears it and so do my daughters." She snorted: "Every time."

"I'm beginning to see," I said, standing because the dry-cleaning lady had beckoned me, "what you're up to."

"Don't give yourself," she said to my back, "too much credit."

Instead of spinning around, as I should have, I picked up my boxes of dry cleaning and the thick bundle of hangers and walked them to my car, which I'd left unlocked because this town and the suburbs of the town where the Laundromat was were nowhere. The thieves were weakened stock; no one had any oomph, even for crime, which is not as easy as people think. It is a real cardiac-stroke career, if it doesn't get you a slug in the back or a year in the slammer (to say it the way Mrs. Dick's husband might in the barroom or sitting at home in his recliner talking to his son-in-law or to the neighbor just finished cutting the grass.)

Into the car my clothes went, but there was still the bag of laundered things, which, when I re-entered, was missing.

Mrs. Dick was tending her bulk dryer, waiting for the tumbling to stop, and sticking a hand in to fetch, within that egg white of braided cloth, the slurry in the center, hoping that the pain would be worth it. But out came not the rayons and nylons and Dacrons and polyesters that dry fast, shrink, and harden, but an oddment or two: face cloth—throw it back in—hankie and bra—keep them out, and so forth. She was shaking the plucking hand to cool it.

"Not worth it," I said. "Let 'em fry."

"Yeah, let 'em," she said. "I got your laundry here," she said, pointing to a basket on wheels. And of course, there it was.

"That was very nice of you," I said. "I thought for a minute—"

"I know what you thought. I could see it in your face, even though you were too polite to blurt it out, and, for all that, my hand was killing me, I didn't have time for you. But now," she said, shutting the dryer porthole and letting it hump, churn, and whirl. We watched. "But now, I do," she went on, when we had sat down again.

"Thanks."

"Say nothing of it."

"How can I repay your kindness?" I said, because I'm the type whom a politeness, a courtesy, a favor undoes: my bones weaken and my heart slows. I go right back to the beginning, the pure trustfulness of a baby out of the womb just long enough to appreciate the air and the service.

"Well, sit," she said. "Cool your heels. I don't see why you were in such a hurry. Where do you have to go to that you can't wait till I'm finished and see what I might like to do next? Time is heavy on my hands, see. I say my beads two, three times; I clean up after myself and him; I do my grocery shopping, twice a week laundry, kill a little time here and there up at the Y or the senior center. My sister lives up the road, my daughter a mile away. I can fill up a day, believe you me, but look what I have to fill it with. Just these dribs and drabs. I see out that window that you've got a spanking new car and all your hubcaps. You're sitting here writing something and having things done for you. That's nice. I can appreciate that."

"You can?" I said. "You can also talk a blue streak when you want to."

"I can, can't I?" she smiled. "See, you've already helped me feel good about myself. You've got it in you. I could tell just the way you didn't jump down my throat when I told you— what did I tell you?—to look alive or smarten up, or something."

"Wait a minute," I said. "You didn't say that to me."

"I didn't?"

"Nothing that rough," I said. "Or I'd be a fool not to take offense, which I did, if you remember, but you couldn't keep your mind on what you were saying."

"I can't remember. Maybe you're right." She shook a finger at me. "But I could tell you're the type that respects its elders. You can see it in the way you sit with your feet and legs tucked in so tight. You couldn't hurt a fly."

"Want to split a candy bar?" I said, pointing to the machines and fishing a dollar fifty or whatever it took.

"They got free coffee. Did you notice?" she said, thumbing toward the dry-clean wall, where I had noticed the stomach-turning black brew, there since Christmas, and the packets of creemola and—now that I was looking—a hobnailed glass sugar bowl—a nice touch, I thought.

"Yes," I said. "Thoughtful."

"Oh, they're very thoughtful here. Sometimes there's sandwiches, donuts once in a while, a dish of candy—something just to tide you over."

I sat back.

"Go back to work," she said. "You were writing something, a symptom or a souvenir—I forget what you said. It looked like a poem to me."

I was pleased by that: thoughtful and precise. So I did cool my heels, return to my work, help Mrs. Henly fold the red-hot sheets and thin, scruffy towels, the like of which I hadn't seen in thirty years, when my mother used them as scrub rags. I'm a good folder, and Mrs. Henly learned a few tricks, like socking corner into corner of a fitted sheet, or making a stocking ball, which she knew but had abandoned in favor of stocking knots. She showed me some: panties folded in four, a nice chunk of tight cloth; heavy, rubberized bras with the cups nested; dishcloths and towels rolled. When we were done and had packed the trunk of her cream four-door with two baskets, we drove, caravan-style to Dunkin' Donuts and had coffee and crullers. She smoked a cigarette.

"Look," she said, when I asked. "I'm not going to tell you my sob story. I'm sick of it, and you wouldn't see much in it."

"How do you know?"

"What I know, you've seen, if—as you say—your mother lives hereabouts, close enough for you to run her laundry up to the Fluffer."

"Yeah?"

"Why don't you tell me *your* story?"

"It's not that simple," I said.

"Did I say it was?"

"It's not easy to tell without touchstones."

"What are those?" She pushed up the sleeves of her bulky knit and rested her face on her hands.

*A*nd that's how we began. First there were touchstones, then mediation, the anxiety of influence, raw bits of iconography, and the different kind of living: in flats or large, shabby houses decorated ultra-modern or a sham kind of late nineteenth century—reflections on the Empire. Pro-seminar, traveling fellowships, and all the machinery and grime and sweat in the head.

"It sounds like a whole lot of nothing to me, but," she held out her hands in defense, "what do I know? You know what my husband calls my family? Peons. We're peons, he says. I don't like it, but he could be right."

"It might sound like nothing, but it fills up the days." I looked out the window at the drive-up for coffee-to-go. "In my life there's not quite as much motion."

"I'd hate that," she said. "Change of scene, get in the car and take a ride, go up to the apple orchard, make-your-own-sundae, flea market—all of this you're missing, I guess. Are you at the books all day long? Can you take a break?"

"Yes and no," I said, for why shouldn't I give a fair account? Was she going to talk to the dean?

"No! That's inhuman, even if it is nothing that you're doing."

"For us a break would be for you the work. Doing laundry, cleaning the sink, buying the meat and vegetables, and getting the oil changed. All that's for breaks."

"Stinks, in my book."

"Well, you're not understanding it yet. I'm not even sure you're trying."

"It could be your fault too," she said.

"For not spelling it out, or talking your language?"

"You're speaking English, aren't you?"

"I'm speaking English, but I often form my sentences in Latin."

"Wowee!"

"Yes," I said, "so it takes me a long time to say anything."

"Do you hear in English and send it back to Latin?"

"No, I leave it be. I like people's voices and their words."

"I do, too, but I get sick of the repetition."

"That's the curse of your life."

"What's yours?"

"Muscular deterioration and a thing they call in animal physiology "tetanus." It's like lockjaw of the brain. And we also tend to get old fast."

"Yeah, well that's common."

"But it's a kind of old you might not know. I'm not even sure I know it."

"You're young."

"Parts of me are older than you."

"How funny you are. Odd—you know?"

We agreed to meet a couple of days later and go to the real city, a place she hadn't been to since "the element" crept in and drove the ethnics to the suburbs. No one went to the city, and all the department stores closed down. There was nothing there but crime and filth and vice—the city had gone to the dogs—so why did I want to go? Everything run down, she went on (before I could answer), rats and drugs, and when she was a kid, people would wear gloves—pink, beige or white, sometimes black—before you'd even think to board the bus to "go downtown"—imagine.

I wanted to go, I said, because the city, notwithstanding its decline, was still the heart of it. And there she gave me the benefit of the doubt because, before my time, and even before her time, it *was* the heart—everyone was there, every house and building filled: streetcars, kiosks, tearooms, Chinese restaurants, merchandise to make and to sell, rivers full of trade. At noon, Exchange Place, a sea of hats; at 6:00, at 11:00, the diners (Silvertop, Havens, Miss Little Rhody, Streamline, 20th Century) crushed with custom, after they were pulled in by horses.

"Hearts," she said, "are all right by me."

But, in the interval, from Friday to Friday week, when the sentimental journey was booked, the poem began to grow, to bristle; it took on a sex. My mother had cleared a table for my use. On it: dictionaries, art books, clean pads, ball point and ink pens, and a special ruled paper for the roots and branching and sometimes even the diseased bundling and boling of translation—it isn't a one-to-one operation. In between two languages, dead or alive, is a terrain of termini and culs-de-sac, flood plains, tar pits, and mazes. You make maps of the worst sections, and it fills ten pages, unless you have the special kind of layered, translucent, cut-out paper pad with lots of redeemable glue.

For that week, I sat on a kitchen chair with a little braided seatpad and watched my poem conjugate into a hundred versions, one worse than the last. I wouldn't have a hair left on my head if my mother—a version, as I said, of Mrs. Henly—hadn't patted me on the back every once in a while, right before I was going to blow my top. What had happened to my delicate art?

So, enmeshed, I called Mrs. Henly and asked for a raincheck.

"Oh no," she said, "don't be a flat-leaver. You promised. Pretty please. I had my heart set on it."

Why the pressure? I wondered. I tested it, but she was firm. "My husband told me, 'Don't take no for an answer.'"

"How did he know," I asked, "that you'd be getting a no?"

"Oh, he knew. Life is like that. As he said, 'Can't count on nothin'.'"

So I felt bad enough, with the hundred-odd ruins and now this, a crushed heart, or even an artful stab at one. "You win," I said. "You're on."

So, I made the last grisly tentative on the poem, whose latest whimsy was slipping back into its Latin hole and pulling the lid over; it was recovering itself. For every moth-eaten, cobwebby English skin I opened for it, it slicked through and back into Latin. English was not Latin. Latin was quiet and rock-hard; the empire was in it: the Caesars, the terrible foreign queens, and all those speeches, jokes, and lamentations. How hard a rusk and thick a rind, and the poem could not be pulled out of it.

"Helly," my mother said, "go easy, hon."

"How can I?" I said in a tearful rage.

"Put it up, then."

I didn't. I slapped and strained, and, always, it slithered back. So, out came my hat and coat and, calling Mrs. Henly to move the date up to the very minute, off to Providence.

"I see something's eating you, Ducks," she said, as we hit the freeway.

"Call me Helen, or Hel. Most people call me that."

"Hell?"

"One ell."

We drove past the jewelry factories, the shipyard, the exterminator with the blue bug, big as a Buick, and there ahead was the city of Providence with a river slicing through it. Dome, towers, and steeples. "See," I said to Mrs. Henly.

"Yeah, I recognize it. I lived here all my life, you know: 45 Acorn Street, near Triggs."

"I remember Triggs."

Then she said: "How can you drive with your eyes closed?"

And I said, "I was thinking," because I was. The word "phalarope" came to mind and jiggered its way into a pulpy part of my brain where the English mucked with the Latin. I began to see the Latin poem seaming apart along certain heart-stopping lines. "I gotta get off the road," I said.

"Do you want me to drive?"

"No," I said. "No, I'll keep going." And with my teeth clenched like that, I barreled on into the city taking the Gano Street ramp and left on Angell. "This is one wing of the city," I said to my partner, looking out her window.

"Where are we?" she said, as we rocketed down the hill and past river and river park, a Versailles of orderliness spread to our right. "What happened to the old train tracks?" she said, "the municipal parking, the nothing that was here, and the garbage that began in front of the URI annex?"

"New," I said.

"It's not the same," she said, "although I can still imagine the old. It wasn't so bad."

"It wasn't bad at all," I said, "but here's Venice on the Moshassuck and Woonasquatucket."

"Okay," she said thoughtfully.

"I've never been to Rome, but look, Mrs. Henly, it's the Vatican, the Palatine corso. All those freeways knotted over there—nothing but chariot raceways. Okay? Feel like a sundae and a flavored Coke?"

"Sure." And we went to McGarry's restaurant, there for fifty-odd years, and sat by the window looking into Exchange Place. French-empire city hall, the park of the Revolutionary soldiers, the golden-yellow Renaissance facade of train depot and outbuildings.

"See?" I said, as the waitress laid out silver dishes on pedestals.

"It was always pretty here, but gray. Remember how gray it was, Hel, when the buses came under the dark tunnel or bridge, near the Biltmore?"

"It's still gray," I said. "It's a gray place. Gray is its dignity, although all this white granite, white marble is mighty fine as an accent."

"You don't have an accent."

"I lost it," I said. "Or, it fell away."

"Too bad," she said. "Your voice doesn't sound like one of ours."

"And yet," I said, sinking my spoon into the mound of white frozen custard—as they used to call it—"I sound like here, away from here."

"No kidding," she said.

By and by, we drove along Atwells, up Federal Hill, and down to the old neighborhood.

"Oh," she said.

"Yes?"

"It's exactly the same."

A spirit of quietness came over the car. We listened to each other's breathing. She was first to sigh. We were passing the brick Catholic church, cleaned when I was a kid, and still a burnt red, too large—an ark, as my mother would say—on its puny lot. With her thumb she marked crosses on her forehead and chest, bowing her head as she muttered the words Jesus, Mary and Joseph.

"Wanna pay a visit?" she said.

I parked on Fairview, and we walked past Supinski's funeral home for the Polish, and up the steep steps to the porch of Blessed Sacrament, or BS, as we all called it, and into the marble—damp, cool, and smelling of candle wax and incense. I sat, she knelt. Time passed. The clerestory windows gave us beaded light—wine-bottle green, vigil-light red, and the blue of life after death. As we walked out, our heels clacking on the stone tiles, tears were washing down her elderly, pink-powdered cheeks.

"How come?" I said when we were outside, on the top step, but she didn't hear me, entering, as we both were, into the fastnesses of the past, when the world was contained in six square blocks—the sweetness and the deadly boredom, the swearing, the masses, the schoolyard, the A&P, the clotheslines, the FCJs, the cigar shops, beauty parlor, and Castle Theater, Castle spa. She was gripping my bony arm.

"I forgot your name," she said.

I patted her hand. "Do you remember," I said, pointing to the statue of Our Lady of Fatima, "when we built that with our mission money?"

"My kids," she said, her voice had a flutey note in it, showing how the mystery of loss was being solved by figments of past arts and labors, all the color of it not yet gray, not all glossy black and white and still forever. She was holding my hand now as we stepped down, one by one, the grand entrance staircase, steps to make the BS the summit of the space.

"Nothing is over," I said, as I unlocked the car door.

"It's all over," she said.

"It's over," I said, "yes, but it's not done with."

"It's almost over."

"That's a fair statement."

We bypassed the city, taking Route 10 past the old rubber company. "Rotten eggs!" we said together, before a silence enveloped us, and the fluid air parted to pass us through and close up behind.

Paris

The last time I saw Paris, my husband was there with his girl-friend. Henry skipped over there with the woman he loved and left me with just the thought: walking along the Seine, left bank, right bank, smoking a cigarette, stealing a kiss, letting their eyes rest on a gargoyle or a stream of traffic, while their feelings coiled around each other. Pressure built, and they were soon in bed in a cheapish hotel—American and within the budget since the girlfriend was paying the whole freight—locked in each others' arms, although I know my husband—"ex," I suppose I should say—and he was feeling the cheap, starched sheets under his sensitive hide and wondering how clean the pillows were and what his feet had picked up from the sticky rug and whether that slight throb—not in his loins but in his left temple—was the onset of the migraine to end all migraines. In this thicket of worry, the dimpled darling with the heavy chest was just part of it, and a small part—but that she couldn't yet know—although we do know, don't we, the minute the attention of love flicks off, like a magnet changing poles. I love it. I watch it unfold, right here in my room where I was left to learn how not to count my chickens.

What did I count—about a thousand? He laughed to think of it, I'm sure, as they flew over Labrador with their dinner trays—no wine for him, please, he doesn't drink with the medications, the painkillers, the tranquilizers, the pep pills, the anti-anxiety tablets, and whatever extras he'd cadged from the twelve physicians who each thought he was operating alone on a patient whose "dependence" needed to be watched.

Oh, Henry, I felt; oh, Henry. I counted a thousand chickens and a million birds in the bush, and how many were there? None. Or just the one flying over Labrador in the tight skirt, striped top, and spike heels. Oh, Henry. Why did you play me such a trick?

So I cashed in my movables and convertibles and flew after them on the next jet, about twenty hours behind. I don't know the city. Name a city I don't know, and it would have to be Paris. And it was nothing of what I thought it would be. Noisy, filthy, streaming with the horde of summer vacaters and teeming with natives, noses in the air, taking no guff. It was dusty, hot, with nothing in the air but benzene, diesel, and CO_1. Sickening, especially to my lungs and fine immigrant nose, bred on trade winds and rotting seaweed, piney woods and fresh developments—buzz saw on greenwood, shaving the air with mortal bosc. Paris stank. In other words, they left no trail. Nothing like crumbs on the Orly tarmac or some luminous signing, but I didn't need it. Paris was big, huge even, but not infinite, and the doctors of philosophy and their forbidden fruit congregate in a few well-known pockets, in certain quarters where they can see the sights they came for: the quality stuff, the smaller museums, the bookshops, the subsections crumbling with age and none but native students. Prior to takeoff, I had apprised myself of these schoolmen lairs, and I had a good map.

After cabbing in and getting stiffed, I parked myself in a flea-bag up near the graveyard, Father Chair, and sucked up a few coffees and *fines* the way you're supposed to after you learn how to flush the toilet (that button on the top pulls out) and unlock the door.

At the sidewalk cafe, suffocating on fumes, I rehearsed the ultimate moments of my ill-starred marriage, my marriage to Henry, and maybe he was Henry eights, sure, but he was only at five or six by my count. Henry was a field of torment, a walking hornet's nest, but inside the stinging buzz, the motion without aim, was a hard pleasure place, a miniature, and he carried it between his two, close-set eyes, because it was a thing, as I told the waiter, only of the mind. In France, though, mind is high-sexed, so the waiter regarded me with nothing but puzzlement, beside feeling ill-used by a strange customer, a woman of a certain age, looking to ease her pain with a dose of French bread and *cafe au lait* and whatever *jambon* some born-yesterday *garçon* could spare: an entanglement. But he wasn't nasty. He listened, in between carrying cups and throwing a rag over his shoulder. There was much I couldn't explain. Why would this hornet's nest, this sphere of self-centricity, of magnetic oneness, allow a cool cube like myself, a pound of white margarine or plain yoghurt, to sit next? Sure there was fruit at the bottom and a prize wrapped in silver foil, but compare the difference. Compare and contrast, I said to the waiter, who, baffled, returned to his station by the bar, but he looked at me from there. In France, *la belle,* outsiders are meaningless: they give, they take away nothing. One's eye falls upon them only as a resting place from *la belle de jour* when ennui makes *la joie de vivre fade, tiède.* Even then, I swear it, nothing is registered on the French brain or inside the eyelids. Pigs, gnats, even mosquitoes and roaches have their function; some are revered. But these *outre-mer* visitants are the pure invisible, the thing that no one needs. But still he stared. Maybe because I was still talking.

The mystery of it, I was saying, was not that he had left (Henry, I meant) but that he had swarmed into my summer kitchen at all, my butter house, which was dark, blue and silent. He said to me, this Henry: Who d'ya think you are, little Nell in the churchyard? And then the bees would fly screaming like dive bombers. The bees. *Les abeilles,* I explained to my waiter—Philippe his name was—were long an object of pastoral interest, but these were not the same kind of bees

DREAM DATE

as Keats's or Virgil's: these were, in effect, mechanical bees; bees, I insist, on wire threads. A haunt of machine bees. Enough, he said, and of course, he was right. The day was young and the love pair still abed, Henry with the pillow over his head, facing away, locking in his sweet moments of unconsciousness from the caresses and tenders of the new one, a goddess of heat—like jam still on the stove. Heat or cool, Henry craved his sleep: there was little enough of it with the nightwork he had to accomplish, the old grudges and pains to review, the lost fortunes, the meals not eaten, the drinks not drunk, the pleasure receding day by cheating day.

Philippe by now had given me a key to his flat. He and his *copains* would assist. They knew the grids and swirls of Paris and were capable of ferreting out *les puces.* I should lock myself into the room. Philippe-*mère* would bring to me all that I required. I was to sit tight. They would bring the *salaud* and the *putain.*

Dream on, I told myself. The chief of the business was mine; it was my pleasure and my part. Before I bogged down with the definition of my aim, I hit the streets, changed money, darkened my glasses with clip-ons, and marched toward the chief American landmark, *la tour.* I would fan out from there.

First I called. Hen-ree-ee. Hen-ree-ee. But before the *flics* could pick me up, pack me away, and even while I was hearing the klaxons, I scuttled away. It was just a gesture, a *beau geste,* thinking that the warmth of ten years matched up together, knee to bending knee, breathing each other's hair, bringing in the first coffees, jabbering at each other the livelong day—each trying to implant the full brain, history, and emotional template onto the other. Kick that other stuff out, the trivialities of your own life, those useless and worn-out schematics, and put in THIS. Also, sharing the same towel, the same dishes, picking tissues out of the same box, and sitting side by side in the blue car, as if all that soul melting into soul, cell into cell, would awaken him from his dreams, or his *rêves,* if you prefer, and clock his steps to mine under the tower we all recognize equals Paris.

But penetrating signal that I issued notwithstanding, no one came flying up the Champs, or sailed down on the elevator, or tracked in on the back of the *poubelles,* no one, nothing. Please come flying. So I slipped into the real streets, the narrows, but soon was distracted by memories, small chunks and big twiny stories, from the thousand French novels that had created an inner Paris, a mental Paris for me all these years. Oh, this street and that, Henry James and Honoré de Balzac, Mr. Flaubert and Marcel P., Gaby Colette, the gang, including the shrimps from *Amerique du nord,* like Ernest and Gert, or from Dub, like Jim and Sammy Beckett. The playwrights, the poets—to me they're still scribbling now, waiting for their ships to come in, counting, like me, their chickens. But it was their city, and who was I to see it without them? And anyway I couldn't. I lost a week this way—strolling, *flânning,* snorkeling up more *fines* and *boks,* ordinary *vins,* coffee by the tank. In that week, so happy, *contente de moi,* that I forgot why I was there. Or would have, if Philippe hadn't reminded me every day at the small lunch I took at his joint.

"Mrs.," he'd say, "why do you tarry?" or however quaint it translated.

So, one week in, I was back on the scent. You'll say the scent was buried in time's dusty ruin, but no. Paris love has its first week, and its second is always different, diluted by the touring. After all we're here, why not go see the sights, and Henry was a glutton for fine food and oil-paint odalisques. He liked a thrill, a succulent treat, something he couldn't get so easily at home, so by second week, I knew they were on the move and ready to fall, thus, into my trap.

I waited at the Louvre: I was Christopher Newman, I was Milly Theale. I stacked my weight in a deep, inner room, in front of a Barbizon also-ran, my back to the crowd, and sure enough, I waited five minutes to an hour, but no more than an hour and a half, and in they came. I felt the air move. I listened but heard no sound, tenders or informat. This new woman—I called her the salamander, making up to her in species what I had taken away in genus—was a scholar of painting in the French schools and would be giving of her labels and dates and fine aspects to her learned friend, if that were the kind of tidbit they exchanged on an all-love diet.

But hearing nothing, not a note, I twisted my thin neck on its pole and saw exactly what I didn't mean or even want to see. Yes, it was she, the *louche,* but where was he? Alone, surfing on a tide of period art, and coming up short on distraction, she stood before each square, skipping mine, and making a good job of it, if a little too fast. She was blind to my presence—or, if she had taken in the block of my flesh statue, she misidentified it, seeing in it nothing but empty categories. Or so I thought. Hying out of that room, and with a certain speed, she was nearly gone, but—I coughed, choked, sunk to the floor, gagged, and squirmed.

"Water," I said. "*Au secours!*" I added, just in case.

It brought her to her knees beside me, where, because of paroxysms, she could not yet see who was there suffering, maybe dying, on that cold floor.

I squeezed my eyes and knotted my face, but looking, and looking more—holding my hand in case I was dying—she saw. "Holy cow!" she mumbled, or "*Sacre coeur,*" or something. It was too late to fake it, so I opened my cow-like blues and fixed her almond blacks.

"How," I said, "how could you do it?"

The blacks rolled up a little and the brain ticked or ratcheted, because I could hear it, whatever it was. But then a veil covered over all this mental laboring; first a veil, then a thick curtain, a plastic mask, the hardest face I've seen, and I've seen everything.

"Grr," I heard, "ssss," and I hustled myself upright because my ivory neck, soft, clean, and narrow as a straw, was there to tempt her claws.

"Don't try to reverse roles," I said. "Try to keep things straight." Then I formed my face into a question so as not to be too pushy.

"I never understood you," she said, rolling back on her heels.

"Did I ask you to?" I said. "How do you like, for example, the pictures in this room? It's all the same to me, either way, because I am not to you the *chose inconnue*. Yes, maybe I am," I corrected myself, "but it's none of your business, see?"

The hard mug was reformatting, and the blacks oiled over with spite.

"No, you don't," I said. "At least keep that much straight."

"What, exactly?" she said, rising to stand on her big, thin feet, so up I came, too, because I didn't want any footprints on my body.

"Stealer!" I said.

"Let's go have a smoke," she said. "You bore me, but I haven't had a conversation in seven days, and you're better than nothing. That much I'll take on faith."

So we padded out, Rose Red and Snow White, east and west, new versus old, and caught a metro to what I explained was the noisiest corner of Paris and the skankiest place for good coffee, fine service, and dense pollution.

"Your pick," she said, "and your nickel."

"Don't try to sound like me," I said, "for if you did really sound like me, how can you be as different as you look, and do what you did? Moreover," I said, in the din of the tube, "why would he move from me to you if you sounded like me?"

"What?"

"He sounded like me, too," I mused. "He was sick of it. All my pet phrases were in play, and none of his."

"I know them. I know them!" she said.

We were quiet and absorbed the bumping and speeding and

chattering windows and screeching brakes. I took her hand in mine to show her, in sweetness, there were no extra hard feelings, but she threw the hand off.

"Don't go overboard," she said.

"Yeah, that's one of them," I noted, talking only to myself. "Don't overdo. Don't kill the job. Don't blow it. That applies a little differently."

"Stuff it for a minute, will you? Can I have five minutes' peace?"

"I thought you wanted conversation, *badinage,* or whatever it is."

"You may not be capable of it," she said, as we alighted and climbed the steps, passing under the nouveau art, wrought-iron gatehead, Père LaChaise.

"Don't high-hat me," I said, "or I'm gone. I didn't buzz over here, leaving my life behind me, to be abused by the likes of you. I came for my mystery man. Never a mystery before, but now," I nodded, "yes, a mystery."

"You said a mouthful."

"See! Another!"

"I can speak French, too, and fast."

We settled at an outdoor table near the traffic and out in the hot sun. When Philippe came to our table, his jaw dropped.

"She's no babe," he said in our own lingo, a Yiddish pig latin, prepared for just this occasion.

"What did he say? Does he know me?"

"He said, 'Welcome, ladies. What is your pleasure?'"

"By 'ladies,' was there anything else implied?"

"Hmm," I said, "Maybe. But take it as a compliment," I said. Even the whores of Paris are rich silk-satin brocade (under my breath) compared to the dusters of the states, not to mention, honey babe, your ilk, hard-hat pedagogues, *tu sais*?

That made us both depressed. It was too much truth, and the sun was hurting my eyes, so we went inside, and Philippe puttered around us, haunting us, until the new one said, "*Va t'en, garçon.*"

"Scram," I added. "Beat it," giving Philippe a wink.

Both her arms, up to the elbows, were just then on the tabletop. It was time for turkey talk. "Why," I said, "just tell me why, and if I understand," I went on, "I'll go home and leave you in peace." Or, that's what I think I'll do, I said under my breath.

"Why?" she echoed. "Is there ever an answer to why? Let me rephrase," she said, with her arms now resting on elbows. "Is there an answer that you want to hear?"

"And that you want to tell," I added.

"And that I *can* tell," she said, sharpening it. "That can come out of both sides of my mouth and sound like one."

"Well, let's put it this way," I said. "Is there one answer for each of us three?"

"Oh, no," she said. "Not so fast. *Garçon,*" and Philippe pulled up. "Two *eaux-de-vie* and a salami plate. Big bottle of water." After he left, she said, "Not three stories, two."

Why two and not three?"

"Because," and here she folded her hands together and waggled them at me, "his and mine are the same, and yours is different. That's how it works."

"Perhaps."

"No 'perhaps.' That's how it works. That's why you're here. That's why your face has aged a hundred years and eyes sunk in your head with gloom and even your skull dented a little where the brain gasped for air."

"How do you know so well?" I asked, "say, if you're right, which I'm not saying."

"Don't ask unnecessary questions, if you want to go home squared."

"*You,*" I said, my voice sparkling with wonder, "are going to square *me?*"

"It's not a job I chose, but I did want him and he was yours, although let me tell you something right now: he said he never was yours. He never felt that way, or acted that way, not the way he acts and feels with me."

"Or so he says."

"Or so I feel. He gave you nothing of what he really is."

"How much do you get?"

A look of such fierce hunger, of desolation, of defeat—I had to look away. "Shall we change the subject?" I said.

"No," she said, pulling herself together. "Not until you get the picture, and you haven't so far."

"What's the picture?" I said, "that I don't already know, because," I went on, "I was there first, my love, and there was one before me."

"Point taken," she said, and our food and drinks arrived. We both sighed. We drank a little, nibbled on the meat with dusty chunks of stale bread. We ordered coffees and then began an alternation—booze and *café*—so we were loose enough to talk and tight enough to stay firm in our chairs with logic on our side at least 10 percent of the time."

It boiled down to this: I was skunked, shafted a little before my time.

"Only a little?" I said. "Was there a timetable?"

So she said, "Your days were numbered from the day even before he met me."

"Even then?" I said. "What about yours?" Lowering her eyelids while I watched the silver tears snake down the thin cheeks: "They're already over!" I screamed.

Philippe brought a towelette for her runny eyes and nose. "Let it out," I said. "You're with friends. Philippe, another round, and take a chair yourself. This is Philippe," I said to the crying head, "and he was on my side, but consider him yours." Her eyelids flicked and bright plums cleared, but looking closer at poor Philippe—fifty if he was a day and not a specimen Paris man—cheered her up. He was mine and less than she required or would even accept. She was way ahead of me, but sorrow has its own claims.

"All ready?" I said, checking my facts.

She sighed, and out it flowed. "I can't, don't you see, keep his attention."

"You're smarter than I am," I said, "and faster."

"No," she said. "He stole a book of your diaries, and I read it. It spoiled everything, but in this, I can't blame you."

My mouth was still open. "My what?"

"He Xeroxed all your diaries, and, at first, we read them for laughs. You take yourself so seriously, or at least you used to. And little reportings on your little self. It reminded me of samplers or paint-by-number. We know you like a book. But you knew him. And knowing you, I learned, and it was all spoiled after that."

"I ruined it?"

She sighed.

"Say."

"Not 'ruined,' just 'spoiled.' Just like learning how things work at any level closes them off from view."

"I never felt that way."

"Clearly," she said, "because you could write it, but not learn it."

"And why is that?" I said. It was getting dark and decisions must be made.

"Don't ask me. That's just you. That's one of the reasons he had to get away. You had the goods, but when were you going to use them? He stayed awake nights wondering. Why do you think he took all those pills?"

I was soaking this in. "Is he still reading the diaries?"

"Too depressing," she said. "We read about four pages and took the rest to the incinerator. *Auto da fé*. Didn't matter. Damage was done. I'm pregnant, you know, with the baby that should be half yours."

"What baby?" I said.

She stood and I saw where it lived, no bigger than a minnow. "Is that yours?" I said.

"Sort of," she answered. "Aren't you getting hungry for dinner?"

"That was awfully fast," I said.

"You don't want to hear why. It'll just hurt your feelings," she said, pulling me out a cigarette.

"I can add 2 and 2," I said, "and more power to you, by the way. So it's half yours and half his?"

"And a little bit of it," she said, raising her eyes to my stunned face (I'm not faker with a hard mask), "is yours."

That's when I paid the bill, hugged and kissed her—the way ladies do, or sisters, and had Phil see her to the taxi, waved, ate some onion soup and drank a bottle of something a sight better than cheapo or table, packed my bag, and rolled to the airport.

Wave bye-bye to Paris, I said. It diminishes. You know how it diminishes? Time and space make it small.

So I mounted my bird, buried my axe, and returned myself to my home, formerly ours. Here I sit. What did you say? Speak up. Oh, yeah, you took the words right out of my mouth.

The Last Time

Gertrude Stein wrote all night and I sleep all night and most of the day. When I get up—slowly, grudgingly—what do I do? Nothing. Gertrude is in the kitchen making fresh pasta and I'm stretching out on the divan, tired from brushing my teeth with that special brush whose nubs are mohair and fold right down to the ebony stick so nothing but fluff touches my sensitive whites. On the divan I study the pattern of the ceiling and all the time that's gone by since this style of ornament—fruits and plants and curly-headed boys—was in fashion, long before Gertrude's day, and Alice's too. Alice is typing last night's pages. Typing doesn't irritate me, so the door to the tiny study is left open and she can see me and I her and we exchange signals and reports on Gertrude's latest infamies. But all of it done with a wink and sweet smile.

Soon the *déjeuner* is ready and Gertrude sets the table under the canopy on the terrace. We eat from the five food groups and drink from the sixth group, wine, and sometimes the seventh, coffee. For the eighth, we just smoke, careful not to blow directly into each other's faces.

Gertrude is just thirty-five and has all her hair and Alice never looked worse or better. She has a suit on and sits low in her chair, although her legs are actually very long. She kneels for pictures and tucks the long shanks under her suit skirt. Gertrude is not tall, nor is she fat. That's another trick. Once they've served me and I've eaten my fill of farina, polenta, noodles, rice and had my aromatherapy, I settle in the leather armchair to look at pictures. I'm fond of two artists, neither of whom became a household name. But all their paintings they gave to me and Gertrude had them bound in these large books, so I could while away the hour between lunch and *café* flipping through the canvasses, or unraveling them if I feel like it: just pulling a string and, over time, there's nothing left. Our days together are long and fruitful. After pictures, I'm dressed in my pure silks, and fine pumps are put on my feet, a green umbrella or a pink parasol, depending on *le temps fait beau* or *mal,* and a small corsage is purchased on the street corner. Gertrude ties it on my left wrist and takes my hand in hers. Alice walks behind us and does the marketing.

Five full days pass before our next visit with Picasso, who comes alone. He's an irritable guy and we're all—me included—walking on eggs until he's taken off his cap and ironed out some of the wrinkles that hatch his face.

"Mr. Picasso," Alice says, "a cup of tea or a drop of wine?" That gives him something to think about while we skitter about picking our chairs, and last one gets that low stool near the fireplace.

"I don't know," he says and looks around the room until he finds me sitting up straight in a ladder back chair. "Who's that?" he says.

"As if you didn't know," I say so fast that the words are like arrows on their target before they even spring the bow.

"What did she say?" he asks in Spanish, the only language I don't have, or so he thinks. He eyes me, but my face and narrow form, much sought after by Mr. Klee and Mr. Miro, are just popular filler to him, although perhaps—in the back of his mind—a thin cat.

Trouble begins to boil. The two ladies offer Mr. Picasso fifty dollars so he can buy his own lunch and rent a studio on Avenue des Pompiers for the next ten years, so he's satisfied, in a sense, and doesn't go away angry or empty-handed, but of course, he fails to say goodbye to me, or even salute me for my birthday, which is next week, so I curse and swear in every written language until Gertrude comes with the syringe and gives me my first shot of Evening in Paris.

It turns out Gertrude has to pay them all, and more now that I'm here, big as life, a fly in their ointment.

"Why," I ask Alice after we both hear Hemingway wiping his feet on the doormat, ready to knock with that ham fist, "am I a fly in their ointment?"

"Shh, darlin'," she says. "Wait now." And that day, I do, tucking my feet under my skirt which covers my legs just to the ankles.

Hem comes alone. He's in uniform but the war's been over for five, six years. In he comes with thick boots and a big, toothy smile. "*Miracolo,*" he says. And that means, Alice whispers in my ear, another sentence has been written, pulled like a tooth rooted in the jawbone, or even in the ribcage, or rooted in the feet, for that matter.

"Okay," I say. "Celebration." And we take a colorless, odorless liquid of a lethal proof and each drinks to art, to grandeur, to manhood and to the three ladies of the rue de Fleurus, with their pink faces and easy ways, especially the ways of Alice, whose fingers curl around mine to boost my spirits. Hemingway has never liked me and his big mug shows the ugliness of his feelings as soon as he sees that I'm not going anywhere. I can count the fleas on his collar and the hairs on his head, if I felt like it, and in a game or marbles or tic-tac-toe, he'd eat the dust. Hangman is my true sentence. But I'm nice, I'm friendly, I ignore the puss with its strained, false smile that he puts on just to keep Gertrude from sinking her teeth in his neck. Gertrude and Hem have been at war since '06, which may be why he wears the uniform. It's up to Alice—it's always up to Alice—to make the peace.

We each give the writer and telegraph artist a ration

ticket—mine is actually an old chance in a turkey raffle—so Hem can buy the can of milk for Hadley's brat and a night of peace in that hovel, so Hem leaves, saluting the chief and wearing his welcome very thin indeed by a sneer toward me that comes in range of Alice's strong eyes.

"To hell with him," I say, as the door slams shut.

But Gertrude is wild and throws over her shoulders her velvet writing garment—even though the Paris sun has not set on the '20's—and begins a little earlier that day to drain the ink tanks of Western Europe and then on to the carbon pencils and eat all that paper, too, while she's at it.

That's the spell that Hemingway, the old fraud, casts on our house, or fog maybe I should say, or plague. The sky darkens and Gertrude thinks it's nighttime; factory whistle blows and the mill must be turned.

Thank heavens, at that moment, Ez Po and Bill Williams show up with hotdogs and cupcakes, enough for all, and the Chinese characters to go with them.

"Hi, Bill," I say. "Hello, Mr. Pound."

"Hiya, Betty," says Bill, but Ez's head is all beehive and he's praying to the seventeen god families of known history for a blessing on the canto of tomorrow; a curse has clearly dogged the canto of today and we know about last week and a month of Sundays before that.

"I said hello, Professor Doctor Pound," but Gertrude cuts me off, proffering a silver salver of confetti, those delicious stale almonds packed in a coat of sugar, and EP fills his pockets. Bill sits down beside me, but without a word. We shake hands, kiss cheeks, punch shoulders, pat backs and rub each other's forearms. I take a hotdog and break it in half.

"Take. Eat," I say.

"Thanks, Pal. Don't mind if I do," is his reply and with it, Ezra's eyes pop open.

"Hot dog!" he says, and sits, eyes burning, with fifty ideas slotted behind them. Happy to be filled in the head, he eats his fill of dogs (Where had they gotten them? The *patisserie*? The *boulangerie*?) while Alice's busy hand peels the papers on a couple of black-and-white cupcakes, the kind you can get up around Boston and Fall River. We eat in peace, although Gertrude doesn't touch the stuff. Pickled onions for her and a quarter of a pickled egg for my darling Alice, with wine in those dirty flasks.

Once filled, we circulated papers. (It was so nice not to be despised). Essays, poems, a libretto, four tiny short stories, a recipe, and blank page from me. We read, first silently, then with closed eyes, shut tight. Ezra read from one of his indoor screens, a canto or a little bit of rubbish that collected there. Bill had his banjo and everything with us was American fourth of July, for fifteen to twenty minutes, until—pooped—the two men of letters left and the three of us (mostly Alice) were left to clean up the mess and backbite, which was the chief fun for all the work of the Rue de Fleurus.

II.

Some days no one came. The rain fell, the sun shone. Gertrude wrote all night until her blood collected in her feet, stuffed into *pantoufles* like the bros. Goncourt wore. Then she passed out. Alice was there, pushed up in a chair next to Gertrude's to take that heavy head on her shoulder. The picture I have in my mind! I was never jealous because I had four or five cats, a litter from Colette's favorite, unnamed pet, stuffed into the cracks between me and the wall. In that way we never felt like a threesome, a sore-pointed triangle. I gave them their space because Alice's love was complete. She was made for love, where Gertrude was made for greatness and I for sleep.

This is compatibility of a sort, and very easy for the folks who visited us, trying to make their way, or bull their way into history. We offered (even Gertrude) no resistance. Why not Gertrude? She salivated for glory, but she also had money, and Alice—don't forget—so these punies who came by, with their crayons and their worn-out Fabers and their flat hats, they did her no harm. Alice had kept the fattest coat of love wrapped around her Gertrude—tough as a walrus skin, thick as a church wall and roomy, for Gertrude was growing, right under our eyes, and under tout Paris, for that matter, or under that part of it that came knocking.

One day, though, and sadly, it all changed. Life is like that; it doesn't tolerate perfection or contentment, even what they had, and what I could get from Colette's cat's litter, and keeping an eye on the pair, and letting them take care of me, an American in Paris.

It started here. One very simple day, the car broke down and overhead, there was a flight of migrating birds ("ducks," I said; "geese," said Gertrude, and "no difference," Alice said, whether she believed it or not). In fact the flying birds or fighting tigers were pigeons from Sacré Coeur on their way to Ile de la Cité for the leavings that were always choicer. At the time, no one understood the meaning of this sign, but more were coming. We hopped a tram, but without tickets, and boy-o-boy, the fur did fly when the trouble started. Down at the station where we were—I want to say "escorted," but arrested and cuffed is more the speed of it—none of the given bracelets quite fit around the meaty bone of Gertrude's fighting arm, so they took her left, which threw everybody off; *flics* and prisoners were all in a foul mood as the paddy carried us, siren-screaming, to the lock-up, a holding pen, I guess it was.

"Name?" asked the desk sergeant.

"Ha!" I said out loud. "Wait'll he hears."

"*Attendes*," he said to me, "*tais-toi.*"

"Name?" He turned to Alice, and together she and Gertrude did the great thing, true American Yankees: they shut their traps tight.

"*Kein Deutsch,*" little Alice said.

"A-la-la," the chief man said. "*Attendez, tout le monde,*" and out he went looking for what we didn't know.

Let me put it in a nutshell. Held all day for questioning until every language cop in the capital had been jerked out of his hideyhole to come translate the three madams until finally the chief inspector, a real character, thought to ask the arresting office what we had done, what all three did to need the people of Paris's police apparatus, beloved institution, to undo it, to get justice or repairs. No one could remember; it hadn't even been written down.

How could it be, since there was no confession, no name, no street address? All was general puzzlement, or the beginning of a dangerous kind of irritation. I had stood that whole time stone silent, my mug all tucked up without its usually juicy expression that gave everybody the bright idea that I could be read like a book, and who knows what kind of book. Well, then I spoke, I said my piece, first words I wasted on the French *flics* or any French.

"This," I said, pointing to my left where Alice stood, tall and Sapphic, "is Gertrude Stein, who owns half of America, and this," I said, pointing to Miss Stein, who still had the car crank in her hand, "is Missy Toklas."

Fine, sure, they said in their own language, but who are you?

"What do you mean who am I? Who are they? Aren't you going to check? Check it out."

They didn't like the tone, I guess, because, in a minute, the pair of sapphs were ushered out the main door, toodle-o, didn't even think to say goodbye, going straight to the *Tabac* to buy a thousand tickets, or as many as they thought they'd need between now and the end. For me, it was different; it was always different.

But I served my time. I saw the butterflies on Devil's Island; I marched in a striped suit to the Bastille. My legs were too skinny and weak for the big ball, so they found a child's ball. (That's what they do in France.) It was pretty but heavy and I carried it in my own arms and wept bitter tears of auld acquaintance be forgot, but by the end of the first month, Mr.

Camus showed up. He'd gotten wind of it and thought to spring me by offering the name and address of someone they really wanted. So out I went and off I trotted. Mr. Camus, a tough guy—no pulp in him the Algerian ragazzi hadn't beaten out of him—squired me up to the flat he kept with Beckett's ex and put me up for a few days till I stopped crying and could lap up some chocolate, because I was so meatless by then it sounded like bones dropping when I fainted dead away two or three times *par jour* from sheer inanition. Mrs. Beckett, a nurse, tried to pep me up, feeding me with an eye dropper from her own cup, chocolate with a stinger of Armagnac. Little by little, I pulled what I had together and rose off my lit-ter at the foot of Mr. Camus's own litter, and sometimes right next to his, and sometimes pulled over so there was no dif-ference between what was his and what was mine. (And Mrs. Becket was in bed, too, or out on call.)

"Alice and Gertrude," I started to say when I found my voice, but so weak it was that it barely crossed the barrier of my soft teeth.

"Alice and Gertrude what?" said Mr. Camus, lighting my and his cigarette. We smoked like fiends.

"Do you mean," I said, "what is their last name or what was I going to say about them?"

But his eyes glazed over. Something was eating him. His hair was turning white, just individual hairs, but I could count them when he pressed me to him so tight that his hair was in my eyes, and being me, I opened them.

"My sadness," I said, "my cutie," because we were in love, "what ails you?"

He lifted those oily eyes, mud-color, to shine on my still-emaciated face and said, "*Au jourd'hui*—"

I stopped him dead. "I've already heard that one before," I said.

"Maman," he went on, as if the words were putty in his

mouth, but then he stopped because he could tell that I *did* know it.

"Etcetera, etcetera," he said.

And we took the day off—a boatride up the Seine, *une pique-nique,* a little music and boozing. He carried me home in his arms, just a pile of bones I was, with a bocce ball. This was not the life for me, too heroic, so I packed a few things—nothing, really—in a baggage and traced my steps back to where it won't surprise you to hear I was going.

Love was fine, but I'd gotten my fill of it. I left Mr. Camus a suicide note, so he wouldn't come snooping, a tip for Mrs. Beckett (her life was hard), and hoofed it over to Rue de Fleurus. Gazing up at the windows, I saw a TO LET sign. What I didn't know—or didn't know yet—was Paris was yesterday. Alice and Gert had started out for the south with Picasso and Fernande and that trip was just the first in the slope toward the end. I sat on the doorstep. Little by little, no one came. Hem, a little bird told me, was in Spain; Bill and Ez had parted company, and even Mr. Fitzgerald was less frequenting the Ritz bar and had pulled in his horns for the nonce. The work had really started, the fun was over. For me, the fun was just beginning.

Nighttime had not yet fallen on Lutèce, but Jean Rhys came clicking by to look me up. A laugh a minute she wasn't, but at the Brasserie Lipp, where her connections were, she led me to Fordie, to Joe Conrad, and, on off-days, to Eddie Dahlberg and Mr. Miller. Such were the joys. The end was in sight, just the three chimneys of the Queen Mary, or maybe it was the Lusitania, but over I went with steamer trunk of memories. I was delivered with the rest to the bottom of the sea, five fathoms, and here I lie, my father's eyes are still my eyes, my time is now my own. I think of Alice, and for a long time before going to bed early, I know she thought of me.

Acknowledgments

The author gratefully acknowledges publication of "The Secret of His Sleep," "Partly Him" (as "The Ice Patriots"), "The Thin Man," and "Body and Soul" in *Boulevard;* of "The Maestro" and "Among the Philistines" in *The Yale Review;* and of "With Her" in *Southwest Review.*

Ever grateful, the author acknowledges the vigilant eye of her best editor and great friend, John T. Irwin.

Jean McGarry was born in Providence, Rhode Island, and educated in parochial schools. She received a B.A. from Harvard University and an M.A. from the Johns Hopkins University. *Dream Date* is her sixth book of fiction, following *Gallagher's Travels, Home at Last, The Courage of Girls, The Very Rich Hours,* and *Airs of Providence.* She teaches in the Writing Seminars at Johns Hopkins.

FICTION TITLES IN THE SERIES

Guy Davenport, *Da Vinci's Bicycle: Ten Stories*

Stephen Dixon, *Fourteen Stories*

Jack Matthews, *Dubious Persuasions*

Guy Davenport, *Tatlin!*

Joe Ashby Porter, *The Kentucky Stories*

Stephen Dixon, *Time to Go*

Jack Matthews, *Crazy Women*

Jean McGarry, *Airs of Providence*

Jack Matthews, *Ghostly Populations*

Jean McGarry, *The Very Rich Hours*

Steve Barthelme, *And He Tells the Little Horse the Whole Story*

Michael Martone, *Safety Patrol*

Jerry Klinkowitz, *"Short Season"and Other Stories*

James Boylan, *Remind Me to Murder You Later*

Frances Sherwood, *Everything You've Heard Is True*

Stephen Dixon, *All Gone: Eighteen Short Stories*

Jack Matthews, *Dirty Tricks*

Joe Ashby Porter, *Lithuania*

Robert Nichols, *In the Air*

Ellen Akins, *World Like a Knife*

Greg Johnson, *Friendly Deceit*

Guy Davenport, *The Jules Verne Steam Balloon*

Guy Davenport, *Eclogues*

Jack Matthews, *"Storyhood as We Know It"and Other Tales*

Stephen Dixon, *Long Made Short*

Jean McGarry, *Home at Last*

Jerry Klinkowitz, *Basepaths*

Greg Johnson, *I Am Dangerous*

Josephine Jacobsen, *What Goes without Saying: Collected Stories*

Jean McGarry, *Gallagher's Travels*

Richard Burgin, *Fear of Blue Skies*

Avery Chenoweth, *Wingtips*

Judith Grossman, *How Aliens Think*

Glenn Blake, *Drowned Moon*

Robley Wilson, *The Book of Lost Fathers: Stories*

Richard Burgin, *The Spirit Returns: Stories*

Jean McGarry, *Dream Date*